BONDS

COMMAND

FOUR POWERFUL AND DOMINATING BILLIONAIRES
ONE UNBREAKABLE BOND

SIERRA
CARTWRIGHT

USA TODAY BESTSELLING AUTHOR

COMMAND

First E-book Publication: July 2021

Adult Reading Material

Disclaimer: This work of fiction is for mature (18+) audiences only and contains strong sexual content and situations.

It is a standalone with my guarantee of satisfying happily ever after.

DEDICATION

For Sierra's Super Stars. You are simply the best! And for Shayna whose name should always be in lights! Especially for January Apted whose tireless support is so very much appreciated. For Miss Whit and Angie who are always there. Cathy with the constant and daily inspiration and vision. For ELF who had the guts to say, "Wanna know how you can be better?" And for BAB, who's always the biggest cheerleader and greatest friend. For bloggers everywhere —your passion for books inspires me.

And most especially YOU, yes, YOU, who picked up this book and love the written word as much as I do.

CHAPTER ONE

"How's your love life?"

"My…?" Aria Dewitt sat back in her chair and stared at her boss and friend, Julien Bonds. In the time she'd known him, he'd asked some ridiculous questions. But this had to be the most audacious. "What the hell has my love life got to do with anything? And it's none of your business. It's illegal to ask."

"Is it? This isn't a job interview."

"Details."

"Sue me." He picked up a bright red, organic apple from his desk and tossed it into the air. Without looking, he caught it in one hand. "But first, give me the details."

Aria felt as she'd stepped into an alternate reality. Which wasn't all that unusual when walking into Julien's office. "There are no details."

"Ha! I knew it sucked."

"It doesn't suck," she protested.

"Yeah, it does."

Because he was right, she exhaled instead of arguing. "Has anyone ever told you you're an asshat?"

"All day. Every day." He grinned.

She looked at him. Unable to discern anything in the steadiness of his gaze, she asked, "Why did you really call me here?"

"It's time we had a talk." Julien's tone was flat.

She gripped the bottom of her chair. She knew how to react to his exuberance as well as his frustration. But she knew that when he lacked emotion, he often had bad news.

Desperately she raced through snippets of recent events, trying to think of where she'd screwed up. She came up with nothing. Her focus was as intense as it had ever been. She was logging more than sixty hours a week at the office. Her phone was always on, and she made sure she was available on nights and weekends. She met all her deadlines while managing to push a group of creatives toward ever-higher levels of technical genius.

"I'm sending you to Los Alamos to work with Grant." Julien remained unmoving, letting the implications of his statement ricochet in her brain.

"Grant Kingston?" she asked, despite knowing there wasn't any other Grant in her boss's inner circle. Julien was reputed to be one of the most creative, brilliant people on the planet. Until this moment, she'd shared that opinion. "That's worse than working with you."

"I'm not sure whether to feel insulted or flattered."

"Neither. Both."

"He's stalled. And I need him to take a more active role at Bonds. That's where you come in."

Julien's suggestion was, at best, ludicrous. "This is a joke, right?"

"I think it's a spectacular idea," he assured her. "One of many I've had today. And when you come back to California, you're going to thank me for the opportunity."

For a few seconds—an absolute eternity for Aria—she was rendered speechless. "I've heard he lives in a cave."

"It's a very nice cave." His words were light, but he didn't smile. "And it's more like a...house built into a mountain. Not actually a cave, really."

Dread slithered through her stomach. He was serious.

Six years ago, Julien had contacted her for the first time. He'd said he'd been following her career. At twenty-four, barely out of college, she'd joined an Internet retailer that was in danger of becoming obsolete. She'd worked her way up the corporate ranks, and her vision for same-day delivery of products had helped them to raise the funding needed to increase their business and compete on a global level.

When she'd received the text message inviting her to a clandestine after-hours meeting at 1, Bonds Street in Cupertino, she'd refused.

But Julien Bonds was not easily dissuaded when he wanted something.

For a year, he'd relentlessly pursued her.

Finally, Aria had become disenchanted with her company's egotistical CEO. Evidently Julien had heard about the falling out. The next time he'd approached her, she'd agreed to meet with him.

When he'd sent his jet to shuttle her from Los Angeles to northern California, she'd been star-struck.

Everyone in the industry had heard rumors about Julien's astounding headquarters, but the first view of his round building at night had made her mouth drop. Even though it was after eight p.m., lights had blazed from almost every window. The campus had been teeming with activity.

The moment she'd stepped inside the architectural wonder, she'd understood him perfectly. To him, creativity wasn't just a concept, it was a demand—an expectation—and she'd instinctively responded to that consuming challenge.

He'd promised her that, as Director of Global Strategy at Bonds, she'd have autonomy, a ridiculously large salary, unbelievable benefits and her own staff. In return, she'd have objectives, and they would be damn difficult to meet. The job would come with stress, long hours and a demanding boss.

And that was where she operated best—at the intersection of impossible and imperative.

As she'd listened to him, she'd realized he'd studied her like he did any problem, figuring out her talents and what she needed in terms of money and challenge before he'd made an offer.

Aria had accepted on the spot.

During the ensuing years, she and Julien had spent significant time together. They had shared numerous successes and a couple of not-so glorious product debuts overseas. Over time, she'd come to think of him as more than a boss. He was also a friend and confidante.

"I don't understand." She shook her head. "Did I screw up?" Why the hell else was she being banished from the inner circle to... Jesus H. She didn't even know where the cave was. "It's in this country, isn't it? In the bowels of a mountain somewhere."

"New Mexico," he supplied helpfully. "Yes, that's in the United States. Near Colorado—and Arizona, I think. Gorgeous this time of the year."

"You'd have said that no matter what time of the year it was."

"True. But just picture it, a layer of snow will make it refreshing and...pure."

"Snow? *Snow?*" She struggled to hold onto her temper. "Come on, Julien. We live in California. I don't do cold."

"Didn't," he countered. "You do now. Temporarily." He tossed the apple in the air again. "The change will be good for you. It will allow you to see product development, understand more of what's involved in getting something to market. Think of it as cross-training."

"With someone I've never met."

"He's a friend of mine. We went to college together."

"Is that supposed to be a recommendation?"

He opened his mouth, but then closed it again. He contemplated the apple before responding. "You have a point."

She narrowed her eyes as she realized he hadn't answered her question about screwing up. And he'd asked about her love life. "This is about Simon, isn't it?"

"Yes." The word was sharp, its trajectory exact.

Aria wrapped her arms around herself. *God.* She knew that the fiasco with her former fiancé was going to continue to haunt her.

"But it's not about punishment, Aria. You didn't screw up. I'm doing this for you. Everyone needs an occasional change of focus. You work too hard. Hell, I work too hard. It fucks up relationships, interferes with free time, makes us forget we're human. A break, even an enforced one, clears the mind, helps reset the focus. You'll come back with even more to give."

"I don't need that."

"Don't want it," he corrected.

"Don't want it," she agreed.

To the whole world and to her, it had seemed an ideal match. Simon had been smart, attractive, successful. How the hell could she not want to marry him?

She'd ignored the fact that they really had nothing in common and didn't like to do the same things. Sex was okay, but there'd been no real affection there. They both traveled a lot for work and they were often on different continents and in vastly differing time zones.

As the months had gone on, she'd begun to realize that

she'd originally been caught up in the fantasy that they could have a relationship like some of the power couples she knew. But even after he'd put a ring on her finger, their phone calls had rarely lasted longer than a minute. A few had clocked in at less than twelve seconds. Mostly they'd communicated via text or email.

The wedding dress she'd hung in the closet at her apartment seemed to mock her. Friends and family told her the jitters were normal. But jitters had morphed into the fear that if she got married, it would be a big mistake.

She'd finally gathered the courage to sit down with Simon and confess her misgivings. And it turned out, he wasn't as devastated as she'd feared he would be.

He'd admitted he was mostly going through the motions, too. Get a career, get married. He loved her, but he wasn't crazy about her. He'd agreed that they both deserved better.

The news had relieved her, but she'd been sad, as well. No matter what she'd thought, at least on some level, she'd been a failure. If not because she'd ended the engagement, then from accepting the ring in the first place.

Though they'd issued a joint statement canceling the wedding, it had been too late to stop the invitations from going out. A well-respected online business magazine had made the announcement top-of-the-page news. It had been accompanied by a picture of her smiling, arms folded. The headline had asked, *Fit to lead?* The accompanying article had questioned her decision-making and ability to stick with something for the long term.

When she and Simon had both refused to comment, the enterprising reporter had called Julien for a comment. He'd said he had total confidence in her. She'd appreciated his loyalty, and she would do anything to repay it.

"I'm not giving you a choice in this," Julien said, interrupting her thoughts.

"Are you asking me to resign?"

"No." He tossed the apple and captured it. Repeatedly. Annoyingly.

"Firing me?"

He tossed the apple again.

She scowled, temper unraveling in the least ladylike way possible. "Transferring me?"

"No."

"Okay. Asking me to take a leave of absence?"

"All those would be worse for Bonds in general."

As always, he'd keep the company in mind. But what about her sanity? "I'm confused." She reached to absently twirl her engagement ring. Then, realizing it wasn't there, she laced her fingers, trying to keep them still. It didn't work.

"Don't read anything into this. Have I ever lied to you?"

"No. More like the opposite." Julien Bonds was honest to the point of bluntness.

"It's a temporary reassignment. Nothing more."

That didn't help dim the thrum of her agitation.

"Grant's overextended, not at his best."

"Trying to twist the Theory of Relativity will do that to a man," she said dryly.

"It's the Laws of Physics. I think. But close enough."

Finally irritated into action, she reached out, snatched his apple then slammed it on the pristine surface of his desk. The *thunk* satisfied...and it would leave a mark.

"That was my dinner."

"Put it in a smoothie."

"If it had been grapes, we could have made it into wine."

"This is my fucking life we're talking about, Julien—boss or no boss. Give me the courtesy of being serious for five minutes."

He curled both hands around the apple and drew the fruit toward him. Then he met her gaze. "You're going to Los

Alamos. You're going to spend time with Grant. And you need to snap yourself out of your funk. I think the challenge will be good for you."

"Are you my psychologist now?" Frustration made her edgy.

"Grant needs to refocus, too. Bonds needs him. I need him."

"Wait a minute." All of a sudden, the genius's strategy became clear, the colors vivid. "You're sending me to do something you haven't been able to do."

"I wouldn't say that," he hedged.

"Well?"

"Inspire!" He snapped his fingers. "That's it. You'll inspire him. Be a muse of sorts."

"Julien, please..."

"Svetlana will be ready for you tomorrow morning at eight. Meet her at the airport."

Aria set her chin. "And if I refuse?"

"You won't."

"Are you threatening my job?" Fear left her momentarily immobilized. For the past four years, she'd given everything she had to Bonds. If she was forced out, what the hell would she do? Where would she go? She'd never contemplated a future without her job.

"Stop," he warned. "Whatever the fuck you're thinking, get rid of it. I need you reenergized. You and Grant are two of my best people. It's time for you to work together."

"And my regular responsibilities?"

"I'll have David fill in. He's capable. You've seen to it."

David was her number two. He was a good choice, and he would have been running things during her honeymoon, anyway. Julien was right, but that didn't mean she liked his decision. "How long am I exiled for?"

"Until you have a new product. Two days? Three weeks? Six months?"

The shockwave of fear edged away, replaced by pragmatic reality. "It's not possible for me to stay away from the office, my life, my friends, my parents for that long."

"Then I suggest you work fast." As if unconcerned, he picked up his bruised apple and took a bite.

Her stomach had turned inside out, and he was eating? "Do we have a corporate house or apartment there?" Bonds had interests all over the planet, they owned a number of properties that senior executives or engineers could stay in while traveling. The places made extended stays away from home marginally more pleasant, and employees weren't at the mercy of hotel availability.

"No. When I go to New Mexico, I stay with Grant."

This was getting worse and worse. "You're suggesting I move into a cave with him?"

"It's a very nice—"

"Don't say it."

"More of a mountain retreat," he finished. "You'll like it."

At some point, she expected Julien to crack one of his infamous grins and declare he'd only been having fun. A lot of it, at her expense.

Instead, he continued, "There are hotels nearby, but they're impractical for long-term use. You'd have quite a drive every day. But of course, if that's your preference, we'll make the arrangements." He stood and walked past her.

His knit polo shirt with its embroidered Bonds logo had made her believe he was dressed in casual business attire. In reality, that was illusion. He wore baggy basketball shorts that hung down to his calves. He'd completed the look with gray athletic socks and orange tennis shoes. "Quite the outfit."

"Everyone's a fashion critic. Most people have the courtesy to take a hint and leave before I have to kick them out."

"You're kicking me out?"

He continued through the office and pressed the elevator call button. "You have a thousand details to see to, informing David of the new plan, meeting with your team, packing, paying bills, talking to your parents. I'm not sure how you'll get it done in the next couple of hours, but you're resourceful, and you'll figure it out. You can sleep on the plane tomorrow."

"With Svetlana flying it?"

"She hasn't nicked any mountains." He cocked his head. "Well, not recently, anyway. And it's been ages since she crashed an aircraft. Years, I'm sure. And the Tornado is spectacular. It can practically fly itself."

Aria realized he was trying to ease her mind with the casual banter that defined their relationship. Until now, he'd been the one to help her sort out reality, not distort it. "I'm trying to understand. Am I allowed to be in contact with people?"

"Don't make this complicated, Aria. You're a valuable asset to Bonds and to me personally. It would be catastrophically stupid of me to prohibit you from talking to them. But limit your exposure. I want you focused on your new project."

"I apologize for the wedding fiasco."

"The non-wedding fiasco," he corrected her. After giving her a smile that didn't help mitigate her angst, he added, "Rise to the new-product challenge, and accept this time away from California as the gift it's meant to be."

"I don't know anything about product development."

"You know more than you think you do."

"This feels more like a prison sentence," she admitted.

He gave her an unholy grin. "Marriage to Simon would have been a life sentence."

The elevator arrived. "Are you telling me you think it wouldn't have worked?"

"You're a smart woman."

"So why—"

"He was a wuss. A wimp. He wore tweed jackets with leather patches at the elbows." He gave an exaggerated shudder. "You need someone you can't push around."

"*What?*"

"You chew through weak men as if they're candy, then you complain when you get a toothache."

Her stomach plummeted. No one knew that about her. What the hell had she ever done that made Julien think she needed someone strong?

"Grant is man enough to handle you. Now go."

The longer she stayed, the more false hope she'd fill herself with. Despite his reassurances, she felt as if she were being fired.

Focusing on sorting her million priorities, she entered the car then pushed the button to take her to the lobby.

"Aria?"

Was he offering a reprieve? She shoved out her arm to prevent the doors from closing. "What?"

"It's really fucking cold there. Take boots!"

Scowling at him, she allowed the door to close. As the elevator descended, she could have sworn she heard him add, "You know, those sexy ones that make men forget their names!"

"Are we settled then?"

"What?" Jolted into awareness, Grant Kingston looked up

from his computer monitor. Two minutes ago, the privacy of his workshop had been demolished by Julien's interruption. The smooth jazz background music had faded out and every speaker in his house had blasted a synthesized symphonic piece that could have accompanied a movie. It had been followed by an announcement that a genius was trying to reach him. Most people used a phone or computer connection to talk to people, but not Julien. And as Grant had discovered, keeping out the government was easier than keeping out Julien.

Julien had started their conversation with pleasantries, which, in retrospect, should have made Grant suspicious. Generally his friend made a blunt statement and waited for a response. This time, though, he'd told a story about one of his executives, about her broken engagement and how she needed to get away.

And it wasn't until Julien's question that Grant figured out that it somehow applied to him. Dumbfounded, he asked, "You want her to come here?"

"Putting together two of the smartest people in the company is a brilliant idea."

It sounded as if he'd rehearsed the comment.

"I don't run a bed-and-breakfast."

"I wasn't asking."

"No fucking way." Because he was a partner with Julien—one of his best friends—Grant tolerated a lot of crap. Generally though, he got more in return than he ever gave. But this...? Allowing someone into his home, his work space, his sanctuary? *No.* He barely tolerated Julien's impromptu—but mercifully short—visits.

The surround-sound speakers remained mute.

He wasn't stupid enough to think that meant Julien had accepted his response. "There's a reason I live near Los Alamos. Send your runaway bride somewhere else."

Julien's laughter filtered through the room. "Aria would chew off your balls for that description."

"You're not just interrupting my work, you're starting to piss me off."

"What time is it there?"

"How the hell would I know?" He looked out of a window and saw nothing except the reflection of the room. "Somewhere between dusk and dawn." Grant wasn't quite sure when that had happened. It'd been light the last time he looked.

A spasm rendered his neck immovable. He winced. But rather than waiting for it to pass, he pressed two fingers to the muscle—or was it a tendon?—and massaged it.

"It's after one a.m. in New Mexico," Julien said.

Was it? He looked at the time icon on the bottom of his screen. He'd been up since five this morning. No wonder his muscles were starting to freeze. "And?"

"I took a guess that you'd still be working."

"Tough shit if I had been trying to sleep," Grant remarked.

Julien didn't interrupt often. Most times, when he did, it was with good reason.

The two had met when they'd shared student housing at UT Austin. Like most of their buddies, they'd had a shared interest in coeds and parties, but their friendship went deeper. Over beers and games of pool, he and Julien had discussed ideas, products, ways to change the world.

They'd challenged each other's assumptions and beliefs. When Grant had an idea, Julien would ask a million questions. The result he'd end up with would be different—better—than where he'd started from.

Continuing the alliance after graduation had been natural.

If Julien was the visionary behind Bonds, Grant was its engineer. He'd drawn little salary in the early days, and he'd worked tirelessly to make Julien's visions a reality—still did. Not that the man needed much help. By all rights, he *was* a damn genius. But he needed a friend he trusted implicitly, who gnawed on a problem until it was solved.

"As I was saying—"

"Christ," Grant interrupted. "You didn't go away yet?"

"Pay attention," Julien said.

"I think I told you to fuck off. If I didn't, let me repeat. Fuck off. Send her somewhere else. She's not coming here."

As if Grant had never spoken, Julien continued, "Svetlana will have her there by about ten, maybe eleven. Make yourself presentable."

"Svetlana?" He felt a stupid grin forming on his face. His relationship with the sexy Russian ex-spy was hot and simple.

She had some interesting sexual demands, and he was happy to indulge every single one of them.

Theirs was an unusual friendship, defined by a unique code. They played with each other as long as neither of them was involved with someone else—no attachments, no emotion, no mess. It suited them both.

"Sorry, Grant. This is a touch-and-go."

Meaning Svetlana was delivering her passenger and leaving right away. His smile faded. He always loved having her at his mercy, on her knees.

"You'll get the chance to say hello when you meet Aria."

"I believe I told you no fucking way."

"You have a vehicle. Something big and mean, if I remember."

"Yeah." Tricked out with the latest gadgets, some of which didn't work exactly as hoped yet. "But I don't have time for company. Sorry."

"And I said that's not an option." Julien's voice was very quiet, uncompromising.

Grant dragged his hand across his face and got stubble burn. How long had it been since he'd shaved?

"I'm shutting down the hologram project."

He stared up at a speaker for long moments. Silence echoed back. Obviously Julien was waiting for his words to register.

Slowly at first, then bigger and faster, the ripples went through him. "What?"

"You heard me."

"Video on."

One entire wall had been filled with a soothing picture of his alma mater, the University of Texas at Austin. With barely a ripple, it flickered out and was replaced by an image of Julien holding a bottle of water, seated on a couch in his Cupertino office. As exhausted as Grant suddenly felt, Julien looked worse.

"You're working too hard." Julien's jaw was set in firm resolution.

Grant had seen that kind of intensity directed at others, but never at him.

"I mentioned that to you when we were at Reece's bachelor party," Julien continued. "I'd hoped Mexico would give you a break, encourage you to take a few days off. We waited for you at breakfast the last day, but Svetlana told me she'd flown you home the night before. We thought you were sleeping off a hangover. You were back at work."

"You're getting what you pay for," Grant said. Which was a seven-figure income plus an ownership percentage that was worth more every year.

"Not even close."

He blinked. "What the fuck?"

"I'm paying for the best of you, and I'm getting the dregs."

"That's a fucking unfair assessment, even from you."

"Is it?" Julien slid the water bottle onto the table in front of him. Other than that, he didn't react. "I need you to be fresh, creative, energized—an engineer who's aware of the world around him. I'm getting someone overworked, overextended, who doesn't know what day of the week it is."

"I do."

Julien waited.

"Thursday?"

"On the other side of the International Date Line, maybe." He recapped his bottle. "I tried to give you a vacation. In Mexico. With Svetlana. You wouldn't take it."

"We only have a few months before—"

"You're done."

Jesus. As if the tectonic plates had shifted, Grant reached for a table to hang onto. "You said we need something splashy for the show."

"And we'll have it."

Julien was giving him a fucking headache.

"We have more than one team working on production, so I'm not worried about it. But you and Aria are going to be going to the spring show. And you, Grant, will be doing a presentation."

Cold sweat arrowed down his spine.

"I will continue to do all the yearly debuts, but I need you to step it up. I need you, your help with store openings, some presentations overseas. This isn't a surprise. The logical time for you to step in is when we open the store at Kennedy's State Street Plaza building."

"We've discussed this before. Being in front of people, doing show-and-tell is not my forte."

"It needs to be. People want to see you, to meet you. And Aria is a great coach."

Grant tried again. "But the hologram—"

"Will not be presented. Period."

He met his friend's gaze. "You're serious?"

"Free up your brain. If ideas for the hologram come to you, you can work on it as inspiration strikes. But I want it to be fun for you. A diversion, not a deadline-driven monstrosity."

"We've invested months—"

"You're pushing a nut up a mountain with your nose."

He frowned. "What the hell does that mean?"

"I'm not sure," Julien admitted. "Sounded better in my head before it came out my mouth." He shrugged. "Bonds needs you—your creative energy—for the next fifty years. There's a difference between working on something that ignites you and something you're forcing."

"But now I have nothing to focus on."

"Representing Bonds is what you're going to work on. You'll be working with Aria. You'll like her. Smart. Sassy."

"I work alone."

Julien laced his hands behind his neck. Now he had a big fucking grin on his face.

The two had been friends long enough that Grant recognized Julien's look. The man thought he was being brilliant, as if he alone could see the mysteries of the universe, the way things clicked together to keep the planets in orbit.

"This should be interesting as she likes to be in charge, too."

Looking at his friend, Grant asked, "Does she know anything about me?"

"I didn't really have the words. So I figured I'd let you inform her."

"You're a world-class bastard, Julien."

"Only do something if you're going to be the best at it." He unlaced his hands and leaned forward. "You'll thank me later."

"I'm sure I will."

"Listen, Grant. You need to get out a little. Talk to people. Interact."

"You been reading self-help books again?"

"I never stopped." More seriously, he continued, "I shouldn't have let you live like a possum for years."

"Mole." As if anyone could have stopped him. Knowing he was losing, desperate not to, Grant forced his fingers to uncurl from the desk. "No stress there."

"Different kind of stress. This is the good kind. It'll fire you up." Julien rubbed his hands together in front of his face. "Light up all your cylinders. Enjoy your visitor. I need you, Grant. More than ever. The world… Nay, the universe"—Julien stretched his arms wide—"is yours to command."

"You really have lost your mind." For the first time, he wondered. Since he hated California and loved seclusion, he spent little time with Julien. Even though the back of his home was carved into a mountainside, rumors of Julien's odd behavior, weird eating habits and bizarre demands had reached him. He'd thought Julien cultivated that image to confound people. Now he wasn't sure.

"Keep Aria warm. She hates the snow."

Snow? Grant looked outside again. It was difficult to see with the flood of lights he had in his workshop, but at this time of year, it was conceivable that the white stuff was falling. "I'm starting to see your point. I'll go back to Mexico with Svetlana."

"That ship has sailed."

"Meaning I had my chance?"

"Meaning she's met someone."

He rocked back on his heels. "Someone better than me?"

"Imagine that."

"He's not scared of her?"

"Terrified."

"Those legs." Reputedly, she could break a man's neck.

"I'm not afraid to say I'm a bit careful around her myself," Julien confessed.

"That's part of why you like her."

"I adore women who frighten me." With a wave of his hand, as if it were a magic wand, Julien vanished.

The sudden silence rang in Grant's ears.

Ten minutes ago, every area of his life had seemed secure. Now… Nothing.

Svetlana had moved on. They'd only had an occasional, hot, mind-numbing, tongue-lolling hook-up. It was enough to sustain him for weeks. Months. And one time, even a year.

Genuinely, he was happy for her. Everyone deserved someone. More than he, she yearned for something to complete her. He was lucky he'd been able to play with her as often as he had.

But that, coupled with Julien's pronouncement that Grant was off his pet project, cast him adrift for the first time since he'd left college. He'd always known what the next logical step was in his professional life. Suddenly he wasn't even sure where the floor was.

Now he was expected to take in one of Julien's strays, work with her, disrupt his solitude and his life.

At a loss, he told the computer to save his work before lowering a screen over the large sheet of glass he'd been using for his mathematical equations.

Then he wandered around his workshop, running his fingers over circuit boards, an ancient computer, screwdrivers, wires, precious metals, glass made from sapphires, from diamonds, all the things that made his heart beat.

What now?

Julien might have a point, Grant realized. He wasn't fit for human company. Truthfully he hadn't interacted with many people in the past few years, not since he'd moved—escaped—to New Mexico. He didn't have a group of friends and the only people he saw regularly were those at his favorite restaurant, the grocery store clerks and his housekeeper. Each Tuesday, Daniella swept in like a mini tornado, cleaning, doing laundry, clucking over his lack of companionship, singing as she prepared a few dishes, stocking the kitchen with fresh produce and talking incessantly.

He realized now that he often went for days without talking to another person.

And Julien had decided to change that.

Fuck. How long was Aria staying? At some point, Julien's words had all blurred together, and Grant hadn't heard any of them.

He strode to the console in the corner, pushed the buttons to reconnect with Julien.

The man's voice reverberated through the room. *"The genius is offline. If you've reached this message, you should be too. Unless this is the President of the United States, call back tomorrow. If it is the President of the United States, I would have already been expecting your call so you wouldn't have reached this message. So whoever you are, go the fuck to sleep."* His voice was replaced by soothing music. A lullaby?

Good God.

Grant checked his smart watch. It was too late to call Daniella, but he could text her and ask her to make up the guest room first thing in the morning. Or… "Molly," he said to the home's computer, "remind me to send a message to Daniella to make up the guest room."

"Of course, Your Majesty."

"I'm going to reprogram you if you keep calling me that."

"You always say that, but you never touch my buttons. And I gave up on the knobs months ago."

"Has Julien been in the system again?"

"Genius is as genius does."

He shook his head to clear the gathering headache. Then

he thought about food. He'd have to consider someone other than himself. No doubt she'd want to eat at regular intervals whereas he ate as, and if, the mood struck.

Irritation made his blood pressure rise.

What the hell did he know about having company?

That thought was less important than the next one. *How quickly can I get rid of her?*

Knowing he needed to release tension, he placed his palm against the metal hand plate. The door slid open, and he touched the plate on the outside to close it again.

"I'm done for the day," he informed the computer.

"It's night," Molly corrected.

"So I've been told. Power save mode." Meaning the air conditioning would keep the area at a precise temperature and humidity, and that computers and other electronics would go on standby.

Grant crouched to look at the dog sleeping peacefully beneath a window. They'd been partners for six months. He supposed that, at some point, he should give the pooch a name.

He walked down the hallway. Exercise was Grant's medication, and often, swimming provided the juice to ignite his creativity and help him find his Zen space.

He opened the door to the workout area and instructed Molly to give him forty percent lighting. "Make that thirty," he amended. It was a trick, to make his body think he should actually go to sleep. At the very least, he hoped it would help him shove aside the thoughts worming through his brain.

After grabbing a towel, he walked past the free weights and cardio equipment into the pool area. As always, the sight of the vast New Mexico night sky soothed in a way that nothing else could.

He stripped before diving into the invigorating coolness

and cutting through the water. Generally he lost track of reality and swam past exhaustion into a feeling of peace.

But tonight none of his tricks worked.

The impending arrival of an unwanted houseguest and the knowledge he had been removed from his favorite project unraveled him.

Grant pulled himself from the pool and headed for the hot tub. "Give me bubbles, Molly," he instructed, too lazy to work the control himself.

This time, she did as he said without comment.

As heat seeped into him, his muscles began to relax. He realized that exhaustion was crawling through him, from the inside out.

He refused to admit that he might be stuck, that spending this much time away from other people might not keep him at his sharpest. He'd never intended the move to the Los Alamos area to be permanent, but at the time, getting away had seemed like the only solution. The longer he'd stayed, the less inclined he'd been to return to the city lights, noises, stimulations.

Grant still didn't want to concede Julien's point, even when he went to bed and slept for five blissfully uninterrupted hours for the first time in months.

When Grant had closed his eyes, stars had been winking on an inky sky. Now, muted orange and pinks blended together.

For a minute he simply stared, seeing it as if for the first time.

Part of the appeal of this area was for the wide-open spaces and sky that seemed to go on forever. Absently he wondered when he'd stopped seeing them.

His good mood lasted through his tall, cold glass of

filtered water. Then he remembered he had to pick up his unexpected guest from the airport.

Christ. What time had Julien said he needed to be there?

He grabbed his cell phone. His calendar had been updated by Julien. *Surprise.* And the man had added a personal note —*Be nice to Aria.*

The words were a mandate, Grant knew—one that wasn't going to be easy to follow.

Or so he'd thought.

He arrived at the airport in time to see the Tornado land in all its glory.

The door opened, the airstairs deployed then Aria stepped from the plane.

All of Grant's expectations fractured, as if they were an icicle that slammed onto the concrete.

When he'd thought of her as a runaway bride who didn't like the cold, he'd mentally prepared himself for someone nervous-looking, maybe huddled in a parka, curled up into herself.

Instead...

Instead, this woman had her shoulders back and held her spine regally straight. And she looked down at him as if she owned the planet.

Wind whipped her brunette hair around her face. She wore a tight-fitting black jacket, an indecently short skirt, tights, and spiked-heel boots that went up and up until they disappeared under her hem.

She was temptation and sin wrapped in a tall, fuckable package.

Every male instinct in him flared, and Grant almost tripped over his own libido.

CHAPTER TWO

Aria paused at the top of the airstairs. The man leaning against the side of a nearby SUV stunned her. *Grant Kingston.*

A supple brown leather bomber jacket snuggled his upper body. His jeans were a slightly faded shade of blue, and he wore motorcycle boots. The wind tossed a dark blond lock of hair over his forehead.

As he pushed away from the vehicle and strode toward the plane, he pulled off his sunglasses and placed them on top of his head.

His approach was purposeful.

She adjusted the duffel bag on her shoulder and tightened her grip on her briefcase before descending to the tarmac. She told herself her legs were bit wobbly from sitting next to Svetlana and seeing, up close, how challenging the landing was with the airport's infamous crosswinds. But the truth was, the idea of being in intimate proximity with a man this good-looking for any length of time unnerved her.

After she'd returned home last night, she'd spent an hour online looking up stories about him. For someone who was such a prominent part of the Bonds conglomerate, there were surprisingly few.

He'd received requisite mentions in the business and tech sections, but she saw the same photographs many times, which likely meant the news sources all used the same stock photos.

She'd scoured social media. It didn't appear that he had his own accounts, but she saw a handful of snapshots on Julien's pages. There'd been one at his friend Reece's wedding. Grant had been standing with the groom, Julien and Kennedy Aldrich.

There'd also been an older shot at Julien's birthday party, and the four friends were sporting neon-colored athletic shoes. None of the shots had been a close-up.

On the flight over, Aria had been nosy, asking Svetlana about Grant. The other woman had mysteriously said that he could be intense and liked to be in charge. Intrigued, Aria had pressed for more. Svetlana had said it would take a very special woman to be everything Grant needed. She'd hinted that the two of them had been a bit more than friends, but there had never been anything serious between them.

When Aria had pressed for more information, Svetlana had given one of her famous half-smiles and wished Aria luck finding out for herself. Purposefully, Svetlana had checked the altimeter then changed the subject to talk about her continuing trip to New York to meet with her future husband.

The conversation had left Aria frustrated. The more she'd tried to find out about Grant, the more he seemed like an enigma.

Nothing she'd seen or heard had prepared her for seeing him in person. A shiver ran through her. His features had an old-world ruggedness and his shoulders were impossibly wide. He was more masculine than she'd imagined, more commanding.

"Welcome to New Mexico." His voice was deep, friendly, reassuring, making her insides turn somersaults.

Her immediate, consuming attraction to him surprised her. "Grant Kingston, I presume?"

"At your service."

Even around successful, handsome men, Aria had always been completely confident. Until today. "I didn't expect you to come yourself."

"I'm the only Bonds employee in Los Alamos. You know Julien wouldn't have allowed me to send anyone else. And after everything Julien said about you, I was anxious to meet you. And I'm glad I came." He smiled.

The full power of its seducing effect smacked her. A feminine part of her melted in instinctive recognition. The sensation was as unusual as it was unwelcome.

"I've heard a few things about you, too." And it had made last night's sleep more than a little restless. If her guess was right, she wouldn't rest any easier tonight.

He extended his hand.

She slid her palm against his and found his hand big, his touch warm, reassuring. Nothing could have prepared her for the impact he'd had on her.

Grant held her hand a bit longer than socially acceptable. Maybe it was because of what Julien and Svetlana had said, but she was very much aware of Grant's strength and power. Aria's heart thudded, and she pulled back her palm so she wouldn't be tempted to stay forever.

He was smiling, but she thought there might be something slightly predatory beneath the welcome.

Aria lowered her sunglasses.

Since they stood so close, she noticed how deep and blue his eyes were, reminding her of an arctic lake. And damn, he smelled good. She inhaled the scent of his leather jacket, certainly, but there was more. Musk was layered in, along with the crisp rawness of the outdoors.

Mostly, he radiated power and confidence. To make things clear to both of them, she added, "Thanks for having me. I can't imagine you're happy about having an unwanted houseguest."

"Turns out I might not mind it as much as I thought I might."

Each word had been dragged across sandpaper. For a moment, just a wicked moment, she imagined him whispering her name as he unfastened her shirt.

Aria shook her head to clear it. No doubt she was attracted to him, and he'd made it clear it was mutual, but that didn't mean anything. She was a professional businesswoman, and she had never slept with anyone she'd worked with. She wouldn't allow Grant Kingston to be the first… even if she had to constantly remind herself of that fact. "I'm good at taking care of myself, so you won't need to go out of your way to entertain me. I'll be a good houseguest."

"I'm sure you will."

An airport employee removed Aria's one big suitcase from the jet and hauled it toward the SUV.

"Can I help you with your briefcase or the other bag?" Grant asked.

"Actually, the duffel is for you."

"For me?"

"Svetlana asked me to give it to you. She said it's a gift from Julien."

"In that case, I'll definitely take it. God only knows what's in it."

"Oh? You've made me curious."

"I'll guarantee it would scare the boots right off your feet."

"Now I've got to see."

"No doubt whips, chains, handcuffs."

"You're not serious." She looked at him, unsure whether or not he was joking. And if he wasn't, what then? "Handcuffs?"

"Do you always rush into danger?"

Her pulse missed a beat. "Is that what I'm doing?"

"Yeah. Consider yourself warned."

Was that a statement or a dare? She shivered, and not from the cold, but rather from the anticipation his words sent through her.

He took the bag.

Svetlana headed down the stairs, preventing further conversation.

Despite the watery sunlight, there was no mistaking the wink of the diamond on her left hand or the way Grant looked at it.

Realizing they'd probably appreciate a minute alone, Aria said, "If you'll excuse me, I'll make sure my suitcase gets loaded properly."

"Give me a minute and I'll do it for you," Grant replied.

"I've got it."

"I promise to return the moment the genius gives his approval," Svetlana said to Aria.

Aria glanced at the frozen tundra. "Keep the plane fueled up because I want to get back into my sandals." After another quick thank you to Svetlana, Aria met the airport employee at the car.

The man slid the suitcase in the back of the SUV, and she kept her briefcase with her.

Since Grant had thoughtfully left the engine running, she cranked up the vehicle's heater. Then she grabbed her purse from the briefcase, pulled out her phone and sent a text message to her parents to let them know she'd arrived safely.

As warmth gusted from the vents, she checked the GPS to

get her bearings. No matter how often she traveled, she still got disoriented in an unfamiliar city.

She glanced up in time to see Grant give Svetlana a quick salute before turning and walking toward the vehicle. Svetlana jogged back up the airstairs, obviously anxious to be on her way to her fiancé.

Even before Grant had stowed his duffel on the backseat, the airplane's main entry door had been closed.

"Comfortable?" he asked as he slid behind the wheel.

"I turned up the heat."

"I may have to start taking off clothes."

That wouldn't be all bad.

He fingered a button next to her. "Seat warmer," he explained before checking the surroundings and heading toward the exit. He stopped in front of the security gate and waited for it to slide open.

Within a few seconds, they had turned from Airport Road onto East Road. Everywhere she looked, they were surrounded by mountains, plateaus and a seemingly endless covering of white. The sky, though, sizzled with brightness.

"It's called the Land of Enchantment," he said, with obvious pride.

"I'm not sure why with the cold and snow and gloom. I'm not sure I can even breathe. Just walking to the car left me gasping for air." At least that was her excuse.

"We're a little more than seven thousand feet above sea level," he agreed.

"Almost a mile and a half?"

"You'll acclimate."

She put her head back, but there was no part of her body that was relaxed.

"Roads aren't that icy."

"I'm not concerned about that," she admitted. But that's as

far as she'd take that conversation. "Are we making any stops before we go to your cave?"

"Cave?"

"Ah..."

He waited.

"That wasn't nice." Aria squirmed a little. "I've been told it's a very nice cave."

"It's not bad. Quite livable, in fact."

"I didn't mean to insult you."

He slid her a sideways glance. "I'm wondering what other preconceived notions you have."

She could change the subject, she knew. Make it about business, talk about the weather—or she could find out a thing or two about him. "I thought you'd be a nerd."

"A nerd?" His response was perfect, light, non-confrontational. Friendly. "Does anyone really use that word anymore?"

"Okay. How about geek?"

"You're not apologizing very well."

"I'm not, am I?" She sighed. "Actually, I wasn't even trying."

"In addition to living dangerously, you say what you're thinking."

"I meant that you're not what I expected."

"So I'm not a geek?"

She finger-combed a few stray wisps of hair back from her face. "You probably are. But only in the best sense of the word."

"Now I'm really interested."

"Oh Lord. I mean brainiac." She unzipped her coat a little, and not just because the seat wrapped around her like a warm blanket. "That's a good thing, isn't it? It means you're brilliant. Inquisitive."

"Which makes you astute."

Unable to help herself, she grinned at him.

"And you're right. I thought we should eat and pick up whatever necessities you need from the grocery store before we head home."

Home sounded far too intimate. "It's not too late for me to get a rental car and hotel." The town had a handful, she knew, and a couple were more than suitable for a long-term visit.

"Do you really want to drive back and forth? More snow's due. May make roads challenging—if not impassable—in the next few days. All that could delay us. I think part of Julien's strategy is that we're more likely to interact creatively if we're not constrained by work hours and if we have time for spontaneous interaction."

Spontaneous interaction. She wondered if he'd added the emphasis to the words or if she'd imagined it.

But his argument was sound. If they were snowed in, better it be together than with her stranded in a hotel room across town. "You're right."

"Breakfast?" he offered.

She wondered what went with a side of simmering sensuality. "Is there coffee on the menu?"

"Regular *and* piñon."

"Piñon?"

"It's local. Made from pine nuts."

"Sounds…interesting."

"I thought you were going to live dangerously while you were here." He parallel parked in front of the building then turned off the engine. "Might as well get started. I'll keep your secrets."

Damn. This man was dangerous.

While she slipped her phone into her purse, he came around and opened the vehicle door. "Thanks," she said. "I'm quite capable of doing that myself."

"I'm sure you are."

Though she wouldn't admit it to him, or even herself, she appreciated the courtesy. A sudden wind gusted around them, shattering the moment. No doubt the weather predictions were accurate, and she zipped up her coat.

She preceded him into the restaurant.

A number of enticing scents wrapped around her. Eggs. Bacon. Green chile. *And, yes there is a God,* coffee. "I love it." She surveyed the scarred black-and-white checkered-linoleum tiles on the floor. A portion of one wall was decorated with broken pieces of cups and plates, designed and glued in a mosaic style. Other walls had family photos and scenic landscapes.

There were a couple of dozen tables in the dining room.

"It's been here since World War II. The Montoya family has owned it the entire time."

"Hey, handsome!" a woman called out. "Sit anywhere. I'll be right with you."

He waved in acknowledgment then picked up a menu from the front counter and led Aria to a booth near the window.

She shrugged, unzipped her coat and tried not to stare as he shrugged from his.

He wore a long-sleeved navy shirt that made his eyes look even more startling.

Aria had sworn off men, and it was a good thing. He was definitely the type of man to whom she was attracted. Tall. Rugged. Independent. Assertive. Damn it. Damn Julien.

As soon as they sat, the woman slid a mug of steaming coffee in front of Grant. That he didn't need to order showed Aria he was a regular.

"A hundred thousand blessings on you," he said.

Another thing they had in common. Love of the almighty brew.

"Blanca," he said after taking a sip. "I'd like to introduce my colleague, Aria DeWitt."

"Do you also work for Mr. Bonds?" Blanca asked Aria.

"I do. You've met him?"

"A few times. He's...delicious."

"Delicious?" Aria repeated. Clearly the woman was attracted to Julien. And who wouldn't be?

"I mean he's interesting."

"Now *that's* an understatement," Aria said.

"He says he only works with smart people who are able to solve problems."

The compliment made her suspicious. "Why do I feel as if I'm being set up here?" Aria shot a glance in Grant's direction.

"I have nothing to do with it." He took a drink then sat back.

Aria was very much aware of his gaze, as if he were watching the way she interacted with his friend.

"I need a program for my phone that lets me sync responsibilities with other people in my family and in the business."

Because of her position at Bonds, Aria didn't get to interact with end users the way she would like, and this opportunity thrilled her. Leaning forward, she invited, "Tell me more."

"*Mi abuela* takes seven or eight different medications. She has physical therapy, doctors' appointments and she needs to run personal errands, like grocery shopping and going to the beauty salon. Family members spend a lot of time calling each other to see if someone picked up meds at the pharmacy, who is taking her to see the doctor, does she have follow-up visits scheduled...that sort of thing." Blanca exhaled a whiff of breath. "Then with the restaurant. Did we get food ordered? When is it scheduled to arrive? Who's opening? Who's closing? Whose turn is it to roast the chiles? It gets complicated."

"So it's more than just a calendar you can all access?"

"It's for the business. It's for our family members. Yes."

"Let me think about it," Aria said. "Checklists. Accessible by a number of people. Real-time synchronization. Reminders. Notes." She nodded as ideas formed and coalesced. This was the type of challenge she loved. If she could figure it out, she could make a real difference in people's lives. "Maybe the ability to add handwritten entries."

Aria pulled out her oversized phone, removed the stylus from the side then tapped open an app and scrawled ideas on the screen. "Can I get your contact information?"

Blanca gave it, and Aria entered it into her address book.

"I'll have something for you in the next couple of weeks."

"Thank you," Blanca said. "Can I get you something to drink? Coffee?"

"I'd take a pot of it," she admitted.

"Piñon?"

"I…"

"Try mine," Grant offered.

Sharing was intimate, maybe more so than she wanted to be. He slid the cup toward her. A bit reluctantly, she wrapped her hand around the cup. Before tasting the brew, she wrinkled her nose.

"Her first visit to New Mexico, I think," Grant said.

"It is," Aria acknowledged.

"Wait till we get some agave in her," Blanca teased.

"Agave?"

"Otherwise known as tequila," Grant supplied. "Try the coffee."

She took a drink. The dark brew wasn't as bitter as she expected, and it did have a slightly nutty flavor. "It's different."

"I can get you a cup of that or I can bring a Colombian roast."

"Live dangerously," Grant reminded her.

"Okay. I'll have the piñon," Aria agreed.

"I recommend *huevos rancheros* for breakfast," Grant said before Blanca left. "And we could take home some tamales."

"I'm not sure I've had either, but I'm willing to try."

"Eggs over -medium?"

Aria nodded, and he told Blanca, "Two of them."

"You don't have an electronic system?" Aria asked when Blanca scribbled down the order.

"We're still old fashioned." Blanca shrugged.

"Are you interested?"

"We looked into it once. It was too expensive."

"What's expensive is the kitchen misunderstanding orders—or running out of products."

Blanca winced and looked at Grant. "Speaking of that, I sold the last piece of sour cherry apple pie last night."

He put his hand over his heart. "But I live for it."

"I bet Ms. DeWitt can keep you going." Blanca pocketed her pad.

"I'm here for work."

"Oh. I thought..."

"No," Aria said firmly. No matter how tempting, she refused to consider the idea. "We're coworkers, nothing more. But I might be able to help you out. Imagine this... You enter the order directly on your phone. The kitchen receives it before you leave the table. The inventory system is alerted and tracks the reorder point. You could allow your customers to swipe their credit card on your phone, or better yet, they could use a payment system, if they'd rather. Unless they want to, people won't need to wait in line to pay at the front cash register."

"Just think," Grant told Blanca, "if you were using Aria's ordering system, our food would already be on its way."

"You're hungry? Sorry," Blanca said insincerely.

"And I'd be enjoying a second cup of coffee."

"Some customers had better leave a really big tip."

Aria grinned at the exchange between the two of them.

Without another word, Blanca scooted off.

Having breakfast in the restaurant allowed Aria to see Grant interact with other people. He was obviously at ease with Blanca, in a casual place. And with the way they joked, it was obvious he was well regarded. All of a sudden, he wasn't just an enigma or adversary, but a fully formed person with a sense of humor that she appreciated.

After delivering the coffee, Blanca hustled over to the kitchen, ripped the top piece of paper from her pad, affixed it to a rickety-looking metal wheel and spun it toward the kitchen as she shouted, "Order up!"

"We can make the process so much easier for them," Aria observed.

"You'll lose all this character if you convert them to an electronic system."

"You're sounding crotchety, and not at all what I would expect from a technical guru." Aria touched the send button on her phone then slid her stylus back into its spot. "You should be thinking about what they'll gain, rather than what we'll lose. Add Internet ordering, even an app. People can call ahead, order online and have their food ready when they arrive. Like in the big city."

"Do you attack all problems like this?"

"I don't like to waste time or opportunities." She wrapped her hands around the coffee mug and pulled it toward her. "I love working on practical applications," she said. "Ways to make life better, easier for people. Don't misunderstand. I love flashy things, gadgets, but for me, my heart is in those small things that you realize you can't live without."

He nodded. "Nothing wrong with flashy things."

A server slid a basket of chips and a dish of salsa onto the table.

"Like the hologram project?"

He'd been reaching for a chip, but he lowered his hand. "What do you know about the hologram project?"

"Not much. I'm told it's stalled. I've heard there's some real-world challenges with it." She regarded him.

"It has practical applications," he said, sounding a little defensive. "Have you seen Julien enter a meeting via hologram yet?"

She shook her head. "But there are Laws of Physics, relativity, that sort of stuff."

"Minor constraints."

He was like a man possessed. Suddenly she saw why Julien was concerned.

"No matter what he says, he's not going to be able to live without it."

"It's fun. It's a diversion. Maybe it should stay that way."

"I've spent months on it."

She understood his frustration, especially if a solution felt close. She also knew the danger of staying with a project too long.

Blanca arrived with their meals, scattering the tension.

"Is it rude to dip my tortilla in the egg?" Aria asked.

"Yes. Unconscionably," he said.

"It's perfectly fine," Blanca corrected. "Don't listen to him."

But he was grinning as he tore a strip from his tortilla.

"See?" Blanca asked.

Aria ate every single bite of her meal. "Okay, so I'm starting to see the appeal of New Mexico."

"*Sopapillas* or flan for dessert?" Blanca asked, returning to scoop up the empty plates. "Maybe some *tres leches* cake?"

"I'm not sure what that is."

"Literally? Three milks. It's *mi abuela's* recipe. We make it with sweetened condensed milk, evaporated milk and cream."

Even though she'd already eaten, Aria's mouth watered. "All that calcium has to be good for my bones."

"Two forks?" Blanca asked.

"One," Grant responded.

Blanca went behind a counter, and Aria watched the woman cut one of the biggest slices she'd ever seen.

"No one has dessert after breakfast," Grant protested when the plate was placed in front of her.

"We're living dangerously, remember? And I never pass up the opportunity to eat on someone else's expense account."

"Who said I'm buying?"

"No one. I'm putting it on my Bonds' credit card," she said with a grin. "When Julien gets the bill for this trip, he'll think twice about making me leave California at this time of the year." Then she added a quart of green chile and a dozen tortillas to go along with Grant's tamale order. "Julien is buying all that, too."

After she'd polished off the last bite, Grant looked at her over the rim of his coffee cup. "Where do you put it all?"

There was no mistaking the expression of appreciation in his gaze. She hadn't been wrong about the pulse of attraction she felt earlier.

She knew she carried a few extra pounds, but it seemed he either didn't notice or care—or maybe he even appreciated it. "I exercise. Some would say compulsively."

"I've got a workout room at my place."

Judging by the size of his biceps, he used the equipment.

To distract herself, she wriggled back into her jacket and didn't look his direction.

At the front register, she paid the bill and promised to stay in touch with Blanca.

As she was already coming to expect, he opened the vehicle's door for her before putting their to-go order in the back, near that curiosity-inducing duffel bag.

"We have a co-op and a regular grocery store." He checked the rearview mirror. "Which do you prefer?"

"Does the co-op have junk food?"

"The grocery store it is."

She filled the cart with cereal, cookies, potato chips, her favorite double caffeine, high-sugar soda, two more bags of coffee and a container of artificially flavored creamer.

"Pumpkin pie spice?" he asked.

She plucked a second one from the shelf. "And vanilla latte. Don't tell me... Your body's a temple. You never put anything sugared, artificially sweetened or laced with preservatives in it."

"Do you eat anything good for you?" he countered when she stopped in front of the frozen food section.

"I've got to keep up my energy." She grabbed a double pepperoni pizza.

"Vegetables and meat give you energy."

"I thought we were planning on working. And by the way, I really don't cook."

"I do."

"You...cook?"

"Not always. Rarely, in fact. But I can manage something. Put the pizza back."

"I don't think you understand. It has cheese in the crust."

He plucked the brightly colored carton from her hands.

"Wait. It's comfort food."

"You can eat as many of them as you want when you get back to California." He shuddered.

"Are you always so damn bossy?"

"Aria, you have no idea." With that, he took hold of the cart and wheeled it toward the produce section.

"I don't eat asparagus," she said when he reached for a bunch of the green, sword-like stalks.

"You haven't had it prepared well, in that case."

He picked up lettuce, specialty cheeses, olives and a gorgeous-looking loaf of bread before heading to the checkout lanes.

When they had loaded up the car, he asked, "Anything else you need?"

"Wine?"

"We've got plenty."

"In that case, I might survive for a few days."

He drove away from the city and into the surrounding mountain area.

"It's quiet here," she observed about fifteen minutes later. The homes were more spread out, and they passed fewer and fewer cars.

"Peaceful," he agreed.

Her cell signal bars had faded to nothing before he turned off the road and onto a narrow paved driveway that sloped down then appeared to vanish around a corner. She didn't see a house, just a random tree, some cactus, and lots of rock and potential for a sharp drop down the sheer mountainside. "Ah…"

"Relax. It's not as death-defying as it appears."

She gripped the handle in front of her.

"I installed grappling hooks to the undercarriage. They'll grab the rock so we don't fall off the road."

"I'm not sure if you're kidding."

"About which part?"

No more than thirty seconds later he braked to a stop in front of a set of metal gates. They were set into a thick adobe fence with a rounded top. The gates were teal in color with spikes jutting out from a figure that resembled a humped-back flute player.

"Kokopelli," he said when she asked about it. A moment later, the gates swung open. "Along with the sun found on our state flag, you'll see a lot of him in New Mexico. He's a Hopi god, if I have my anthropology correct. He represents fertility."

"You're making that up."

"Am I?"

From his tone, she had no idea whether or not he was joking.

Grant drove through the opening into a large courtyard and she saw his house for the first time. It, too, was adobe, light tan in color. The home had a slight curve to it so it conformed more naturally to the surroundings. A number of narrow floor-to-ceiling windows added a unique touch.

"Not bad for a cave?" he asked, his voice light with a tease.

She felt a blush creep up her cheeks. "I apologized for that comment—or at least I think I did."

"You shouldn't have. The house is built partially into the mountain."

"It's spectacular, Grant." Off to right side was an outdoor living area with a tall, concrete fountain and several seating areas, complete with lounge chairs and assorted-sized tables. Several planters were filled with small trees and perhaps lavender.

As the gates eased closed behind them, she felt as if they were being sealed off from the rest of the world.

He parked in front of a detached two-car garage. "Let's go in, get you out of the wind. I'll come back for your luggage."

"And your duffel bag?"

"Definitely that."

After zipping up her jacket, she grabbed her briefcase and a couple of grocery bags before following him across flagstones toward the intricately carved double doors. Two lighting sconces flanked the entrance, each bearing a weathered-metal Kokopelli.

Without him touching anything, she heard a lock turn. "I'm confused," she said.

"I like my security to be unobtrusive. Retina scan."

"Wait… I didn't see you do anything at the gates. Do they just open automatically?"

He shook his head. "There's a sensor on the undercarriage of the car."

"Near the grappling hooks."

"Exactly." He grinned and indicated she should enter. "We'll get your vitals scanned."

"Ah…"

"Or I can give you a key." He closed the door behind them, and she heard the lock fall back into place.

"Hi, honey! You're home."

Aria couldn't make out where the woman's voice was coming from, even though she looked around.

"Aria, say hello to Molly."

"Molly?"

"My electronic assistant. She controls all the functions in the house. You can tell her what to do and she'll do it."

"Within reason," Molly responded. *"I don't do laundry. The washer agitates me."*

He groaned.

"Your sense of humor, I take it?" Aria asked. "It needs some work."

"Molly, say hello to our guest."

"Helllllllo, Genius," the disembodied voice with a sexy hint of an Irish brogue all but purred. *"I missed you."*

"Programmed for Julien. Sorry. Molly, say hello to Aria."

"Oh. I apologize. So the genius hasn't come to save me yet?"

"Molly…say hello to Aria."

"Isn't that a musical term?"

"Very good, Molly. And spelled the same way. But in this case, it's my guest's name."

"Oh. Hello, Aria. Welcome to Kingston Castle."

"Kingston Castle?" Aria grinned when she saw him wince. The more she saw of Grant, and his idiosyncrasies, the more she liked him.

"That's our secret, Molly. What are you supposed to do with things that are secret?"

"Oh. I know. Sorry." Then, in a whisper, she repeated, *"Welcome to Kingston Castle."*

He shook his head. "I'm about to shut you down," he threatened.

"Touchy, touchy, Your Majesty."

Given the amount of time she'd spent at Bonds headquarters, Aria knew she should no longer be shocked by the toys and gadgets the company dreamed up, but this was a whole new level of electronic interaction. And because Molly had a personality, Aria found it more charming than intrusive. That could be the key, she realized, to moving the technology forward. It needed to be integrated, easy to interact with and it would be especially appealing if it was also fun.

When they'd entered the house, it had been into a large, open space. Several hooks hung from the wall, and a wooden table stood nearby, and next to it, a large yellow Labrador. "You didn't tell me you had a dog." Its tail wagged. "What's his name?"

"He doesn't have one."

"What? Dogs are supposed to have names." She bent to pet the animal, but her hand passed through the air without stopping.

"Hologram," he explained before she could ask.

"He looks so real."

"Thank you."

"That's a little freaky," she said.

"But he doesn't eat or need to go outside. You're welcome to leave your briefcase

She took a moment to drink in her surroundings. The kitchen appeared to be off to the left, and a table with six chairs was in front of it. A couple of banks of windows comprised most of the far wall, and they were separated by a gigantic fireplace. The ceilings were vaulted, and she guessed they were fifteen feet high at the tallest spots.

Warm honey hardwood floors were accented with large, Southwestern-inspired throw rugs, and a leather sectional couch was arranged in front of the hearth.

"Molly, open the blinds."

By slow measures, the windows were revealed.

Everything seemed to draw Aria's gaze toward the awe-inspiring grandeur of the outdoors. "Good heavens."

"That was my reaction, as well, the first time I walked in."

The view of the snow-dusted plateaus stole her breath, and it seemed as if the house dangled from the side of the mountain. "Land of Enchantment," she said, understanding what he'd meant earlier. She looked at him in time to see his smile.

"Yeah," he said. "Now you get it."

"It's awe-inspiring."

"It is indeed." He nodded. "This way."

As she took the first couple of steps into the house, a wave of vertigo washed over her. "Tell me that's optical illusion."

"You're not going to fall," he promised, "but the view is not an optical illusion. We're anchored to granite. The couple who had this built hired a brilliant architect and a well-respected engineering firm."

"It's spectacular."

"There's a deck through that sliding glass door."

Since the deck had glass walls, she hadn't noticed it right away. "I'm not sure I'm brave enough."

"You can always sit in the courtyard." He grinned. "You wouldn't be the first. Let me show you the kitchen then I'll get the rest of the things from the car."

She followed him. The space was larger than she'd guessed, galley-style with quartz countertops and a bar separating it from the dining area. The way it was designed meant that even the cooktop offered a view out of the windows.

For the first time in months, she felt as if she could truly breathe, not just physically, but mentally. Being here, in the grandeur and peace, was already changing her.

"I'm really not sure how you get anything done," she said. "I could sit and stare for hours."

"I don't always take the time to appreciate it. I should." He placed his bags on the countertop and she put a couple alongside them.

He pointed out the location of glasses and mugs, along with the coffeepot. "Since you're going to be here for an indefinite amount of time, you'll want to make yourself comfortable. Help yourself to anything you want, including the wine. I'm not particular. I buy what I want to drink, so I'm not saving any for a special occasion. Can I offer you anything?"

"Water, please. I think it's the altitude." Along with the view and the very sexy man she was temporarily staying with.

He grabbed a bottle for her and uncapped it. "Yeah. I know you can do it yourself."

"Am I that bad?"

"You are."

Maybe she was, she realized. And perhaps it was okay to accept help from time to time. "In that case, I'll say thank you."

Their gazes met and held for a few seconds as he passed the drink to her. A connection arced, formed. And she forced herself to look away rather than lean into it.

"I'll be right back with your luggage." Before she could protest, he added, "No, you don't need to help."

While he was gone, she walked toward a window then retreated a few steps. Aria had never been afraid of heights. She told herself it was no different from being in a skyscraper, but the illusion of hanging off the side of a mountain changed something for her, even though the trepidation wasn't logical.

She took a drink of water before putting the bottle down and going back to the foyer. As she was hanging up her coat, she heard him outside. The knob jostled, so she opened the door for him.

The dog began to wag its tail again. She wasn't sure how long it would take to get used to that.

Grant came inside, accompanied by a burst of cold air.

"I don't think anyone's ever let me in my own house before," he said.

"You said to make myself comfortable."

"I'm glad you did."

Grant was creating an air or intimacy that she'd never experienced with another man. It told her she'd been right to cancel the wedding, despite all the upset and doubts.

He left her belongings in the foyer then she accompanied him back to the kitchen to help put away the groceries and takeout food.

When they were finished, he said, "Let me show you the

rest of the house, give you a chance to get settled."

After hanging up his jacket, he grabbed her suitcase and his duffel bag before leading the way down the hall. She could become accustomed to his chivalry.

"As you've already surmised, the house is more of a rectangle than a square. And not just for the view, but to cut down the wind exposure."

She nodded. "It seems the builder thought of every detail."

He pointed out a powder room, then added, "I remodeled a little in order to accommodate the exercise room and my workshop. So there are only two bedrooms. This one is yours."

He opened the door and wheeled her suitcase into the closet.

The space was bigger than her master bedroom at home.

"You've got blinds and a blackout panel to keep out the sun if you want to sleep in."

A queen-sized bed stood on a thick white rug and was flanked by two nightstands. A small television was mounted to the wall. An upholstered chaise longue had a reading lamp nearby. "It's lovely," she said. "Any electronic surprises I should know about?"

"If I spy on you, it will be the old-fashioned way."

"Does the door have a lock?"

"Spoilsport." But his grin was easy and contagious. "Let me show you the rest. You can use this bathroom."

As she'd come to expect, it was nice, using local stone and accented with the turquoise-blue that she already associated with New Mexico.

The stall was large enough for two people, and she didn't see a showerhead.

"More like a rainfall," he explained, answering her unasked question. "Lots of holes in the top. The towel rack will heat up the moment you turn on the water. And the temperature and pressure control is right here. Waterproof. Select your temperature. Molly will tell you when it's the right temperature. It won't take long, since we have a tankless heater."

So maybe Julien wasn't completely without feeling. This punishment came with a few niceties.

"Exercise room is next. Lights on, Molly, one hundred percent. Blinds open."

"Exercise room?" Aria repeated when he opened the door. "Isn't that a bit of an understatement?"

"I don't want to drive to town to get my workout in," he said. "So I've tried to make this as appealing as possible. Towels are over there. Wet ones go in the hamper. There's a shower on that wall."

She followed him in, bypassing the equipment so she could see the pool and hot tub. "I thought I saw a hot tub when we were outside."

"You did."

"You have two?"

"There's nothing like a summer night outside."

"I've stayed in hotels that weren't this nice."

"See why I can't get rid of Julien?"

"And maybe me," she added.

"*Mi casa es su casa.*" Then he translated. "My house is your house. Feel free use the amenities at any time."

"Thank you. *Grazie.*"

"*Gracias.*" His correction was accompanied by an easy smile. "Wrong language."

"I learned *tres leches* already."

"Why doesn't it surprise me that you speak fluent cake?"

She appreciated his teasing answer. "Dessert is my first language." When Julien had given her this assignment, she hadn't anticipated she'd like Grant, but he was easier to be around than she'd imagined, odd sense of humor included.

"Would you like to see my room?"

"That seems nosy."

"But?"

"I'm nosy. It's a serious character flaw."

He bypassed a closed door. Next to it was a keypad and a metal plate. "My workshop," he said.

She was reminded that he was a chief engineer for Bonds. As such, he developed a number of gadgets in secrecy.

"I'll show it to you later."

The master bedroom was at the end of the hall, obviously so that two walls could have floor-to-ceiling windows. And the one directly in front of her had French doors that exited onto another deck.

But it was the portrait propped on an easel in the corner that riveted her. Track lighting illuminated it, and it was obvious he meant the picture to be enjoyed.

The pastel was of a nude. The woman knelt on a rug that was much like the one in the guest room. The model's buttocks rested on her calves. Her shoulders were rolled forward, head bowed, hair falling around her face. "Is that your girlfriend?" she asked, turning in time to see him put the duffel bag on the bed.

Until this moment, it hadn't occurred to her to ask if he was seeing anyone. It wasn't any of her business, and it wouldn't matter either way.

"I don't have a girlfriend." He moved in closer. "The model isn't anyone I know. I saw this painting in a gallery in Santa Fe."

"It's..." She was at a loss for words. Over the years, she'd seen a lot of art, but nothing that she'd been inspired to pay a lot of money for. Her apartment was decorated with a handful of posters from her travels. "Do you mind if I have a better look?"

"As long as you're aware that you're living dangerously again."

She glanced up at him. That wasn't something she was accustomed to. With her height, and the boost from three-inch heels, she looked most men directly in the eye.

"Which is something I'd like to encourage in you."

Aria's heart had added a couple of extra beats. Despite that, she walked toward the easel. The woman's pose made her look serene, and her hands, palm up on her thighs, appeared as if she were anticipating something.

"I've never seen anything like it." She leaned in to read the engraved metal plate. *Submitted.* Aria looked from the picture back to Grant.

"I warned you," he said.

"You…" Her mouth dried. Suddenly she felt unnerved and wished she'd held onto the water bottle so that she had something to do with her hands.

"Prefer my women submissive," he finished for her.

That word certainly didn't apply to her.

"And I mean sexually," he went on. "And what's interesting about that is the way I love strong women. The more headstrong, the better."

"How can that be?"

"When she gives herself over to me, the feeling is humbling."

Over the years, she'd had friends who were involved in BDSM, but she'd never been with a man who practiced it. Until now, it was something she thought was interesting but didn't apply to her. Now a dozen thoughts crowded through her mind, not least of all the confusion he'd created with his seemingly incompatible ideas. "The picture"—she glanced back at it—"seems so…" She struggled for the right word.

Rather than saying anything, he waited.

She refocused on him, hoping he'd understand. "Gentle."

"Tell me what you mean by that," he encouraged.

Part of her couldn't believe they were standing in his bedroom, in front of a portrait of a naked woman, having an intellectual conversation. "From what I've heard… I associate submission and dominance with something more intense."

"And you believe this isn't? Can you imagine what she's thinking? She's waiting with infinite patience, but we don't know whether she's been doing it for five minutes or five hours. She has no idea what will happen once her Dominant arrives. Yet she appears peaceful, at ease. I get the idea that she's filled with trust, that she knows her devotion will be rewarded. That takes real strength. Discipline."

His gaze was intently focused on her. It took all her effort not to shiver. Had she ever had a man look at her like that? As if noticing her every movement, paying exquisite attention to *her?*

She was starting to see what Julien talked about with regards to Grant. The man was passionate about the things that captivated him. She wasn't sure that her presence would achieve the results Julien hoped for. Distraction might be the last thing Grant needed.

"From her expression, it's obvious that the relationship she has with her partner is complex and rewarding. But I don't fool myself that any of that is easy. It means she has to still her mind, much like in meditation, prayer, even study. Waiting with such composure while you're filled with expectation and anticipation is difficult. And what she's doing is transcending all of that, putting their mutual desire above her own wants." He turned from the portrait to face her. "I find it commendable. Moreover, I respect and appreciate her for the effort."

"Is that what you want in a relationship?"

"Ultimately, yes."

Aria wondered why she was suddenly seeing herself on

her knees.

"But I recognize that most people never find something like that."

She ignored the little tingle of arousal. "That's a lot to expect from a woman."

"It's a lot to expect from both of them," he corrected. "Her Dom has to be worthy of that kind of devotion. I can't imagine she'd do that a second time if he didn't make it worth her while. A successful relationship, be it vanilla or extra spicy, requires each person to put the other first."

"Is that something you've had? Or an ideal you aspire to?" She searched his gaze. The blue depths seemed darker than they had earlier. She knew she was asking questions she didn't have a right to, but she truly wanted to know him better.

He moved his head slightly, as if considering his answer. "For a while, I thought I had it."

"Would you have a relationship where submission wasn't a requirement?"

"If the question is, would I date a woman who wasn't interested in being tied up while I drove her to the edge of an orgasm and used my tongue to keep her there for a very, very long time...?"

Aria waited, pulse hammering.

"The answer is certainly."

Suddenly she could barely swallow, and stringing a coherent thought together was almost impossible. Was he talking about her? *Them?*

"But I'd need to be clear that it would never progress beyond dating."

His voice had a layer of steel that warned her she was tiptoeing close to very personal information. But they were colleagues, potentially friends—nothing more—so she pressed on. "Why is that?"

"I tried. I was engaged. We'd talked about it and, for me, she tried, but it didn't work for her. I loved her enough to deny what I needed. Eventually we realized we weren't compatible."

He might appear nonchalant, but he couldn't disguise the layer of hurt woven in the words. It made her squirm. Nosy was one thing, exposing someone's pain was another. "I apologize. You don't have to tell me all this."

"Unless you've changed your mind and don't want to know the answer, I'm happy to tell you."

"Do you have any secrets?" she asked drily.

"Not many, but I'm greedy. I don't let women I'm involved with have them, either. I want everything out there —raw, carnal, exposed. So the answer is, if I met a woman and she was interested in fucking and if there was mutual attraction, I'd spend the night pleasing her in every way she wanted—and I'd cook her breakfast in the morning. But in the long-term, I would never again propose to a woman who wasn't interested in submission."

She cast a glance back at the portrait. "She's an ideal, then?"

"As well as a constant reminder of what I expect, what I should hold out for. Yes."

"The picture serves as a warning, as well. To the women who see her."

Grant followed her gaze then shrugged. "I hadn't thought of it that way. Perhaps. You tell me. You're the only woman who's ever seen it."

"Well, I'd say you're honest about what you want. So it's both a warning as well as a promise."

"Promise?"

"If a woman is into it, wants it, she knows you'll deliver it."

He nodded. "Well said. Have you ever been spanked,

Aria?"

She was caught off guard, and she sucked in a breath.

Outside, snow had started to drift down, but she knew her shiver had nothing to do with the outside elements. "Once. And I didn't much like it. It hurt like hell and I honestly wondered what the fuss was all about. I was underwhelmed."

"Then I can tell you, your man didn't know what he was doing. If you were over my knee, you'd get your ass warmed and your clit would throb so hard you'd be afraid it had turned white. And when you came? You'd scream. If I was really good, you'd be crying, but only because the force of the orgasm left you otherwise unable to function."

She wondered if she would choke on her own breath. He'd melted her brain circuits until they'd flatlined. "I'd say it's a good thing we're colleagues and nothing more."

"I take it you've seen enough of my bedroom?" Grant smiled.

"Thanks. Yes."

"My workshop isn't as scary," he informed her. "But you might want to avoid going into the outdoor shed."

"What is it, a dungeon?"

When he didn't reply, the feeling of vertigo flooded her again. Julien's words about her needing a strong man echoed in her head. "Does Julien know about your...tastes?"

"Yes."

"So the duffel bag really does have handcuffs and..."

"Probably." He flicked a glance at it. "Do you want to open it up and find out?"

Julien said she needed to be involved with more complicated men. If he'd meant Grant, he was wrong. Grant was considerably more complex than anyone she'd dated. Uncomfortably so. What the hell had Julien been thinking in sending her here?

CHAPTER THREE

"Well?" Grant prompted.

"Actually, I'm good with leaving it alone." Her voice was bit breathless.

He enjoyed watching emotions play across Aria's face. After she'd seen the name of the portrait, she'd cocked her head to look at him. When he'd asked if she'd ever been spanked, a small frown had buried itself between her eyebrows. And when he'd offered to let her open the bag, her mouth had parted in shock.

But he didn't see fear in her rich green eyes. A small degree of curiosity, maybe. Anything beyond that might be wishful thinking on his part, but what a wish. He'd love to have this woman's bare skin exposed to his lash. He wanted to see her body jerk from the pleasure only a strip of leather could deliver. And to her screams of pleasure...? "There you have it. Transparency. Everything there is to know about me. You know where I stand and what I like."

"Maybe a few things I'd be better off not knowing. Do you share this with all of your coworkers?"

"No. Julien is the only guest I've had here. And even he

hasn't seen the portrait of the submissive. Other than my housekeeper and my designer, you're the only person who's ever been inside my bedroom. Honestly, Aria? You're the first coworker I've ever been attracted to. And I want you to know what you're getting yourself into if you decide." Deliberately, he left the end of the sentence vague. He gave her the opportunity to either begin or end the conversation.

She was silent for a few moments before quietly asking, "Decide what?"

"To give me a sign that I should act on what I'm thinking."

Again, a ridiculously long amount of time passed before she picked up the thread he was using to weave his images. "What are you thinking about?"

"Kissing you. I'm imagining that your lips feel as full and as soft as they look. But I'm also wondering how you taste." He already knew that her scent reminded him of the earth after a cleansing storm. In just the short time she'd been here, his perception had been altered. Her bag was in his guest room. Her coat was on a peg near his. Her purse sat on his entry table. His refrigerator was stocked with artificially sweetened creamer to ruin a perfectly good cup of coffee—and he didn't mind any of it. For someone who didn't like having his space disturbed, he was enjoying the feminine touches. "I'm picturing your mouth parting in an unspoken welcome as I stroke my thumb up the column of your neck and pull back your hair."

"That's not happening."

"You're not even the least bit curious?"

She hesitated a long, rewarding moment before answering. "No."

"In that case, let me show you my workshop." He stepped aside.

Aria took another quick look at the portrait before passing him.

Her boots echoed off the wood floor as she walked up the hallway. If he'd ever heard a sexier sound, he suddenly couldn't remember it.

He was man enough to notice the sway of her hips and the way the skirt hugged her body. Her legs seemed to go on forever. And, not for the first time, he pictured them wrapped around his waist.

Maybe he should get out more, much as he hated to admit that Julien might be right.

Aria stopped near the door, and Grant moved in and put his hand near the palm print scanner.

"Can't Molly just let you in?"

"Not into this room. We wanted the best security available. I've set up the system so that my print must match, and it must be at normal body temperature."

"Overkill?"

"I always hope. It's doubtful anyone would get past my fence—"

"How hard can it be to go over? Or, even wiggle under?"

He grinned. "That's not happening unless there's a power outage and my generator fails."

"It's electric, also?"

"Among other things. As I was saying, the things I develop for Bonds in my workshop have practical applications for other businesses, governments, the military. So with this sensor factored in, I don't have to worry about someone having a hand cut off and used on the scanner—at least theoretically."

She wrinkled her nose.

"But some people in charge of security do. You know all that, though."

She shook her head. "I may have the title of Director of Global Strategy, but my focus is on the consumer level. There's a whole geek language I can't speak."

"Well, you can't have everything. And after all, you are fluent in dessert."

Aria smiled at him, and he was a goner. Her green eyes turned the color of molten jade, seducing him in a way that was beyond sex. He already liked her quick wit and her curiosity. It wouldn't be long, he surmised, before the urge to live a little more dangerously called to her. When it did, he'd happily be the one to introduce her to its seductions.

He pressed his hand fully against the palm plate. "A lot of this never makes it out of testing. And some of it's done on a proprietary level. Certain companies don't want anyone to know what they've got."

"You trust me with this?"

"Julien sent you here. That's all the endorsement I need." The scanner cleared him and the door slid open.

"That looks like something out of a science fiction movie."

"It is." He grinned. "When I was growing up, watching *Star Trek,* I dreamed of having a door like this. So the first chance I had, I installed one. At first, I would go in and out. Just because I could."

"So why the keypad?"

"I thought it looked cool."

"It's nonfunctional?"

"You'll get a jolt from it. Want to try?"

She curled her hands at her sides. "What is it with you and electricity?"

"It has sixty-three thousand different uses. Four of them are sensual."

Her breath seemed to catch, and he watched the way she forced the air out of her lungs.

"After you."

She seemed drawn to the middle of the room, and she slowly spun while he sealed the door closed.

"Part of it looks like an operating room," she observed. "And the other..." She looked at the piles, the glass, the broken pieces, the half-finished prototypes, designs sketched directly on tables with marker.

"I call it Idea Heaven," he said.

"It's... Your workspace has an institutional feel to it. I mean with all the metal, the bare floors, no paintings or knickknacks, mementos... You don't even have plants. Do you spend a lot of time in here?"

"Most of my waking hours."

"The view is incredible, but the surroundings seem a little sterile. Austere maybe."

"Maybe at first glance. But it reflects my moods." When he thought of it. Lately that hadn't been often. More and more, he was seeing how right Julien was in his assessment. How long would he have been willing to go on that way? Work had become his life. And at some point, it had stopped being fun. "Molly, why don't we show Aria the Caribbean."

A wall shimmered as an image of white sand appeared. An island followed, taking shape, with palm trees and a hammock, a bird he couldn't name. Then came the water, three different shades of blue, the color intensifying the farther it moved away from shore. Yellow fish darted beneath the surface. In the three-dimensional distance, a yacht drifted.

"Well. Wow."

"Don't worry. I can switch it to the arctic if you prefer."

She wrapped her arms around her, warding off an invisible chill.

"Or San Francisco, if you're homesick. Or my dungeon, if you're brave."

"Are you ever serious?"

"Almost always. You want to think I'm joking because it seems safer for you that way."

"Ah..."

"You're wondering. What it would be like if I kissed you. In fact, outside, in the hallway, you were hoping I'd lean in."

"Dreamer."

He shrugged.

"I bet in high school you were able to talk girls out of their panties."

"I rarely tried." He met her gaze.

She was frowning skeptically.

"Wasn't till college, and I met Julien and our other friends that I got invited to parties. Before that, I didn't mingle much with the opposite sex."

"You were a fast learner."

"Not really."

"You went from not really dating to wanting to be in charge. Isn't that a big leap?"

"No. There was a natural progression, like most things in life. Come here. Let's get your palm print set up."

"I'm not sure whether I trust you or not."

"It won't hurt a bit," he promised. He pulled out a metal barstool and beckoned her forward. "Come here, little girl," he said in his best mad-scientist voice.

"There's something about you..." Then they spoke simultaneously.

"...That you're finding difficult to resist," he said.

"...That scares me a little," she said.

He grinned. "Good."

"Good?"

"A bit of fear or uncertainty is intriguing. It's the elixir of arousal. I just don't want to terrify you. Yet."

He saw her shift her weight as she crossed her feet. What he'd said had an impact on her. Unless he missed his guess—which wasn't likely—she wanted to know more. It might take her a while, but she'd walk into the net he was creating with his words and actions. Aria would need to feel safe before she'd move forward, which meant he had to take it slow as well.

"Should I be scared of you?"

"Maybe," he replied.

"That wasn't reassuring."

"It wasn't meant to be." He waited a few seconds before patting the top of the stool.

She licked her lower lip, betraying her confused emotions.

With the portrait and their ensuing discussions, he'd given her a hell of a lot to think about. So he decided to change her focus.

Once she took her seat, he moved in next to her. "Are you right-hand dominant?"

"Yes." Aria's body was rigid.

"One thing you need to know is that I won't do anything you don't ask for."

She turned toward him. They were only inches apart.

"But I love it when a sub asks. It's sexy. That's not to say things don't naturally evolve, but when you ask, even beg, that's what I live for."

It took her a minute to respond. "I think you have me confused with some other woman."

"Perhaps I do," he conceded. "Put your palm on the glass. When it has a good scan, the light will turn green. I want you to do it about a dozen times. Pick your hand up, put it back down with your fingers in different spots, more weight on the heel of your hand, then more on your fingertips, on your thumb. You won't touch the palm plate in exactly in the same place or in the same way every time, so I want to be sure we get a good prints." When he was satisfied, he lifted her hand back off the scanner. "Give me a minute." He entered a few commands on a keyboard. The screen in front of them showed a series of whorls and lines and impact points, all in luminescent green.

"That's quite impressive, Mr. Kingston."

"Think of the potential to avoid fraud with this thing. But like you said, probably overkill for most applications—and way too expensive for the vast majority of firms."

"But that doesn't stop your eyes from lighting up."

"Yeah. I love this shit." The screen blanked, then displayed a picture of her print. "Got it. Let's test it. Try to leave the room."

She slid from the stool and moved to the doorway. When he nodded, she put her palm on the plate.

Nothing happened.

With a frown, she turned back to face him. "Something wrong?"

He hit a key on the computer. The system turned green and the door whisked open.

"You did that on purpose."

"Just making sure I can keep you hostage if I want."

She shook her head and removed her hand. The door slid shut. "You're right. It's cool."

Just then, music blasted from the speakers.

Obviously shocked, Aria spun back to face him. "What the hell is that? It sounds like something from a blockbuster movie."

"Julien's theme."

"You're kidding me."

The words, "A genius is trying to reach you," overlaid the music.

"You're not kidding me."

"Man likes to make an entrance, even when he's not there physically."

"Hence the hologram."

He pointed at her. "Exactly."

"Greetings, earthlings," Julien said.

"You could have waited for me to answer," Grant replied.

"But then you might not have."

Grant considered that. "Probably true. Video on."

Julien sat behind the desk in his office. An ugly-looking green concoction filled a glass in front of him. Probably spinach and kale and broccoli all whirred and blended.

"I see you made it safely, Aria." Judging by the grin on his face, he was pleased with himself. "You're staying with Grant, I take it. I noticed you bought groceries and a nice meal, but you didn't put a hotel stay on my card."

"Nothing gets past a genius," she said. "By the way, is the team working on the project for the restaurant?"

"It is for Blanca, is it not?"

"Meaning it's first on your priority list?"

"Above all things in the heavens. Radar shows a storm is brewing. So I won't be shocked if I don't hear from you for a few days. Take a little time to relax, get to know each other. Talk about what you've been working on, Grant. Can't wait to see what you two cook up together." He lifted his glass in salute. "Toodles." Julien leaned forward, and Grant saw Julien hit the disconnect key.

"Did he really say toodles?"

"He has a way with words." Grant shook his head.

For the next couple of hours as the wind whipped up and snow fell with fury, he showed Aria some of the things he was developing. She asked a number of astute questions that showed both a grasp of technology and the considerations for the market.

Finally, he instructed her how to interact with Molly from the console and from an app.

"But watch this." He touched an icon on the screen. "This is where Molly makes your grocery list. She'll even check expiration dates on your dairy products. I'm able to call up the shopping list if I'm arriving back in town after an extended absence. She can also turn on the dishwasher. In a different sort of way, this is the kind of thing you're trying to do for Blanca at the restaurant. Taking separate elements and making them work together."

Aria nodded. "I'd be impressed if Molly could do the shopping for you."

"She can. She interfaces with the store's computer and arranges to have me pick it up or she can enter my credit information and have it delivered."

"I may need a Molly—or a Michael. I want to tell a guy what to do. Could I have a Michael?"

"Indeed. It could be whatever you want."

"Celebrity voices?"

"Can't see why not, beyond the logistics of getting them to agree."

"Have we moved beyond research and development here?"

"No. At this point, I'm toying with it because I enjoy it and want my life to be easier."

"There's hundreds of thousands of people—millions even —who are stretched for time," she reminded him.

"I agree with that. At the basic level, this technology has been around for years, but in terms of its potential, it's still in its infancy. And here's the challenge... The systems that do exist are proprietary, meaning if you bought a thermostat from a hardware store and an alarm from an installation company, you need to access different sites to view the settings or make changes. Molly's level of integration is unique."

She slid from her seat and paced in front of the window.

"Let's go back to the shopping application," he continued. "I don't want to go online and click a box or select a picture matching the products I want. I want the refrigerator to tell

Molly what it needs, then have Molly convey the information to the store. I've been working on this to make my life easier, but actual implementation is more complicated."

He grabbed a stool and dragged it over, sitting on the opposite side of the metal lab table. It was good to talk this out. Aria had been with Bonds long enough that she knew the objections Julien would have to working with dozens of other companies. It would take time, energy, effort, and the expense would have to be well worth it. "If we could sell the required sensors and write all the code, Molly would be extraordinary and perform with fewer technical issues."

"I get it," she said. She stopped and folded her arms across her chest.

Part of him was tuned in professionally. Part of him couldn't help but notice her against the view, fading light and gentle snow.

Aria continued, "If I record my favorite television show, that's done through my cable or satellite subscription service."

"And none of that factors in the human element." With a nod, he refocused. "It needs to be easy to set up, intuitive to work with. For example, if you have six kids, being on the last gallon of milk could be an emergency. But if you're single, a pint might be enough. Molly, or Michael, can't know that."

"Unless the system learns as it goes. You have to add your brand of artificial intelligence to it. Well, maybe not your offbeat humor, but the ability to adapt. If the computer is smart enough, it can learn that you typically arrive home at five o'clock every day and it can have the house at a perfect temperature when you arrive. Of course, you could override that. Maybe it sends out an alert to remind you if you're not home by six. People who want to program the system can. Those who don't can allow her to learn their habits. And there can always be an option to change anything at any point. People who start using it will fall in love and wonder how they managed without it."

She returned to the lab table and propped one hip on the top of the stool. "Start small and inexpensive, enough to be disruptive. Enough for consumers to demand the cable system talk to Molly. Make her personal, somewhat customizable. Imagine a commercial, 'Say hello to Molly' and Molly responding to them, making their lives easier in a number of ways. Damn, Grant, she can start your dishwasher, inform you when your kids come home from school, maybe even feed your pets and keep track of whether you paid your credit card bill. I mentioned she could run the dishwasher, didn't I?"

"Spoken like someone who forgets to do that?"

She shrugged. "Every day."

"We've got a million issues here, Aria. Security. Privacy."

"So what? None of those challenges are insurmountable. We provide a central hub. Stores and businesses can opt in, for a fee. They're difficult, but even you know that if you have an idea and an objective, you can find a solution. You've got the best minds in the universe at your disposal."

"I see why Julien likes you. You don't stop in the face of challenges."

"If you've had this idea, someone else will, too. Do we want to be first? Or a do we want to be a latecomer?"

"Do we want to be involved at all?"

"You could keep it to yourself," she agreed. "That's always the big question, isn't it? What project, what things are worth the investment and yield the biggest payoff?"

Most companies would run an expensive analysis on the potential, but Julien didn't operate that way. Analysis paralysis, he'd proclaim. And he'd add that some companies needed to pull their heads out of their asses and move. His anxiousness to keep moving forward was one of the reasons he'd yet to take Bonds public. Even though the company was growing every year, he ran it by instinct and had little desire to listen to any expert analysis. It earned him some bad write-ups in the financial press, but also the respect of his employees. And besides, Julien had filters on everything he read so that he never saw anything negative about himself.

Aria rolled her shoulders and sat up straight.

"I've kept you working too long." Weren't his work habits something Julien complained about? It had not been his intention. He'd thought he'd show her the house then let her get settled in, maybe have a shower and change out of her travel clothes. Instead they'd seamlessly flowed from tour to work. "How about we take a break?"

"My *tres leches* is wearing off," she admitted.

"I'll pour you a glass of wine while I make dinner."

"Those sound like two of my favorite things."

He had her use the palm plate to let them out of the room.

She preceded him down the hallway, and she almost missed a step when she saw the dog curled up in front of the fireplace. "That's still freaky," she said.

She stopped, and Grant did the same, standing next to her.

"From here, it actually looks like he's breathing."

"He is. Molly, have the dog lift up his head."

"Yes, Your Majesty."

The animal lifted its head, looked around then put it back down on the rug.

"I still think he needs a name," Aria said.

"Feel free."

"It needs to represent who he is. Maybe a play on words."

"Why does it matter to you?"

She got quiet. "I guess it shouldn't, but for some reason, it does. He's part of the family."

That comment surprised him. "Is he?"

"Molly has a name," she countered.

"And?"

"It makes things feel more personal."

"That's important to you?"

He began to think she wouldn't answer. "I've thought about getting a dog, but I just never seem to get around to it. I keep thinking that one day I'll be less busy."

"And?" he prompted gently. He suspected she was revealing considerably more about herself than she had originally planned.

"I've spent a lot of years focused on where I'm going that I wonder if I have sight of what's really important. My friends, my parents…"

She paused. He waited.

"I spend time with them, but I could probably nurture the connections more. Maybe I should think about getting a pet. But not a hologram one."

He appreciated what she'd shared. He, too, knew the trade-offs, the questions. The fact she'd opened up made him question some of his own decisions. Her visit was impacting him in ways he would have never thought possible.

"Dinner?" she prompted.

He was surprised by how much he wanted to cook a meal and share it with her.

Once they were in the kitchen, she said, "What can I do to help?"

"Be properly appreciative of my culinary skills."

"That, I can do. Applause? Or just sounds of approval?"

"All of that." He grinned. "Just relax."

"You're serious?" She leaned her hips against the counter and crossed one foot over the other. "I came here to work, not to take a vacation."

"You can cook another time."

"I'll wait until the snow clears then have Molly arrange for take-out pizza."

"How did I know you'd say that?"

"I'm an excellent helper, though. Don't they call the person who runs and fetches a sous chef?"

"I've got other ideas of roles for you to fill."

His tone told her exactly what they were. Like it had earlier, the idea intrigued her, but she wished it didn't. She shoved the images aside. She wasn't here to be his lover, and definitely not his submissive.

"Any preference on wine?" he asked, crouching to open the built-in wine refrigerator.

"Anything is fine." Just something to distract her or, better yet, take away the sudden edge of desire.

"Red or white?"

"White."

"Sweet or dry?" He glanced up.

"Could you make this any more complicated?"

"I like to take care of my guests."

"I can only imagine," she said. "Sweet. The wine, that is. Not your innuendos."

"In case you were confused, that was an invitation, not an innuendo." He grabbed a bottle. "Chardonnay, it is."

"I'll get the glasses." She took two from a cupboard.

When Julien had told him she was arriving, he hadn't expected to feel this easy with her being in his space. He wasn't missing work, in fact, his mind was going in a couple of new directions since talking to her.

He uncorked the bottle and set it aside while she went around to sit on the other side of the counter.

"What are we having?"

"Tarragon chicken and boiled red potatoes."

"Did you just decide that?"

"Yeah. If you'd have selected a red wine, I'd have made a beef dish."

"What if I chose to skip dinner and just have dessert?"

"Innuendo?"

"A legitimate question," she replied, apparently realizing she'd played along with him.

Oh, yes, she was an appealing woman. Smart. Sassy. "If you had said you wanted chocolate, I'd have chosen a nice Malbec." He laid out crackers, cheese and olives to snack on then poured her a glass of the wine.

"Really, Grant. You'll never get rid of me this way."

No reason they shouldn't both feel the attraction. "Good."

She sucked in a little breath. "I..."

"Have a sip."

After she did, she closed her eyes in appreciation. "Thank you. It's wonderful."

He prepped the chicken then cooked it for five minutes on each side in olive oil until the skin was a golden color. Grant popped the iron skillet in a hot oven then got to work on the potatoes.

"I think you should get your own cooking show," she said, giving him the requested applause.

"Problem is, I have about six meals then I start repeating them."

She laughed. "That's about the same number I have in my rotation, too."

Once the water was boiling, he spread some brie on a few crackers. She snuck in and grabbed one before he could eat it.

"I like your style," he approved.

After their earlier, more emotionally real conversation, she kept the discussion light, chatting about her responsibilities for Bonds. Personally, he preferred her as she'd been earlier...more revealing Aria. The glimpse of her inner thoughts had made him hungry for more. "If you still want to help, you could get the plates and silverware," he suggested while refilling her glass.

"Happy to." She eased off the stool. "Do you normally at the counter?"

"Most times just standing up," he admitted. "So let's use the table. I wouldn't take time to appreciate it if you weren't here."

Their gazes held for a moment. "Perfect."

"How about some music?"

"Jazz?" she suggested.

"Good choice. Molly, find us some jazz to listen to."

"My pleasure. Are you in the mood for something lively or maybe sexxxxy?*"*

"Neither," he said to Molly. But Aria was grinning. To her, he added, "Are you beginning to see the problems with artificial intelligence?"

"What is it you plan on using the music for, Your Majesty? If you want to get jiggy, I could suggest some Marvin Gaye, perhaps start with a little Sexual Healing*—"*

"Miles Davis," he interrupted.

"*Sexual Healing*?" Aria repeated. "That's on your playlist? Do you have her choose that every time you have a woman over?"

"I told you that you're the first woman I've had out here. Molly, cue Miles Davis. Something instrumental, and turn up the volume." Then he added, "Now."

The opening notes of *So What* flowed through the living area, and, as he'd requested, quite loudly.

"Sorry," he said to Aria as he cupped his ear. "What were you saying? I'm having trouble hearing you."

Her grin became laughter. He could honestly say he'd never enjoyed having a woman around more. It felt easy.

Natural. Maybe because they were coworkers? No expectations.

Right.

He enjoyed that they shared a passion for their work. They both wanted to carve their mark on the future and make people's lives easier.

Her hips were swaying in time to the music as she set the table. Male that he was, he stood there for a second and enjoyed the view. She seemed uninhibited. And those legs, in the tights and boots…

Distraction.

He needed a distraction.

He moved to the home's control panel and used the manual touchscreen to countermand his order to Molly and set the music at a level that would make talking possible. Then he pushed the icon to turn on the fireplace. In response, the dog moved slightly closer to the warmth.

"Impressive," she said, glancing over.

"The image isn't perfect. Probably never will be."

"Isn't the quest its own reward?"

"I prefer accomplishment," he said.

"Forever restless."

"My eternal conundrum," he agreed. "I like the Zen philosophy. Yet, it too is a quest. For me, the act of seeking it causes it to be out of reach." Odd, until now, he hadn't put that together.

He noticed that she'd placed a setting at the head of the table, another to the left. It occurred to him that part of the reason he didn't take the time to enjoy the dining room was that he always ate alone, most often standing in the kitchen. Having her here was turning out to be more instructive than intrusive.

Grant drained the potatoes, buttered them and added

parsley, a dash of salt and a sprinkle of pepper before pulling out the chicken and placing it on a serving platter.

"How about more wine?" she asked before topping off the glasses.

He joined her at the table where she was already seated.

"When Julien told me he was sending me here, I felt like it was a bit of a punishment," she confessed.

"And now?"

"It's quiet. Peaceful. And not in a bad way, but more in a way that allows you the space to think." She glanced out of the window. "Except for the snow and the wind."

"I can give you the Caribbean in your bedroom."

"I may take you up on that."

When the plates were pushed aside, she sat back and ran her finger around the rim of her glass. He waited.

"I'm curious."

As he'd hoped she would be. He'd given her a lot of information about what he liked, his tastes. It was up to her to decide which way to take this evening.

"How did you figure out you liked submissive women, the whole BDSM kinky thing?"

"That was in college. I met Julien, and he introduced me to his other friends, Reece and Kennedy. Kennedy liked going to clubs—but not nightclubs, more like dungeons."

"Places like that really exist?"

"I assure you, they do. The first time I went, I was intrigued. There was a couple, she was a Domme. She had a submissive —" He broke off. "Are you sure you want to hear this?"

She leaned back in her chair. "I didn't think I'd be interested, but I am."

"That's the first rule of BDSM—consent. Many times, people think it's about tying up your partner or turning her over your knee and giving her a few spanks. But everything in BDSM is talked about, limits set, safe words discussed." It had been a long time since he'd introduced a woman to his world, and he hadn't remembered it being this stimulating. "At any point, you're welcome to tell me to stop talking."

"Wait, that doesn't happen in most relationships. I've had times I'd rather gouge out my eyes than continue listening to another self-serving story."

"I promise you I'll shut up the moment you find me boring."

"Well, I'm not bored. Yet."

He turned his chair and stretched his legs in front of him. He wanted to see her better, read her expression.

"The woman," Aria prompted.

"I'll never forget her. She was wearing a brocade jacket and leggings, and her submissive was wearing just a thong. As she was attaching him—"

"Wait. The submissive was a man?"

"Shattered some of my preconceived notions, too," he admitted. "But I'll never forget the way she interacted with him, touching his body the whole time that she attached him to the St. Andrew's cross, speaking directly into his ear. It was as if the two of them were alone in the club. The flogging she gave him went on for a long, long time. It seemed more like she was caressing him than anything else. And he seemed completely enraptured by the experience. When it was over, she continued to touch him. I'd never seen a couple look at each other like that. And I decided that I wanted something similar."

"Did you...?" Aria squirmed in her chair.

"No questions are off-limits," he said.

"Did you want to be him? Secretly?"

"No. I wanted to be the one giving the pleasure."

"You call that pleasure?"

"I do. And the respect, the adoration. I wanted it all."

"You want to be adored? That sounds a bit egotistical."

"No. I want to do the adoring, with my whip, my flogger, my paddle, my crop."

"I'm not sure that's the way I'd want to be adored." She scowled and twirled the globe of her glass between her hands. "So then you went looking for a submissive?"

"For me, it wasn't that simple. The club was always looking for Dungeon Monitors. In this case, it was volunteers who would walk around, watch scenes, make sure nothing got out of control, that safe words were honored. DMs don't generally participate. They observe. Kennedy gave me pointers, and a few times I helped out at events. I didn't have a steady girlfriend, mainly because I was obsessed with my inventions. And when I did go out, I didn't have patience for chitchat and games. So I put my name forward for membership in the club. I had to attend five events before I was eligible for membership. Like the owner said, if we're all going to get naked together, we need to know each other. I spent a lot of evenings at munches and at classes, talking about the obligations and responsibilities of being a Dom."

"Sounds like a support group for Doms."

"In a way, it was."

"Is there one for subs?"

"Absolutely. There are also sites online that have groups and chats, questions and answers—that type of thing."

"You're not kidding me, are you?"

"Not at all. People take their kink very seriously. And there are subs who are looking for a play partner. I was happy to be one. I dated one woman after that, but we had little in common besides the fact she liked to be tied up and I liked to do the tying. After that, we played together on occasion, but we drifted apart. All very amicable."

"And the woman you mentioned earlier? The one you were engaged to?"

Even with Julien, Grant hadn't discussed Kathleen much. The failure of the relationship—along with the resulting damage—meant letting go hadn't been easy. The hurt had originally driven him to New Mexico. Driven him? More like he'd escaped. And it had taken him months to move on, even longer to recognize that he'd rather be alone than not have everything he demanded in a relationship.

Yet… Grant told himself it couldn't hurt to talk about it. He appreciated her openness. How could he give less? And if he hoped to move beyond an easy camaraderie, she had a right to know what drove him and what had honed his resolution. "Kathleen and I had a lot in common. She was a software engineer, too. But she was incapable of elevating the physical part of our relationship to the level I demanded. She was happy to get a dozen orgasms a night. If she was in the right mood, she'd agreed to get tied up. Occasionally she'd let me flog her. But when she wasn't in the mood, she could go for days, even weeks, without sex. She didn't need it like I did. For her, sex was fun. For me, in a relationship, it's necessary—vital even. It's about connection. It's who I am."

Aria opened her mouth then closed it without speaking. She settled for sliding her glass back onto the table.

"It's okay," he encouraged her. Encouraged himself, as well.

"I don't want to be rude." She shook her head back, then finger-combed her hair with both hands. "But I feel like you're leaving something out."

"You are bold."

"And?"

He'd told her he liked strong women, and he did. Better to be challenged than to leave questions simmering, maybe undermining the honesty he said he wanted. "You're right. There's more. Kathleen tried to like submission, the protocol of the whole thing. When I realized she only liked a small amount of it, that for her it was nothing more than acting an occasional part in the bedroom, I tried to pretend it didn't matter to me. I was in love, and I was willing to do what it took for the relationship to work. Eventually, though, there was friction. A lot of it. We'd argue about it. She'd say she just wanted to be treated like a princess. But my way was the only way I knew to show her I thought she was one."

Even now, the frustration gnawed at him. "Eventually she ended up throwing things, breaking plates, smashing a photo frame with our picture in it. She equated the drama with passion. Maybe on some level I did too. And then she'd apologize and be loving, contrite for a while. The truth is, I wanted too much from her and she needed me to be less intense. In the end, it ruined us both."

He paused. Words didn't come close to explaining the trauma—how badly it had affected him, and her. How two people who wanted different things could be in love, yet cause so much emotional damage to each other. "At the end, it was fucked up. One night..."

Aria waited.

He thought about whether he wanted to continue. But how could she understand if he stopped? "One night, after I'd gotten back from a trip with Julien, she wanted to start a fight about how I was never home, never there for her, always working. I hadn't gotten home early enough to go to a party she wanted to attend. I was exhausted, wasn't in the mood for her theatrics. So I told her to take them elsewhere. She did. She left, driving her sports car too fucking fast."

"Grant..."

"She wouldn't answer her phone. Went over to a girlfriend's house. They had a bottle of wine, then a second. Then Kathleen drove home—or tried to. She put her car around a telephone poll. She was shaken up. Bruised, but no serious injuries. Even after that, it took three months, maybe more, to stop the insanity and admit we couldn't work it out."

"That's when you moved here," she guessed.

"Peace," he agreed. "Solitude. A way to break the pattern and make sure I didn't repeat it."

Aria took a sip of the chardonnay, and he noticed that her hand shook just a little. "I'm sorry I pried," she whispered. "I had no right."

"You did. I wouldn't have told you if I hadn't thought it was important for you to understand who I am. I regret the way things ended with Kathleen. But I don't regret the good times—or the experience."

"That sounds a bit romantic."

"Maybe. Does that make you uncomfortable?"

She shifted. "I'm not sure I believe in romance anymore. Even if I do, I won't let myself be swayed by it in the future."

Grant decided not to tell her he knew about the relationship she'd run away from. He wanted to hear about it from her. "Oh?"

"Long story."

"With this weather, we're not going anywhere. We've got all night."

She reached for the stem of her glass and swirled the wine without tasting it. After stalling for a minute, she said, "My parents are awesome, but they wanted a large family. They got me."

"They probably would say they did okay."

"You're right, and I love them to pieces, couldn't survive without them. But all their expectations were directed toward me. I'm not whining about it. They worked their asses off so I could have everything I wanted."

"And?"

"I thought I'd found it. But I discovered it was an illusion. Wishing for something doesn't necessarily make it come true." She paused before continuing, "I guess I've always followed the path that's been set for me. After college, all my friends started to get married. They seemed happy. I thought I should want that, too."

"You want to make your own choices."

She let go of the glass and looked him in the eye. For the first time, he saw a layer of hurt in the verdant depths.

"One of my friends introduced me to her boyfriend's brother. And honestly, Simon was—is—nice enough. Everyone told us we were perfect together, and I started to believe it. But as time went on, I ended up feeling suffocated," she admitted. "I would wake up in the morning and wonder if that was all there was to my life. I spent a lot of time telling myself—trying to convince myself—that I was happy enough. But on some level, I..." She took a large gulp of her wine, draining the glass. "You don't need to hear all this."

"I do," he countered. "Just like I told you about Kathleen. I want to know everything about you."

"This is the dark stuff." She sighed. "Things I don't tell anyone else. The thoughts I'm not proud of. Thoughts I'm not proud of. Honestly, Grant, I'm a bit embarrassed."

"I think you're being hard on yourself."

She gave a tentative, obviously forced, smile. "That wouldn't be the first time. After a certain point, I realized the truth, but even then, I still put on a smile and pretended everything was okay. The unhappier I was, the more I would throw myself into my work, sign up for conferences that would take me away from home, volunteer for travel. And when I got to the point where I didn't want to go back home at all, that's when I had to be truthful with myself. See, not very noble or honorable."

"Better to have gone ahead and gotten married and potentially ended up divorced?"

"My mom tried to tell me it was jitters. Happens to every bride."

"It doesn't matter what anyone else says. Only you know the truth."

He watched her turn her fork over and over again. Finally she released it and gave a half-smile. "They weren't jitters."

"Then be grateful you had the courage to walk away."

"Having that discussion with Simon was one of the most challenging things I'd ever done. I felt like a fraud and a failure, as if the relationship—and he—should be enough. I knew I was letting him and our families down."

"Better than dragging it out." Like he'd done. "Facing it, owning your mistake? It's less messy. No matter what you think, it's nobler than having gone through with it just for appearances' sake."

"That's one way to look at it. And that's also what Simon said. He wasn't destroyed when we broke it off."

"Courage can look very different, given the circumstances. Deep down, you know what you want and aren't willing to settle. I admire that." He'd noticed the way she'd looked at the portrait in his room and their ensuing discussion. He wondered if, deep down, the relationship with Simon hadn't been enough for her. Maybe it had been about more than expectations. Maybe it had also been about boredom.

Perhaps she simply needed a man who would challenge her.

Standing, she started to gather their plates, effectively ending the conversation.

Grant understood the impulse to shut down when others ventured into territory that felt emotionally vulnerable. "You're welcome to sit in front of the fire, and I'll join you. Or feel free to escape to your room for a little peace and quiet."

"You cooked. I can at least help clean. Then spending a few more minutes together sounds nice."

That was the last thing he expected her to say. And it proved she didn't run when things were tough, no matter what she believed about herself.

She collected the serving dishes while he was rinsing the plates, and he noticed that she was swaying to the sounds of Miles Davis. Suddenly Grant realized he was staring at her.

He pulled himself back to the task at hand and busied himself with putting away the spices while she wiped the counters. "More wine?" he offered. "Irish coffee? A brandy?"

"I'm fine, thanks. And thank you for making dinner. The food was excellent, and the fact you cooked is very much appreciated. I would have been happy just eating the appetizers you selected."

It'd been a long time since he'd prepared a meal. Her company and her appreciation, applause and all, made the effort worthwhile.

She crossed into the living room and curled up in a corner of the sectional, facing the fire. It surprised him how comfortable she seemed, and how natural it felt to him.

He poured the remaining chardonnay from the bottle into his glass then turned off the kitchen lights before joining her. "Do you dance?" he asked.

"Not well. Well, I can do the line dances at a wedding. And I do an excellent limbo at the roller-skating rink. Or, well, I did when I was ten. But somehow I still keep that image in my mind."

"Ah, to be as good as we've convinced ourselves we once were."

"Exactly." She grinned. "And you? Are you good at it?"

"Dreadful." He slid his drink on top of the mantel. The dog lifted his head and put it back down as if slightly annoyed. "So let's not dance well together. I've already promised that I'll keep your secrets." What he lacked in skill, he made up for in enthusiasm. Since he'd spent more time with electronics than with women in the early college years, he'd missed out on a lot of opportunities to go to clubs and formals.

Julien's mother had told him that the most important thing was trying. She'd added that women liked to be asked, held and talked to. Those things, he'd managed to figure out.

He moved closer to Aria, held out his hand and waited, telling himself he wouldn't be disappointed if she refused. But that was a complete lie. He wanted her in his arms, against his chest. And he knew he'd use whatever method it took to get her where he needed her to be.

CHAPTER FOUR

Common sense urged Aria to run.

She should make excuses and lock herself in her bedroom. If she were smart, that's exactly what she would do.

Instead she was considering it.

He was impossibly tall, impossibly handsome, impossibly seductive. Like her, he hadn't changed clothes when they'd arrived home. So he still wore those bad-ass black boots, jeans that showed an ass that was tighter than it had a right to be. The long-sleeved black T-shirt that he'd tucked into his waistband behaved as a second skin since it emphasized the shape of his biceps and the breadth of his shoulders.

Outside, the wind whipped across the valley, driving snow into the windows. But in his living room, a warm fire, a wonderful dinner, a nice wine, intimate conversation and the lure of temptation wove an indelible spell around her.

She reminded herself that this man was a Dominant. He'd said he could sleep with a woman without having to tie her up. But if she were honest with herself, images of the portrait in his bedroom had flitted through her mind all day, even while they'd been working. The model had seemed peaceful, and the hint of a smile on her lips had radiated the confidence.

Grant made her nervous. Despite herself, she was curious what it might be like to have sex with him, to fall under his powerful, masculine spell. And she knew that, if only for a moment, she would be as appreciated as the woman in the portrait. The way he was looking at her now told her that.

Nerves flooded her, making her giddy as she admitted the truth to herself. Part of her wanted to be tied up by him.

With seemingly infinite patience, he remained where he was, not pushing for a response, but she knew that taking this step might lead to something more. She also sensed that he'd allow her to move at her speed. Finally, she gave voice to her fears. She wondered who she was hoping to convince. Him? Or herself? "Dancing with you could be an insanely bad idea."

"It could."

"We're coworkers."

"Also true."

"Sleeping together might really muck things up."

"Another valid point."

"I wish you'd try to talk me into this," she said, "or out of it, for that matter. Something."

He grinned. "A dance doesn't have to lead to sex."

"But it probably will."

"If you want it." He swept his gaze over her. "Because I sure as hell do."

His words turned her on. But it wasn't just what he'd said or the way he continually looked at her. It was more. Sexual attraction. And it had been building since she'd stepped off the plane and saw him standing there, leaning against the SUV, confident and powerful.

In his bedroom, he'd described BDSM as if it were an

elevated form of sex. To him, it obviously was. Grant had also been brutally frank with her about his failed engagement and his own part in it. She felt she knew him better than most men she'd been with. Aria rationalized that the attraction was an inevitable result of their enforced close quarters and their candid conversations. But it didn't matter. All she knew was that she desired him, needed him.

Her pulse did a slow burn as she stood.

"Molly, bump the volume up a bit."

This time, it appeared the computer's artificial intelligence worked as he instructed, and she took a couple of steps toward him then accepted his hand.

"Perfect," he said. "Standing behind you earlier, when we were getting your palm print, was torture. Inhaling your scent, not being able to touch you... Then being in the kitchen with you... Watching you set the table, leaning over, sashaying your hips as you walked toward—"

"I don't sashay," she interrupted, but at a whisper. The man was seducing her verbally, reducing her objections to a cool pile of ash.

"Oh, yes, Aria. You most certainly do."

She expected him to pull her close, but he didn't. Instead, he held her at a respectful distance then began leading her around the hardwood floor. He was very good, fluid, using the right pressure, making her feel as if they'd done this a dozen times together. "You lied."

"About?"

"This. You're a good dancer."

"Julien's mom taught me a couple of steps."

"His mother?"

"Yeah. We went to school at UT, Austin. His mom moved there when he was accepted. It was the main reason he ended up living with me. Anyway, she took pity on me one evening before we went to a nightclub and showed me a couple of steps. Embarrassing at the time, but now I'm grateful. I broke Julien's phone that night because he videoed it."

She laughed, liking the glimpse of Julien and their friendship. "To me, he's always been a Silicon Valley legend."

"I have trouble picturing him as anything other than the friend who stayed up half the night with me dreaming up ideas. We had no idea that we couldn't take over the world."

"It looks as if you're making some strides."

"So I think, until I interact with Molly. She humbles me."

The music segued into something a little more seductive, and he took the opportunity to draw her in. Willingly, without resistance, she went. She appreciated his strength, the way he naturally took charge. It should have frightened her. Instead, it ensnared her. "I'm curious."

"Go on," he encouraged.

She'd wanted to ask at dinner, but this way, not looking directly into his eyes, was easier. "How would you introduce someone to your BDSM world?"

"I already have."

Adrenaline skittered through her.

He placed a hand on her derrière and brought her against him. Then she felt his fingertips skim the bottom of her skirt. His touch on her legs was intimate and it made her hungry for more. Desperately, she wanted him to lift the material out of the way. She felt breathless, anxious.

Without missing a beat, he moved his other hand behind her and closed it in her hair, then gently tugged so that she was forced to look at him.

This man, clearly, didn't let women hide.

"And for a more complete answer, if I brought it up and she knew something about it, I'd encourage her to talk about her experiences, share her opinions, what she'd liked and hadn't liked, what she'd tried, what she'd like to try. If she knew nothing about it, I'd keep it cerebral for a bit. After all, a woman gets turned-on in her brain first. I'd want her to feel emotionally safe before I ever touched her physically. I'd like her to know what to expect if she wanted to take the first step."

Despite her trepidation, she wanted to hear more. "You want her trust."

"That's not something I would demand. I'd encourage it, but I know that it's a set of building blocks, something I have to earn step by step. I'd start with a kiss before moving on, to a touch, easy-to-follow commands then restraints or a gentle spanking."

"When does the good, old-fashioned sex happen?" she asked.

"All along. When a sub scenes with a Dom, she—or he—is offering not just their body, but their heart and emotional wellbeing. There is no greater gift, and therefore, no weightier obligation to the Dom. He or she—and in this case, me—needs to be aware of that significance and respect it."

Each of his statements made an image form in her mind, and she hungered for the experience, even the spanking, although she hadn't liked it with her first real boyfriend.

"I cherish the women who submit to me."

"Cherish isn't the word I expected to hear in this context."

"To be fair, it isn't for some people. There are couples where the sub is a masochist. Every relationship is unique, but I believe expectations need to be clear so there's no confusion. I'm not talking about anyone but you and me. I want to kiss you, Aria."

Her step faltered, but he was there, supporting her as they swayed to a stop. "Yes," she said. "I want it, too."

He released his grip on her hair and cupped her head with his palm. "I've been thinking about this." He stroked the column of her throat, up and down, pausing to feel her pulse. "So have you."

"How could I not?" she admitted.

"Open your mouth."

Grant eased his thumb across her lower lip. Then, when she responded, he moved in. He brushed her lips with his, once, twice.

"Yeah," he said.

The moment their tongues touched, a jolt of electricity went through her. He retreated for a second, making her long for him, then he touched her again, swirling his tongue around hers.

Within seconds, she opened her mouth wider in invitation.

Obviously Grant needed no further encouragement. What had been gentle now ratcheted into something carnal, weakening her knees and taking her resistance with it.

He tasted of the wine, and more, of possession. Suddenly, she knew that whatever he was offering, she wanted it.

Grant pressed one hand to the small of her back for support then he eased her backward a little, making it clear he was in charge.

Grant turned a kiss into an art form. He teased, tantalized, took, plundered.

It went on forever, and ended too soon, leaving her breathless. Her lips felt swollen, and arousal careened through her, demanding satiation.

Her knees were a little weak, and he helped her to stand back up.

"That was—"

"Only the beginning." He pulled up the hem of her sweater, baring her midriff.

Part of her thought they were moving too fast. The naughtier side of her insisted he get on with it.

She raised her hands over her head so he could tug the garment all the way off, and he tossed it onto the couch.

"Keep your hands where they are," he instructed, voice soft, reassuring, demanding.

Everything about his words and actions seemed carefully calculated to bring her to greater levels of arousal.

"You're gorgeous."

He traced his thumbs along the lacy tops of her bra cups, then rested a fingertip on the dainty red bow between her breasts. Unless she was staying in for the day, she always wore nice lingerie. Now she was glad for the little indulgence.

"Turn around for me."

Slowly, she did, stopping with her back to him, anticipating that he'd unhook her bra.

"Keep going," he encouraged.

Wordlessly, she did. Aria finished her pivot and tipped back her head. Odd, she was still mostly dressed, and yet she felt as if he'd seen more of her than any other man ever had.

"I'd like you to show me your breasts."

At this point in a seduction, she was accustomed to a prospective lover helping her along. But he remained in place, and in fact, crossed his arms over his chest. Her mouth dried at his commanding stance.

She unfastened the hooks and shrugged so that the straps fell from her shoulders. Very much aware of the heat that blazed in his eyes, she pulled off the bra and allowed it to dangle from her index finger.

He took the lingerie from her and tossed it on top of her sweater.

Again, he defied expectation. She expected him to touch, to squeeze, to press her breasts together, but he didn't.

"Molly, turn the fireplace on high."

"Yes, Your Majesty. Different music, as well? I Want Your Sex, *perhaps?"*

He shook his head, and Aria tried to smother a laugh.

"Turn up the heater and set yourself to standby."

"*You ruin all my fun.*" Molly sounded petulant.

"That interaction blows me away," Aria admitted.

"Julien's coding," he said. "He's messing with us. He anticipated a few of my requests to the system and programmed in responses. He's not spying on us."

"Promise?"

"If you wanted to play in public, I'd take you to a club. But otherwise, I assume you want privacy, especially from the boss."

"You're right about that."

"Where were we?" He'd dropped his voice a couple of octaves, weaving his invisible spell again. "Oh, yes. I was admiring your beautiful breasts."

Standing there was a little disconcerting. But she was already learning he did things at his pace.

"Cup them, lift them, draw them together."

"Is this a striptease?"

"Yeah. You strip. I tease."

"I don't think I like your rules."

His eyes seemed to smolder. She'd never been looked at with this sort of appreciation.

"Show me," he reminded her.

Feeling a bit self-conscious, she did as he'd instructed, putting her hands beneath her breasts then lifting them, pressing them together.

"May I touch?" he asked.

"I thought you'd never ask." In her experience, men rarely did.

"Keep them together," he instructed.

He traced each nipple, so lightly that she wondered if she'd only imagined the touch. Her body seemed to hum with energy. Never had a man's touch aroused her so much.

He circled the areolae, then abraded her nipples with his thumbnails. Each thing he did heightened her arousal.

"Do you like to have them pinched?"

"I'm a little sensitive."

"Mind if I gauge?"

She met his gaze. "Go ahead."

He rolled her right nipple between his thumb and forefinger, and she leaned toward him. "You like that." It wasn't a question.

He repeated the action on her left nipple.

This time, she moaned.

"More?"

"I think you might have spent the day figuring out ways to torture me," she confessed.

"You're right." He placed a gentle kiss on top of her head. "Since I saw your reaction to the woman in the painting, I've been imagining this."

His jaw was set, and she wanted to reach out to connect with him. "I can't relate to her," she said. "I'm too impatient. If that's what you expect, you might need to find someone else to interact with."

"You're doing fine."

This time, he squeezed both nipples at the same time.

She gasped and closed her eyes. It was a lot—but not too much. More than she'd had. Not as much as she wanted.

In turn, he sucked each into his mouth, licking away the tiny hurt.

Her toes curled as she sought for balance. It wasn't just his touch or his mouth, but his skill and mastery over her body. With his words, he was working his way inside her brain, as well.

Even though the house was warm, her damp nipples puckered into tiny beads when he stepped back.

"You're more perfect than I could have imagined," he said. "Come back into my arms."

Since she was naked from the waist up, she thought this might feel unnatural. Rather, it felt right.

He wrapped her up in his arms, and she laid her head on his shoulder in unspoken gratitude for a gradual introduction that fed her hunger.

"I like to touch your skin," he said against her ear as he trailed his fingers down her spine. "You're velvet and silk, both at the same time."

Nerve endings fired, sending awareness of him through her. She wanted *more.*

He stepped a little farther away from her, brushed hair back from her face, then traced the outline of her jaw.

"Grant..."

"I know. You've already informed me that you're impatient."

"And?" She exhaled.

"Relax and let me lead, like you did when we were dancing."

"But you want to do a waltz. I want to do a rhumba. So move it, mister."

He grinned and put his thumb beneath her chin. He tipped back her head a little, holding her prisoner. "I'm going to have you naked, Aria, and it's going to be in the next five minutes. Then I'm going to give you an orgasm."

"This isn't the way I'm used to doing things," she admitted. She was a modern woman who knew what pleased her and wasn't afraid of helping things along. Honestly, the sooner she could get it over with, the sooner she'd be able to stop wondering about it. She reached for his crotch and curled her hand around his cock.

He was hard and felt impressive. He was as ready as she was.

"Put your hands behind your back, Aria."

"I…"

"Enjoy the experience," he reminded her.

"I'd enjoy having your dick in me."

"Don't worry. I intend to fuck you. On my timing, not yours."

"We're grown-ups here."

"Do you really not enjoy foreplay? The anticipation?"

"I open all my gifts before Christmas and tape them back up."

"I believe that about you. I know that it might be difficult, but you're not going to make me move quicker. Play by my rules tonight. And tomorrow, if you didn't like it, I'll rip your clothes off and fuck you until you can't remember your name."

His words rocked her back on her heels, so when she answered, she tried to keep it light, rather than let him know how much he affected her. "I can already tell you. I like my way better."

"We'll have a critical analysis of my performance over breakfast."

The reminder that she'd still be here in the morning added another pulse of excitement.

"Agreed?"

She resisted the impulse to fondle his balls. The idea of him taking her hard and fast appealed on so many levels.

"Hands behind your back," he reminded her. *"Do as I say."*

The edge in his voice was different from anything she'd heard from him. It shocked her a little, as if there were two sides to his personality. Just because he said he cherished a woman evidently didn't mean he would tolerate her deviating from his plan.

"From here on, I expect you to do everything I say, without argument."

"That makes me nervous."

"I'm going to prove to you that nothing will happen that you don't like or approve of. If anything is too scary, say the word yellow and we'll slow down or stop. We'll discuss it, or maybe move onto something else. It's my intention to take you to the edge, but not over it."

"Are you a mind reader?"

"I'll be watching every one of your reactions. Tell me how your nipples feel."

"They ache for your touch." He'd strung her tight, already. Although a fresh flood of nerves made her mouth dry, she forced out a breath and put her hands behind her back.

"Put your shoulders back, Aria. Offer your whole body to me."

Her nipples were still damp and hard. She realized she'd never really been seduced before. Simon, her fiancé, had moved straight from kissing to heavy petting. She'd done some touching in return. Before long, they'd ended up in the bedroom. Sex was good, most of the time, but he'd never just looked at her body, talked to her, told her what he intended to do, forced her to wait.

"Keep your hands where they are."

He swept her from her feet and carried her to the couch to place her on the edge of it. Then he knelt in front of her to pull off her boots.

"I can do that," she protested.

"I hear that from you a lot," he said easily. "If I wanted you to, I'd ask you. Relax. Let me."

Damn, he looked so freaking hot, kneeling there, and she had the sudden, vivid image of him putting his mouth on her pussy. Despite his orders and her own intention to let him set the pace, she dug her feet into the floor and lifted her hips.

He ignored her silent protest, which drove her a little

more insane. After tugging off each boot, he helped her to stand.

"I want to look at your body," he said, "inch by inch, as I bare it."

"You're a confounding man."

"Who might go looking for a gag."

She gasped. "You wouldn't!"

"Oh, Aria, yes I would."

Uncertainty made her shut up.

He reached behind her to lower the zipper on her skirt. Then he tugged the material down. It pooled to the floor, but she didn't step out of it or attempt to move.

"You…are damn perfect." Next he hooked his thumbs in the waistband of her tights and lowered them.

Already she knew better than to offer to help. Instinct made her tighten her muscles. That didn't deter him. Rather, he continued what he was doing, crouching as he went on.

Then she was standing and he was on his knees before her.

"Lift each foot."

She did and he removed the tights.

"Your body is so womanly."

By any standards, she wasn't perfect. Her hips were curvy, and her stomach was not flat despite constant working out. But he made her feel as if she were a pin-up model.

"Play with your nipples. I want you pinching, tugging, squeezing. Are you wet, yet?"

"I have been for a while."

He drew her panties down and she stepped out of them.

She felt his warm breath on her lower belly.

Then he placed a finger between her legs and slid back and forth between her labia.

"Damn," she said.

He slid a finger into her pussy and she jerked.

"Keep playing with your nipples."

"They're a little tender."

"Spread your legs as far apart as you can comfortably keep them."

"I…" She wasn't sure what she was really saying, but sensation burned through her as he continued to fuck her with his finger.

He pinched her right thigh.

She yelped.

"I said legs apart, Aria."

She did as he said and was immediately rewarded when he licked her pussy. "Oh, God."

Aria wished she could see his reaction. But all she could see was the top of his head. She'd had men eat her out before, but never while she was standing.

She wanted to grip his shoulders. The experience of him pleasing her without her reciprocating was foreign, and she wasn't sure she liked it.

He brought one hand behind and spread his finger across her buttocks to keep her in place before he tongued her pussy. She cried out and her knees turned wobbly.

He was relentless—nipping, sucking, licking. Then he slipped a second finger inside her.

"Damn. Damn, damn, damn. *Fuck.* I want…"

"You taste so damn good."

He moved a finger until he touched her G-spot.

"I…" She moaned. He had her on the edge and wouldn't let her go over it. "I can't take this." Her words were wrapped in a whimper.

"Say yellow if you need me to slow down," he reminded her. "Otherwise I'm going to finger fuck you till you can't stand, little Aria." He pistoned them into her, but licked her gently at the same time, the juxtaposition making her mind and body misfire as she came.

She reached for him so she didn't fall.

"Steady yourself," he said. "And pull on your gorgeous nipples."

"I want you to do me," she insisted. Her body quivered, but he ignored her totally, continuing to relentlessly drive her toward another orgasm. "I can't."

Again, he said nothing.

"Grant!"

She tried to play with her nipples as he wanted, but sensation overloaded her. Despite her best intentions and his instructions, she screamed as she came, her sex pulsing around his fingers. Unable to stand on her own, Aria pitched forward and grabbed hold of his shoulders.

Even that didn't stop him. "I want you wet," he said.

He put a third finger in her, then thrust them in and out, going deeper, demanding more. He moved his tongue quickly, not letting her absorb one feeling before going onto the next.

"Damn!" This man… Grant… He left her exhausted, unable to function.

Finally, he seemed to take pity on her, and he eased back.

"You're so responsive to my touch, Aria. Perfection." He stood then scooped her from the floor as he did so.

He placed her on the couch then reached down to smooth hair back from her cheeks before saying, "You may be almost ready for me to fuck."

Almost ready…?

Her chest rose and fell, and she couldn't catch a breath.

"Stay where you are."

As if she could move.

"I'll be right back." He plucked a soft and plush throw from the back of the couch and draped it over her.

"I…" Her brain scrambled to keep up with him. She knew he was a Dom, but she hadn't realized that meant he would change her entire expectation about sex. She hadn't seen his body unclothed yet, and she'd already been rocked by orgasm after orgasm. This wasn't just about the physical, she realized. It was emotional, mental, too.

Grant had touched her body as if they were intimate partners rather than recent acquaintances. No one had ever taken this much time to prepare her and make sure she wanted it.

And damn him, if it was already like this, what else did he have in store? He'd urged her to live dangerously and, for the first time, she was tempted.

When he returned, he dropped a condom on the ottoman.

"Finally," she said, propping herself up on her elbows and reaching for him.

"Not so fast."

"I'm really confused about this whole BDSM thing," she admitted.

"I'm listening."

"I thought it was about a woman getting spanked and a man getting his cock worshiped."

"Where did you get your information?"

"It's general knowledge."

"It is, is it?"

"I have friends who are into it. And..." She sighed and turned red from embarrassment. "Fine. I admit it. That piece of information came from a bachelorette party." The more champagne they'd consumed, the more outrageous the stories had become.

"What else did you hear?"

Though she squirmed, he wasn't leaving the conversation alone. "From what I heard, I wasn't all that excited to try kinky things. One woman said that guys get into it because they get to boss women around."

"Well, women are generally in charge, so that's fair."

Aria scowled at him.

"As for the cock worship, you're certainly welcome to get on with it."

At his lascivious grin, she grabbed a pillow and tossed it at him. He dodged and it landed right near the sleeping dog.

"Each relationship is unique, I told you. But yes, you get spanked. As for cock worship, that can be part of it, and I might ask you to suck me off and lick my balls. But you won't have to earn the privilege."

He kept her on the ragged edge.

"Have you ever had your cunt slapped?"

Her insides clenched.

"I'll take that as a no, but I want you to say, not until now, Sir."

Her heart rushed to her toes. If she hadn't been lying down, she might have needed to sit. This was impossible. Erotic. "I'm not sure I even want that."

"Are you willing to try?"

Was she?

His question tumbled through her mind. But he never forced the issue.

"If you are, pull back the blanket, move so you can lie down fully on the chaise." He pointed to indicate the wing part of the sectional on the far right. "I want your feet flat on the ground. I want your pussy completely exposed. This time, I won't tie your legs, unless you want me to."

"No. Thanks for asking, though."

He gave a quick, calculated smile that stopped time for her. "The perfect submissive response is, whatever you please, Sir."

"Sir?" She pursed her lips before continuing. "Is that required?"

"By a lot of Doms, yes. Some prefer Master."

"Sir sounds good."

"A lot of others are comfortable with first names or nicknames. I like Sir just because it will give you a frame of reference for when we're working, having a regular fuck or when we're in a scene."

"Makes sense." As much as any of this did.

"So in addition to doing what I asked, I want you to ask me to spank your pussy. Or you can use the word cunt."

Aria bunched the blanket in her fist. She could say yellow or sit up, or grab her clothes and run like hell. "I'm obviously a novice." But, evidently, a willing student.

"You're doing fine. To be clear, if you want to continue, what will you do? And what will you say?" He stayed where he was, and she saw his erection straining against the front of his jeans.

Trying to make sense of this was somewhat like trying to pull an individual piece of spaghetti out of a boiling pot. "I will pull back the blanket." Which meant releasing her death grip. "I'll scoot to the end of the chaise and lie back, put my feet on the floor and spread my legs." The thought of that tantalized her.

He continued to regard her. She could get lost in the depth of his blue eyes, and she yearned to see approval in them.

Though she was a bit nervous, the emotion was spiced by a smidgeon of *what the hell*. "And I'd ask you to please spank my pussy." She hesitated. "Sir." She realized she wouldn't get any help from him.

Hands shaking, she pulled back the blanket. Then she scooched into position. With the way he stared, spreading her legs took on a whole new level of eroticism.

It took a few seconds for her to repeat his words. The fact she'd said it once didn't help in the least. "Please, spank my pussy, Sir."

"Would you like me to tie your legs?"

In time, she remembered the correct answer, "Whatever pleases you, Sir."

"In that case, no. I want you to stay in position, even if it's demanding. If you break position, I want you to force yourself back into it. If it's absolutely more than you can bear, say yellow."

The mind fuck was unlike anything she'd ever experienced. It seduced her without him ever touching her.

She braced herself by grabbing the sides of the chaise.

"It helps if you relax," he said. "I know it sounds contrary to instinct, but the pain will hurt worse if you're tense."

She shook out her legs and forced out a breath.

Grant put two fingers in front of her mouth and said, "Get them wet."

Her taste was still on his fingers from earlier.

He stroked her pussy. Despite her trepidation, it only took seconds for her natural lubrication to start working.

She forgot to be afraid and, instead, surrendered to the deliciousness.

"Ask me," he prompted.

"Please, spank my cunt, Sir." She wondered if the word shocked him as much as it had her.

"So fucking sexy." His smile made her glad of her bravery.

Surprising her more, he continued to stroke her, tweak her clit, enter her with long, slow strokes.

Now the anticipation was killing her.

He fingered her faster and faster, the way she wanted him to fuck her, making her toss her head, forget about anything but the here and now.

Then he gently smacked her.

She rolled her head to one side, but remained in the position he'd specified.

He went back to those long strokes that only stoked her

need. Then he upped the stakes, moving faster before pulling out and spanking her again with his fingertips.

"Damn," she said. Yes, it stung, but the sensation only lasted a moment before it fractured into pleasure that made her wetter.

She began to anticipate his motions then, so he mixed it up. Fast. Fast. Slow. Quick spank. Fast. "My God. I'm going to come."

"Not yet. Hold onto it," he said. *"Wait."*

Did he have any idea what he was asking for? "But..."

He continued the torture, giving her a decidedly hard slap. She squirmed, desperate to squeeze her legs together and escape, but he'd commanded her to remain in place, and she wanted to please him. Then, just as fast, the pain morphed and she was left panting.

"Your reaction was exactly what I was hoping for."

Her pussy was wet, slick, hot, burning with pain, and her clit throbbed. "I've got to come," she insisted.

Grant responded with his body, changing the rhythm, giving her a dozen gentle pats, then wetting his finger and sliding it across her clit.

"I'm going insane."

He increased the tempo. Spanking her harder, quicker.

"The pain..." She tossed her head from side to side as she tried to escape it and, simultaneously, seek it.

He plunged two fingers deep inside and squeezed her mound, making her arch, making her scream.

"Come now, Aria."

He increased his grip, and almost lifted her from the couch.

The orgasm ripped her apart. She was gasping, panting, and thought was obliterated. It wasn't until later—she wasn't sure how long— that she realized he was sitting and that she was on his lap.

He had a hand dug into her hair, his palm supporting the base of her head.

"Holy hell." She drew a shuddering, steadying breath. "That was hot."

"You can thank me at any time."

She wiggled away from him a bit. "Is that part of it, too?"

"Appreciation?" He shrugged. "Sure."

She noticed he was still fully dressed, in command of the situation and her. Before today, she might have protested that, but she'd never had a man spend the evening doing things to her, for her.

"But I don't require it," he added, then gave her a cheeky grin. "As long as you come, I have everything I need. It's a bonus if I make you scream."

She clenched her buttocks. "In that case, my body told you thank you."

"Yeah," he agreed. "It did."

Aria snuggled against his chest and rested her cheek on the soft cotton of his T-shirt. His breadth and strength were reassuring. "I had no idea I would like something like that."

"Well, we'll have to give it a go your way next time. I think you wanted me to fuck you ragged."

CHAPTER FIVE

Impossible.

No matter what she tried, Aria couldn't sleep.

It wasn't just the strange bed in a new city. She traveled frequently enough that she was accustomed to going straight to sleep, no matter the circumstances.

But she'd never experienced circumstances like these.

She lifted her head and squished and punched the pillow into a different shape, hoping that would help. It didn't.

No matter what she did, she couldn't escape the memory of what she and Grant had shared two hours ago.

After he'd toyed with her and brought her to dizzying climaxes, he'd told her that was enough for their first night. She'd been shocked that they hadn't had actual sex. It felt odd to her that he hadn't received anything out of the experience.

Instead he'd helped her to put her skirt and sweater back on. Then he'd grabbed her boots and undergarments and walked her to her bedroom.

At the doorway, he'd pressed a kiss to her forehead, returned the rest of her clothes then wished her a goodnight.

He hadn't suggested they sleep in the same bed and truthfully, she wasn't ready for that, anyway. Having separate rooms would help her keep boundaries around their relationship—or so she told herself.

Feeling hot, she tossed back the comforter then pulled the sheet around her shoulders.

A few minutes later, she realized that wasn't helping, either.

Giving up the internal struggle, she allowed herself to replay the scene for at least the tenth time. Aria had never felt that exposed during sex before. He'd communicated with her the entire time, and he'd demanded her participation.

The spanks on her pussy had hurt, but that had only intensified the pleasure. She hadn't expected to like his introduction to BDSM, and in fact, she'd been convinced she'd only do it so that they could have sex normal, old-fashioned, man-on-top, jackknifing-like-rabbits sex. That she knew what to do with. She could have intercourse without forming an attachment to a man. But this…?

It was like going to a restaurant and stealing a bite of an unknown food from someone else's plate only to discover a new favorite. Now that she'd had a taste, she wanted other experiences.

Wondering if they'd play again and what they'd do was driving her mad. More, she couldn't escape the constant throbbing in her pussy.

With a huge, frustrated sigh, she tossed back the sheet and climbed from the bed. After grabbing a robe from the closet, she walked to the window and opened the blackout panel without turning on any lights.

It took a second for her vision to adjust. From here, she could only see a few winking lights that indicated where other homes were. She noticed that snow still fell, more gently now.

Being near the window cooled off her overheated body, and she decided to try to sleep one more time.

Half an hour later, she admitted defeat. Sleep was still a long way off and she needed a distraction.

Aria turned on the lamp sitting on the nightstand then grabbed her computer. She curled up on the chaise longue and breezed through the lighter-than-normal number of emails. Obviously, David, her second-in-command, was managing without her, no doubt because Julien had encouraged him to do so.

She opened a book, but when it couldn't keep her interest, she moved on to a game of solitaire. The slow pace allowed her mind to keep chugging along, putting memories together with fantasies and causing anticipation to curl through her.

This wasn't working.

She slammed the lid closed on her computer.

This kind of restlessness only happened when she couldn't settle her mind. Exercise tended to be the only thing that helped. Since Grant had a world-class facility in the house, she decided to avail herself of it. She changed into a pair of yoga pants, tennis shoes and an athletic top then left the bedroom.

When she opened the bedroom door, the hologram of the dog was lying in front of it, almost as if he were protecting her. She realized Grant must have set it up that way to make her feel more secure. The fact he'd thought of her before he'd gone to bed made her heart melt a bit.

She couldn't help but glance down the hallway, half hoping he was still awake, that he'd see her and invite her to join him.

His door was shut, and she didn't see a ribbon of light shining beneath it.

She continued down the hall and realized that Molly was

illuminating the way as she went. Motion sensors. Clever. Grant thought of everything.

Aria entered the workout space.

Except for the gentle sounds from the pool and hot tub, the place was silent. She wasn't sure whether that was soothing or annoying. "Molly, can I get something on the television? A classic movie. Or one of those cooking shows." *Yeah.* "Make it something about food." Maybe she could learn something while sleep evaded her. "Volume low."

She programmed the treadmill for half an hour then started at a casual pace. Once her body loosened up and the male television host sat down in front of a hamburger that was bigger than his head, Aria ramped up the speed until she was running.

To starve oxygen from her overthinking brain, she went through the program a trainer had taught her, running flat out for one minute, then walking for two. When she was particularly stressed, this always helped. She'd used the technique to cope when she was trying to outpace the emotional hurt after she'd run from her upcoming wedding.

By the time she was done, her chest was heaving, but she was still picturing Grant standing over her, arms folded as he promised to fuck her. "Damn it."

After wiping off the sweat with a towel, she told Molly to turn off the television and she walked toward the pool area. She considered a swim, but it was really one of her least favorite forms of exercise. And she hated the initial shock of diving into cool water. As far as she was concerned, the only time to be in a pool was when the weather was gorgeous and she could sit on an underwater stool while a handsome bartender served up a cocktail. Bonus if he stuck an umbrella in it.

The hot tub, though, was an entirely different matter.

Aria glanced around before removing her clothes and dropping them in pile.

She dipped her toe in the water to test the temperature. Since she could see the steam rising from it, she figured it was perfect.

As she expected, the tub was fabulous, and it had subtle curves to support her body. She sank in a bit at a time as her body adjusted to the heat. Eventually, her shoulders were covered.

During the day, the view would no doubt be spectacular. Right now, it just seemed as if the night stretched forever.

Even though sleep evaded her, she was tired from the trip, the long day, the pseudo-fucking. She allowed her eyes to drift closed while she performed some shoulder rolls to release tension.

The peace surrounded her, soothing her. More than ever, she understood why Grant had chosen this spot for a retreat and to heal.

"Am I intruding?"

Heart thundering, she opened her eyes. Grant stood there, wearing a pair of swim trunks. The first view of his nearly naked body didn't disappoint. Even in the dim light, she saw the definition of his biceps, the flatness of his stomach. God, did he have a six-pack? Or was her imagination supplying wished-for details?

His legs were powerful, thighs massive.

Because the trunks were loose-fitting, it was difficult to see whether or not his dick was hard.

Regardless, he unnerved her.

Without conscious thought, she wrapped her arms around herself. Then she realized how ridiculous that notion was. He'd seen her naked, and he'd exposed her more than any other man ever had. "I'm sorry if I disturbed you when I got up," she said.

He shook his head. "I wasn't asleep. Mind if I join you?"

"I've been in here a while, so I was leaving anyway," she said. Lied. To cover her sudden bout of nerves, she gave a half smile. "It's all yours."

"Stay?"

"I..."

He descended the two steps into the tub and sat down across from her. "How are you doing? Everything okay?"

"Strange bed," she hedged. "I was having a difficult time unwinding." At least that was the truth.

"Are you sore?" He paused. "Anything you need to talk about?"

In the past, she had always pretended things were okay, even if they weren't. Somehow, she'd become a master of evasion, something else she wasn't proud of.

She knew her time at Grant's home was limited. They'd made significant progress yesterday, and with the two of them working together, they'd nail down the idea of the virtual assistant. Then Bonds could put an entire team on it to work out the nuances of the artificial intelligence. There were details, certainly, but the gist of the idea was already there.

So if she was ever going to experiment with being bold, now—when there was little emotional risk in a relationship that was naturally short-lived—was the time.

"My pussy is a little tender." Aria uncrossed her arms. "But I was tossing and turning, replaying our scene." Then she admitted the truth, "I was wondering if there'd be a next time."

"Were you hoping there would be?"

Since he'd shown up, the temperature seemed to have increased. She scooped damp hair back from her neck and piled it atop her head, even though it wasn't likely to stay. "I was."

"Was my way okay with you?"

She wriggled around and felt her hair tumble down. "Evidenced by the number of orgasms, yes. I still wanted to have sex, but when you left me alone, I was confused." She looked at him through the steam that rose from the water. "I wondered why."

"Are you wondering if I find you desirable?"

"Honestly? No." She met his gaze. Even if she had doubts, the desire in his eyes would banish them. "I felt your dick through your pants." For her, that comment definitely counted as bold.

He grinned. "Constant hazard when you're around."

"So?" she prompted.

"I'm learning about you, watching your reactions. You're learning about me, my instructions. You're figuring out whether you want to submit to me—and you're probably considering what that might mean. I want to give you experience, but not too fast. Remember the portrait?"

"How did I know you were going to say that?"

"Patience." The smile he gave her was quick, real, disarming. "Foreplay. BDSM and sex are closely intertwined, but they can exist side-by-side. I don't have to fuck everyone I spank."

"This woman, you do. I have rules, too."

Humidity made his hair curl a bit, and that entrancing lock of blond fell across his forehead. "You may not want to have sex with every guy who ties you up. If you're at a club, you may want to try out a different Dom, male or female."

That idea of being with someone at a club was outside her current thinking. And that she might let a female dominate her? "Do you love messing with my paradigms?"

"Is that what you think I'm doing? Messing with them? Then I need to be clearer, Aria. I intend to obliterate them."

An erotic thrill lanced her. So he did plan to continue

playing with her.

"I want to watch you masturbate."

"You're coloring outside my lines again."

"That's what I want," he told her. "And it's what you want, as well."

Until today, until him, she hadn't known she had lines to color outside of. He was showing her dimensions of her own sexuality. It scared her. It thrilled her.

"Get out of the tub and dry off," he instructed her. "Then kneel on a towel and get yourself off."

She let her mouth fall open.

"Get to it."

That tone... Implacable. Response-inducing.

"Coming again will help you to sleep better."

No doubt that was true.

Aware of his intense regard, and grateful for the dim lighting, she moved past him to climb up the steps. She snatched up a towel, dried off, then folded the fluffy cotton and dropped it to the floor. All the while, he stayed in place.

Watching him, her body heated as much from the water as from his command, she knelt.

"Moisten two of your fingers with your mouth."

Never breaking the spell created when they gazed at each other, she put two of her fingers in her mouth and sucked on them.

His jaw was set in a solid line, and she knew she was having an impact on him. The knowledge was heady, and it made it easier for her to do what he'd said.

She got her fingers wet, then moved them between her legs to find her clit. It was still swollen and tender, so the slightest touch made her lean back. "Ah," she said involuntarily.

"Pull back the hood and also spread your labia."

Earlier she'd had the television. Now, there was nothing

to distract her.

Even though he wasn't touching her, she realized he was completely dominating her. That made this even more intense.

She surrendered to the sensation, the moment, sliding her fingers into her pussy, keeping her labia parted, remembering to play with her clit.

Because she'd been thinking about him, her body had been more or less aroused since they'd finished the scene in the living room. It took her only a minute to reach the edge of an orgasm.

"Tell me before you come."

"I…" She moved her left hand so she could pinch her nipples and squeeze her breasts. If he were touching her, she couldn't be more turned on than she was right now.

"Close?"

Her body started to shake.

"That's it, fuck yourself with your fingers, little Aria."

His voice was magic, taking her higher.

Suddenly she could no longer support her weight, and she moved her knees farther apart, getting better leverage. She let go of her breasts, and used her thumb pad to vigorously rub her clit as she fucked herself, inserting her fingers all the way to the knuckles before she pulled them out and drove them back in. "I'm close." His earlier words played in her thoughts, and she amended her statement. "I'm close, Sir."

"I can smell you from here," he said. "Wait. I'll count backward from ten, then you can come."

It wasn't possible to wait, she knew.

"Eight. Wait. Concentrate on what I asked from you rather than on your pleasure."

That was impossible. Aria continued to rub and fuck. She had to squeeze her ass cheeks to fight off the ripples that threatened to explode inside her. Never, ever, had she tried to hold back an orgasm.

The sound of his voice faded, and if he was still counting, she couldn't hear him.

"Now."

She tipped her head back, spilling hair across her shoulders. With a ragged scream, she climaxed, her pussy pulsating around her fingers.

Aria dropped her left hand to the floor to help prop her up.

When the world righted itself and she moved her head back to neutral position, she saw him standing in front of her. She hadn't been aware that he'd even moved.

"Thank you for doing what I said," he said, offering to help her up.

"I've never had this many orgasms in one day."

"Give me your fingers."

Wordlessly, she extended her hand. He sucked the juices from her, prolonging the fuzzy feeling in her psyche.

"You're delicious, Aria. Everything about you. Now let's get you to bed."

He shucked off the water from his body then wrapped a towel around his waist. She scooped her clothes from the floor and walked from the room, aware of him following her, conscious, but not embarrassed by her nudity.

"You're sashaying."

"Yes." She looked at him over her shoulder. "I am."

Outside her bedroom door, she paused. He smacked her butt, hard, igniting nerve endings.

"You might want to behave."

"Or I might not," she replied.

"There's more to come."

"Including your cock?"

"Including my cock."

It'd been a long time, if ever, since he'd had such a physical reaction to a woman. Grant reminded himself that Aria was a neophyte, and that he was enjoying introducing her to his world, but that was only part of it.

The truth was, he liked her, considerably more than he'd anticipated. He liked her bravery, her curiosity, her company, her brain. And hell yes, her womanly, curvy, welcoming body.

Hard to believe that it had only been thirty hours ago that he'd gone for a long swim because he'd been pissed at Julien's interference.

Last night, after she'd gone to bed, he'd been unable to sleep. Ideas for scenes had clamored in his head. For the first time in years, he was thinking about something other than work.

And now, before the sun was even up on a long winter day, he was setting up his makeshift dungeon, and he was filled with energy.

He dragged over a bale of hay and rested it at an angle against a sawhorse. It wasn't a good substitute for a woman's body, but it would allow him to get some practice before he introduced Aria to the feel of his lash. To protect his equipment, he draped a blanket over the hay.

After he'd ended things with Kathleen, he'd all but given up the sexual part of his life. Since then, he'd spent the night with only a couple of ladies. By mutual accord—or really, due to his lack of attention—the relationships had drifted apart and ended amicably.

On occasion, he attended play parties in Santa Fe. While he'd flogged a handful of women, he hadn't gotten them off afterward. And he hadn't sought them out, even though one woman had bluntly knelt in front of him and asked him to be her Dom.

For Grant, it was more complicated than that. He didn't want just a sexual submissive. He wanted a woman who could also be a friend, confidante, partner.

Tall order, he'd told himself.

Even he realized the expectation was absurd and that he was setting himself up for a lifetime of loneliness.

Until now, that hadn't bothered him.

So far, what he was sharing with Aria was different than he'd experienced before. Her reactions were honest. The more he gave her, the more she seemed to want, if her sensuous, intentional sashay had been anything to go by.

He knew his reaction wasn't just from the fact she was residing beneath his roof. Even if they'd met elsewhere, he'd have sought her out. It seemed sex and sass were his new favorite turn-on.

Sending her to bed after spanking her hot little pussy had been difficult. He'd enjoyed holding her after the scenes and —as she'd pointed out—his cock had definitely been hard. He'd ached to sheath himself in her. All along, he'd been intending to do exactly that, and that was why he'd grabbed the condom.

But when he'd returned to her, he'd realized that it wasn't enough to fuck her and send her to bed. He wanted more time together, including an actual scene. He'd already tortured her pussy, and he hadn't been able to resist the temptation to spank the already-swollen flesh, giving her a taste of what she would be getting herself into with him.

From her first question about the portrait, he'd been truthful about his expectations. He realized that his kink wasn't everyone's kink. As he'd said, he could probably have vanilla sex with her and get off. But, with her, that wasn't enough.

After rolling his shoulders, he picked up a flogger—a weighty thing made from elk hide dyed purple. It was a custom-made piece, and he'd bought it at a specialty shop just off the plaza in Santa Fe. He'd never had the opportunity to use it on a submissive's unmarred skin.

He tested its weight, flicking it back and forth a bit.

Then he pictured where he'd need to land it if the hay were actually Aria's curvaceous derrière.

He landed a couple of lashes gently, getting accustomed to the feel, checking how far to stand back, then he practiced his backhand.

For long minutes, he tested his stance, his grip, the pressure.

The next hit was extraordinarily hard. When he repeated that on her body, a searing red stripe would appear on her skin. The image etched itself indelibly on his imagination.

After he was confident with the flogger, he switched to a crop. Honestly that was one of his favorite implements for a more advanced scene. The flapper could work almost like a single-tail, and the rod could be used in place of a cane.

He practiced different positions so that he could land it lengthwise as well as across a sub's body.

Finally comfortable, he grabbed a round piece of felt. He moved it to several different locations to test that he could strike it exactly where he wanted.

Several dozen hits later, he nodded in satisfaction. Now he couldn't wait to see Aria.

He returned his implements to a cabinet that hung on the wall before putting everything else back into storage. After that, he had Molly turn down the heat and reset the room's program. He had a bit of a surprise in store for Aria.

Hoping she was awake, Grant grabbed his coat and headed back to the main house.

When he'd walked over earlier, he'd shoveled the pathway, and since the storm had passed, it was still clear.

Along with the dog standing in the foyer, wagging his tail, the scent of fresh-brewed coffee greeted him. Sharing the house had its advantages. Despite himself, he grinned as he rubbed his hands together.

"Morning," she said.

Aria stood in the kitchen, hands wrapped around a mug he didn't recognize. Her hair was still rumpled, and she wore a robe over a pair of yoga pants. A container of creamer sat on the counter with its lid up. He noticed that she hadn't moved more than six inches away from the coffeepot. Which meant, obviously, she wasn't a morning person.

And he was absurdly happy to see her. "Is it safe to approach?"

"Do you have chocolate?"

For breakfast? He was smart enough not to let the question exit his mouth. "I'll get you as much as you want—if you share the coffee."

"You drive a hard bargain."

"You don't have to pour it. Just step away slowly."

"How far?" She brushed back wayward strands of hair.

All he could think of was wanting to see the locks spread out on his pillow.

"How about I make you chocolate chip pancakes?" he offered.

"You have the ingredients?"

"Probably. Daniella is my housekeeper. She bakes every once in a while when she's here. I keep a stash of her baked goods in the freezer. Top shelf, if you're interested."

She drained her mug and grimaced at him. "Okay, I'll share the coffee," she said grudgingly.

He grabbed a mug and filled it, adding a dollop of organic half and half. He offered his cup in a mock toast. She clinked rims with him.

While he gathered the ingredients for his protein drink and her pancakes, she filled her cup a second time.

"Did you travel with your own mug?"

She showed him the handle. "Big, and it has that notch at the top so I can keep a good grip on it."

"What's the saying?"

"With enough coffee I can rule the world."

"So there's your secret."

Midway through her second cup, as the griddle was sizzling and he dumped his berries and tofu in the blender, she asked, "Can I help with anything?"

"So it does work? Instant human, just add coffee?"

"Precisely."

He was content to have her in the kitchen, even if he did have to work around her at times. By the time he'd transferred the first batch of pancakes to a platter, she'd set the table. He poured an ounce of his drink into a separate glass then began moving food and syrup to the dining room.

"How'd you sleep?" He slid into his seat and put the extra serving of protein drink in front of her.

"Amazing. After everything, I didn't think I would, but with that mattress and the blackout panel, I thought I might stay in bed until noon."

"Any lingering effects?"

"In a bad way? No." She took a bite of her pancakes, then let her shoulders fall as she sighed. "Look, Grant, I'm just telling you straight up, if you want me to leave, ever, you're going to have to stop making food like this."

"I'm glad you approve. Try the protein drink."

"I was afraid that was for me."

"You wrinkled your nose."

She held her fork in front of her. A drop of syrup fell to the plate. "So did you when I asked for chocolate."

"True enough."

After swallowing her bite, she downed the contents of the glass in a single drink. "It's good."

"How do you know? You didn't taste it."

She grinned. Yeah. Sass and sex were his two new turn-ons.

A few minutes later, she finally approached the subject that he'd been waiting for. "I noticed that you cleared a path to the garage and to your dungeon."

"Want to know what I was doing?"

"I'm scared to ask."

"What happened to living dangerously?"

She put down her fork. "You know my imagination goes wild at the idea of a dungeon, right? Whips, chains, torture devices."

"Like a medieval castle."

"Only worse."

"You could be right."

She shuddered.

"It's not quite that bad. I don't have thumbscrews." He finished his breakfast then sat back. "I put it together so that I could host a play party out here when the weather is warmer. But if you want to try it out, you'll be my first guest."

"Thank you for the invitation?" She wrinkled her nose. "I think."

"Torture devices are in the eye of the beholder. You might like it."

"I don't know. Being tied up? Beaten?"

"All of that and more." He finished his smoothie, giving her time to change the subject. Her grip tightened on her empty mug, but she didn't otherwise move. "Until last night, you might have thought you wouldn't like having your pussy spanked."

She pulled the lapels of her robe a little tighter.

"I was practicing with a flogger and a crop."

"I thought about coming out, but I was too nervous."

"We can go and have a look without trying anything. You can ask questions, touch things."

"I think I'll pass. Anyway, I need to shower and get dressed."

If she was hoping the excuse would get her out of it, she was mistaken. "Go ahead. I'll wait. We've got all day."

He cleaned the kitchen while she got ready.

When she returned, her hair was piled on top of her head and clamped into place with some sort of clip. She was wearing painted-on jeans, a black cashmere sweater and she'd selected those lust-inducing boots. "On second thought," he said.

"Oh?"

"Come here."

Her heels made a sound much like a thundering pulse as she moved across the hardwood floor to him. She stopped barely inches away. "While I was in the shower, I was thinking about your dungeon."

"And was it in a good way?"

"Scary. But curious."

"Did you masturbate?"

She looked up at him and seemed to consider her answer. "I thought about it, but I didn't follow through."

"Good. Your orgasms belong to me now."

"I'm not sure I understand what you mean."

"I want you to ask permission before you come."

She opened her mouth, then closed it again. "Wow. I've never had a man demand that from me before."

"It adds another dimension. I'm not into orgasm denial, at least not typically. But I am interested in everything about you, and I may want to give you further instructions. Or I may just want to know you're doing it."

He waited.

"I'm yours to command, Sir."

She might be a little flippant, but to him, her words were with rich with meaning. "I like the way that sounds," he admitted.

To break the sudden tension, he plucked the clip from her hair and allowed the tresses to tumble over her shoulders. Then he tugged off her sweater and dropped it to the floor. "I want you naked," he instructed. "Now."

Aria licked her lower lip. "Right now?"

"Naked," he repeated. "You told me last night you wanted to try it your way, so let's get on with it."

Her green eyes became a shade darker, and he knew his words had caused response to flare in her. This woman was so, so meant for him.

She reached back to unhook her bra before allowing it to fall on top of her sweater. While she unfastened her jeans and fumbled with the zipper, he squeezed her breasts.

He watched her tip her head back and she moaned, driving him on.

Keeping his grip tight, he rolled her nipples between his thumbs and forefingers.

Obviously fighting her own responses, she managed to shove her jeans down past her hips. He lifted her from the floor and sat her on the counter so he could tug off her boots and socks before pulling her jeans off the rest of the way.

"I'm not sure why I bothered getting dressed," she said as she held onto the quartz.

He grabbed hold of her waist and lowered her to the floor. Almost out of patience, he yanked aside the fabric of her panties and pressed a finger against her clit. Her way was definitely working for him.

She sucked in a harsh little breath that further drove him on. When she reached for his waistband, he allowed her to unbuckle his belt and unfasten his fly. "That's it," he said when she maneuvered her hand so that she could grab him through his briefs. "Stroke my dick, little Aria."

Immediately she did, and he gritted his teeth.

She worked her palm back and forth, and she placed her other hand on his shoulder so she could keep her balance as he slid a finger inside her hot pussy.

"Grant, this is so, so..."

If she said anything else, he didn't hear it.

"My bedroom," he told her.

"That's about a jillion miles away," she protested.

"And it will feel like more because you'll be crawling."

She went still and released his cock. "I... What?"

Knowing he'd shocked her, he continued to fondle her, distracting her until he felt her clench her muscles and her pussy began to convulse around him. When he had her on the very edge of an orgasm, he extracted his hand and put a thumb beneath her chin to tip her head back.

Her breath was ragged. Like his.

"Do your sashay thing. All fours." His voice was a little hoarse. He'd never been with a woman where he didn't have complete control, until her.

Even though she worried her lower lip for a moment, she followed his instruction.

He folded his arms across his chest as she tipped her head to the side to look at him through the curtain of her hair.

Then she began to crawl.

The moment her hips began to move and he saw her breasts sway, blood surged into his cock, making it throb. Good thing she'd already lowered his zipper.

Suddenly he agreed with her. His room was about a jillion miles away, and he was anxious to sink deep inside her and fuck her hard.

He followed, enjoying the sight of her delicate, frothy

panties as the material crawled up her buttocks. The fact he could only see the outline of her sex made it even more enticing.

When they reached the entrance to his room, she stopped, and he reached over her to open the door. "Sit on the bed."

She continued crawling, and she was sinuous as she stood, turned then scooted onto the edge of the bed.

Then, tantalizingly, she tossed her head, spilling her hair everywhere before rolling her shoulders. She placed her hands on the mattress a little behind her, forcing out her chest. Evidently she was a quick learner. "Finish undressing me," he commanded.

"I thought you'd never ask." Leaning forward, she pulled the belt from the loops.

"Put that next to you. I have plans for it."

Next, she tugged off his long-sleeved Henley shirt. He bent to remove his motorcycle boots which he tossed beneath the bed.

"Mind if I kneel?" her voice was a bit husky, telling him she was as aroused as he was.

His Aria was a little more submissive than she wanted to believe.

She slid from the bed and knelt in front of him to pull down his jeans. "I've never undressed a man before," she said. "Never knew…"

Grant stepped out of his jeans and kicked them aside, as well.

Without any further encouragement, she worked his briefs down and then gave a little sound of surprise. "You shave your balls?"

"Yeah. And you can take over that little task while you're here."

She looked up at him.

"I'm serious."

"I'm starting to realize you rarely joke, even if I think maybe you are."

"When it comes to things that involve you, you're right." He fed his fingers into her hair and brushed it back to tuck it behind her ears. "Back onto the bed and hand me the belt."

Grant didn't step back, so their bodies brushed as she stood. He offered a hand and she took it.

He noticed the rapid rise and fall of her chest as she picked up the belt. There'd come a time when an instruction like that would settle her in, let her know they were entering a scene. "Turn your palms up and extend your arms, offering it to me."

He half expected a question or a token protest, but she silently did as he requested. "Thank you," he said, accepting the leather. "Now lie back, in the middle of the bed and cross your wrists above your head. While you're at it, spread your legs so I can admire your cunt."

She made a sound that was part sigh, mostly whimper, all feminine and soft.

"You wanted to be fucked, Aria?"

"Yes. Hard."

He wrapped his belt around her wrists several times, making sure she was secure but that he wasn't cutting off circulation.

"I thought we were doing it my way."

"With my signature added," he said. Then he indicated the portrait. "She's a constant reminder to both of us," he told Aria. "Give me a second."

He grabbed two toys and a condom from the closet. "This is a spreader bar. Exactly as it sounds. It will keep your ankles apart."

"What if I wanted to wrap my legs around your waist? Or we wanted to change positions or something?"

He raised his eyebrows and remained silent until she started to squirm.

"Right. Patience," she said, as if talking to herself. "Remember the portrait."

Fighting a grin, he attached her ankles to the far ends of the bars. "Is that comfortable?"

"Barely," she confessed.

"Perfect." Grant opened a tiny box and showed her the four small balls that were nestled against the velvet lining. "Nipple balls," he explained. "I sometimes use clamps, but these are a favorite since they won't fall off, nor is there anything to tug, so they'll stay in place. And they're absolutely beautiful."

"I don't understand how they work."

"They're magnetic." He used his thumb to separate two. In the online advertisement, they looked deceptively simple to use and at first glance, they appeared as if they were capable of only gentle pressure.

He'd practiced using them on the tender flesh between this thumb and forefinger. He'd quickly learned that the buggers moved of their own accord, so they had to be kept separate until he was ready for them to meet up. And the bite was this side of extreme. But since she'd arrived, he'd been desperate to see them on her dusky nipples.

Grant placed the first pair near her right breast. "Have you ever played with nipple clamps?"

"No." She turned her head to the side, apparently to get a better look at the pretty balls. "But sometimes when I use my vibrator, I use clothespins. The plastic ones work best since they don't twist."

"The twisting can be fun. Adds an unexpected dimension of pain."

She looked back at him. "I think you have a diabolically nasty streak."

"And you're at my mercy."

"Yellow still works, right?"

"Always," he promised her. "I'll warn you, these balls are going to be more intense than you're expecting. Harder than your clothespins, probably. Breathe through it. Let me get both sets on before you decide you can't take the pain."

"You're scaring me."

He sucked her right nipple into his mouth, teasing and distending the flesh. "A little fear is good in my submissive."

She squirmed, digging her heels into the bedding.

"Vertical or horizontal?"

"Vertical," she said. "No, wait. Whatever you please, Sir."

"Good girl." Grant picked up the first set of balls and pried them apart. He tugged on the still-damp nipple. Before it could contract, he put one ball on the top, then carefully put the other beneath it. At a certain point, the forces of nature took over and the magnets connected, brutally pinching her flesh.

"Holy fucking hell!" she yelled.

He fingered her pussy and simultaneously licked her nipple. Her body was convulsing, but she slowly settled down. "Can you handle this? For me?"

She forced out a shuddering breath. "Why do I feel like you're a physical trainer? He insists I do one more set when I can't even stand up."

"Seems to me you go looking for sadists, in that case."

Their gazes met, held. "Maybe so. Do your worst… What do I call you? Just Sir?" Before he could answer she continued, "Wait. I've got it. Do your worst, Sir Sadist."

"Oh, little Aria, you haven't been introduced to anything close to that yet." All the while, he continued to play with her pussy and touch her in soothing ways.

Making sure to keep their connection strong, he reached for the second set of balls and put them in place.

This time she whimpered and writhed but didn't scream. Again, he soothed the ache with his mouth. "Stay where you are. I want to show you how sweet your submission is." For a moment, he left her.

"It feels worse when you're not touching me," she told him.

"I'm right here, and I know." Or at least he did now. She needed their bodies to be physically connected. So the idea of her ever being like the woman in the portrait was remote, but if he were truthful, this appealed to him every bit as much. He enjoyed the feel of her skin, her softness, her strength.

In seconds, he returned to her with a mirror. "This isn't going to be easy," he said. "But I want you to sit up." He climbed onto the bed and knelt behind her and helped her into the correct position.

She winced but didn't complain, even though her legs were spread, her hands were bound and magnetic balls bit into her tender skin.

"Perfect. Now bring your shoulder blades together," he said.

After a couple of steadying breaths, she did as he asked.

He kept his body in place to support her then reached around her with the mirror. "Have a look. I want you to see yourself through my eyes."

She inhaled sharply. "I've always played with the idea of getting my nipples pierced."

"And now?"

"They're beautiful, aren't they?"

"You're beautiful. This just enhances it."

Silently, in the mirror, they communicated, her trust and his promise that he'd always earn it.

"Your cock is still hard. Is this when we get to the fucking part?" she asked quietly.

"It is indeed." He helped her to lie down again, and he left the mirror on top of the nightstand, handy in case he wanted to use it again. "You still have your panties on."

"I wondered what you were going to do about that."

He pulled a pair of first-aid scissors from the nightstand drawer.

"Seriously?" she asked, sounding a little scandalized, but mostly turned on. "I like these panties."

"I'll send you a dozen more. But I'll want to cut those off you, as well."

"This is going to be a budget-buster," she warned.

"I'd take out a loan if I needed to," he added before snipping the material from her body, leaving the peach-colored lace in a pile. "Your pussy is swollen."

"Because you spanked it last night."

"I did, indeed." He sat next to her and stroked between the swollen lips. "I think you like those balls more than you might be willing to admit. You're already wet."

"They're hot," she admitted.

"Damn." He leaned over. He used his right hand to separate her labia while he devoured her pussy with his mouth.

Within seconds, he had her jerking again. No woman—even submissives at the club—had ever responded to him this quickly. It was as if they both fed the flames of arousal.

"Every time I move, I feel it in my breasts."

"If you can tolerate it, it's going to drive you wild."

"It is. I want more." Her eyes were wide, beseeching. "Please?"

He reached for the condom and ripped open the package. She kept her gaze on him, and he hurried, aware that she'd soon start to notice the pressure in her nipples. He rolled the condom down his cock, but traced a pattern on her skin so she knew his focus was on her.

After making sure she was still wet, he moved between her legs.

He teased her entrance with his cockhead, then wondered who was really being tormented. He'd hungered for this since he'd first seen her.

"Grant!"

He took several strokes, moving in a little deeper with each. Aria was trying to lift her hips, but the spreader bar prevented her from getting any leverage. She growled in frustration.

They would do this at his speed. No matter whether she'd asked for this or not, he intended to control the scene.

He propped his weight on one elbow, and he curled the other hand around one of her breasts.

Her legs vibrated.

He'd had sex with plenty of women, but not like this, not like her.

"All the way," she urged. "Hard. Do me *hard.*"

He drove his dick all the way into her, joining them completely. She cried out his name. He fucked her, rode her. Devoured her.

"I need to come."

"As often as you want," he replied. He consumed her mouth with a kiss, letting her know how pleased he was that she'd asked.

He sought her tongue, and forced her mouth farther apart with his. He had to have this woman.

She went rigid before turning her head to the side, severing their contact. Aria squeezed her eyes shut and made tiny little sobs as she came in a shuddering climax.

The combination of her sex sounds and her pussy's contractions almost wrung an orgasm from him, but he gritted his back teeth to hold himself back. He wasn't done with her yet.

As soon as her body went limp, he raised himself up a little, but kept his cock inside her. "Deep breath," he warned, and pulled apart the balls on one nipple.

She hissed.

"And again." He removed the second.

"They're hideous," she said.

"And you're hoping I let you take them home with you. Barring that, you hope you can find them in an online kink shop."

"Something like that."

He grinned and shoved both pairs beneath a pillow for safekeeping. "As deep as I was," he said, "as hot as that was, I want more."

"I think my number of orgasms is around one dozen to your zero."

"We'll work out an exact ratio later," he promised. "But only if you put on a schoolgirl outfit. Plaid."

"Ah..."

"That one was a joke." He grinned.

She scowled.

He enjoyed the banter with her, another way in which their relationship was unique. "How are your wrists?"

"The world feels like heaven since you took the balls off." She tested the restraints. "Everything's fine."

"Good, because now I'm really going to fuck you."

"We're not done?"

"As you pointed out, the orgasm to orgasm ratio is a bit skewed." He and moved off her temporarily while he checked her restraints for himself. "I need you to lift your legs."

"Did you spend all morning dreaming up impossible tasks for me?"

He took hold of the spreader bar and helped her to raise her legs. "Keep them in place." Then he moved between her thighs.

"I think this defies physics. At least common sense," she said.

"It does leave you a bit defenseless," he agreed, kissing her forehead. "And you wanted me to fuck you hard. Go ahead and lower your legs."

"I'm afraid I'll clobber you with the bar."

"You won't."

As she shifted, he moved, getting into position so that her knees were resting on his shoulders, the bar was behind him and their bodies were molded against each together.

Slowly, he warmed up her body again, taking it slow until her pussy moistened.

Then he began to thrust. The edge he'd been on since she'd arrived sliced away at his restraint. He intended to possess this woman.

"I like this. So, so much," she said.

She pushed her weight down on her shoulders so she could elevate her bottom, opening herself wider, inviting him even deeper.

He wanted to make it good for her one more time. He shifted his balance onto his elbows. They were skin to skin, need to need.

"My God," she said. "I feel as if I'm..."

He drove into her.

She screamed.

With her eyes closed, she tossed her head. But instead of trying to get away, she used her abdominal muscles to lift her body in silent entreaty.

He obliged. It was impossible not to. The scent of her, arousal layered with a tantalizing vanilla that spoke of promise, made him aware of his masculinity and drove an instinctive need to be with her.

Even though it was difficult, he focused on her, shifting

so that he could reach a hand between them to rub a finger against her swollen clit.

She sobbed, and it sounded like she'd said his name.

"Come for me." He rubbed harder, then moved higher to squeeze her nipple. That shot a response through her, and he felt her body convulse.

That pushed him toward the edge. His balls lifted, became taut. He raised up onto his hands so he didn't crush her, then he stroked once, twice. He arched his back and groaned as he ejaculated deep inside her.

His orgasm went on for long seconds, and he grunted with the raw pleasure.

Strength seemed to have evaporated.

He opened his eyes to see her staring up at him. Her body was as relaxed at it could possibly be given her restraints, and he reached to loosen the belt.

As soon as she was free, she dug her hands into his shoulders, holding on, wordlessly letting him know that whatever he felt, she did as well.

"Let me get you out of the spreader bar, too," he said. Though he'd rather just collapse and gather her close, he adjusted them so that he could put her legs flat on the bed, then he released the ankle cuffs.

He disposed of the condom in a nearby trash bin, then lay next to her and pulled her against his chest, tucking her beneath his chin, spooning his body around hers.

A sheen of perspiration cooled on his skin, and he knew she'd quickly catch a chill. "Molly, temperature at seventy-three degrees. This zone only."

Instead of getting a smart-ass response like he expected from the system, he heard a faint mechanical sound then warm air whispered over them.

"That was…"

"Hard enough?"

"I honestly don't have words," Aria said. "When you suggested this whole kink thing, I honestly wasn't sure."

"And now?"

"Is this ratio thing how it is in every time? Because I've certainly had relationships where it's been tilted a bit in the opposite direction."

"I'm not sure how it is for anyone else," he told her. "But for any submissive of mine, the number's about right."

"Incredible."

He smoothed down her hair. "Is your body okay? Any soreness?"

"Just my pussy."

"From the spanking?" He acknowledged he had been a bit rough with her clit while he'd fucked her. "I could get you a warm compress."

"No, it's more of an internal thing." She winced. "You fucked me hard."

Even though it wasn't polite, he grinned, ridiculously pleased with himself.

"Does this serve as a warning that I should be careful what I ask for?"

"Happy to take care of my lady's needs."

"And even a few she didn't know she had."

Her words had made his ego puff up, and that was definitely not something to be proud of. "How about we get some work done so I can introduce you to the dungeon later? Not to play, just for you to have a look, explore, get comfortable, consider whether it's something you want to take further."

"How am I supposed to do anything other than think about what you have planned?"

"We're in this together," he assured her. Grant was realizing that, quite possibly, he was in deeper than she was.

CHAPTER SIX

"A *genius is trying to reach you."*

"Again? How many times a day does he bother you?" Aria asked, almost having to shout over the sound of Julien's theme music blasting through the workshop. She and Grant had met up about an hour ago. When she'd entered the super-secret space, she'd discovered that he'd made her a fresh cup of coffee and it was in a thermal cup so it stayed warm. It wasn't just his cooking that was making it difficult for her to think of leaving. "How the hell do you get anything done at all?"

"This is unusual," he assured her. "In all the time I've been out here, he's never called three days in a row." Grant shook his head. "He's proud of himself for throwing us together for this project. He needs to see how it's going so he can gloat."

"That's pleasant."

"Wait until he preens."

"He"—her mouth dropped open—"preens?"

"And it's every bit as traumatic as you might imagine. Should we ignore him?"

"Will he call back?"

"Incessantly. And email. And text."

"And sweet talk Molly into letting me use her channels so I can hear every word of what's going on in that house."

"Or that," Grant said easily, giving her a glimpse of how close their friendship really was. "Afternoon, Julien." To Aria, he added, "Shall we turn the video on or make him wonder?"

"I think he should see two of his key people hard at work." As long as she didn't try to move and reveal to him how tender her flesh was from her earlier scenes with Grant.

The image of a lush rainforest faded and was replaced by a picture of Julien. He was standing in his office, hands tucked into the front pockets of his tailored jeans. He wore a white Oxford shirt with the top button unfastened. For once he had on a tie, but the knot was so loose he might as well not have put it on. He rocked back and forth, looking inordinately pleased with himself.

She and Grant exchanged glances.

"You two are doing great," Julien said. "I couldn't be happier."

"Because we're in the workshop having a coffee?" Grant asked.

"No. Because your habits give you away. According to the research I've done, Aria hasn't been complaining to David at all, nor has she called him to try to stick her clever ideas into the department he's running on her behalf. She responded to emails this morning, but didn't generate any new ones other than to check up on the project for Blanca."

That much was true, and she was embarrassed to realize maybe she was guilty of micromanagement to some degree. Like a lot of people, she used work to escape her real-life challenges.

"Radar shows there's been a miserable storm in that part of New Mexico, and she hasn't called out search and rescue to come and get her." He pulled one hand from a pocket and gave a cheeky wave. "Hey, Aria. Nice boots."

She shrugged when Grant looked at her.

"A woman can rule the world in those boots," Julien said. "Heels and leather? Put me six feet under and call me happy." He exaggeratedly rolled his eyes back.

"He did tell me I should wear them," she admitted, feeling a blush creep up her cheeks.

"Good call," Grant told Julien.

"And as for you..." Julien continued, turning to Grant.

Aria couldn't wait.

"You weren't working at two o'clock this morning."

"How would you know that?"

"I pinged you, and you didn't answer. It's been years since something like that happened." He stuck his hand back in his pocket then directed his gaze skyward. "Years. If you were unhappy or brooding—"

"I don't—"

"Oh, please. You've made it an art form," Julien insisted. "As I was saying, you'd have been up all night."

Judging by that standard, she was obviously happy, too. After their rendezvous in the hot tub, she'd slept better than she had in a long time. She wasn't as sure the same thing would hold true tonight.

After he'd fucked her earlier, he'd held on to her for a long time, sharing his body heat. She was the type of woman who enjoyed snuggling, and Simon had not indulged her. After sex, he would roll over and go to sleep, most of the time still naked. If she touched him during the night, he'd move away, insisting he slept 'hot' and that her body heat made it impossible for him to get any rest. Over time, she'd adjusted to sleeping in a pair of pajamas with long pants because he didn't even like to have a blanket on the bed.

The sex with Grant had been astounding, and her

further exploration into BDSM was shattering everything she'd always assumed about sex. She might have to telephone one of her girlfriends later to get some perspective. She'd always wrinkled her nose at the idea of being tied up or spanked, and yet both had happened within a twelve hour period.

After they'd rested for a few minutes, Grant had gotten out of bed and returned with a warm washcloth. She'd reached for it, but he'd moved her hand aside, not even acknowledging her protests that he was spoiling her.

She'd never experienced so many sensations at the same time, from the constriction of her arms to having her legs spread ridiculously far apart. He'd had her completely bound and helpless, but shockingly she hadn't experienced even one ripple of fear.

The vicious bite of the nipple balls had made her eyes water, and she hadn't been sure she could tolerate the pain. But then he'd moved behind her, helped her sit up then picked up a mirror and held it in front of them. Their gazes had connected. At first, she'd seen a reflection of doubt in her own eyes. The magnetic silver balls had looked beautiful. He'd been right about that. Then she'd looked deeper, more closely at him. There'd been approval and encouragement in his blue eyes. And something more. Lust, no doubt. But also something tender as well. A man didn't look at a woman with that expression unless he cared about her.

The combination of regard and need had caused her to transcend the pain, and, in fact, had made her even hotter for him.

"So come on, give it up. Am I a genius, or what?"

"That remains to be seen. We've only been here twenty-four hours." He looked at her.

They had a shared secret, and the reminder made her tingle.

"We haven't come up with anything feasible for Bonds, yet," Grant finished.

She heard the subtext. For them, personally, things were definitely working.

"Our next billion dollars is out there, waiting." Hands still shoved into his pockets, Julien rocked forward onto the balls of his feet.

"No pressure there," Grant said.

"The fate of the world is on your shoulders." Julien's body seemed to vibrate with energy, as if he hadn't slept in days and didn't need to.

"Or the spring show," she added.

"That too," Julien agreed. "But that doesn't sound nearly as dramatic."

"You need to stop watching disaster movie promos," Grant said.

"Hold on," Aria said as realization dawned. The theme music, the way he was talking, the fact he'd sent her into Grant's lair. "You're making a movie."

Grant looked at her, a puzzled frown on his face, darkening his eyes, forcing his eyebrows together. "What are you talking about?"

"Always helps to diversify," Julien replied. "I've always want to attend a premiere."

"Make friends with an actor," Grant suggested.

"Or own the carpet yourself."

"See why I like her?" Julien's grin deepened. "I'm expecting great things from you, and I know you'll deliver." Without another word, the screen went blank.

She and Grant looked at one another for a moment in silence.

"Enlighten me," he prompted.

"Whatever he told us, whatever we believed originally, we were wrong. Don't misunderstand. He adores the fact he can get what he wants—a new project developed especially while he's meddling in our lives—but he's operating from a higher purpose." She waved a hand, indicating Grant's workshop. "He *is* grooming you for a larger role at Bonds. I'm willing to bet he's been telling you that all along. You just haven't wanted to hear him."

"Doesn't matter. Still not interested."

"You're not going to have much of a choice." Everything made perfect sense. If she were Julien, she might have come up with the same idea. "He's diversifying into other areas that intrigue him. Of course he is. He gets bored, restless. But all of a sudden, he's got a million projects going. Even though he is Julien Bonds, there are still only twenty-four hours in a day." She began to pace. "He is interested in movies. And it's time for advances there that are going to come out of Silicon Valley and not Hollywood, or…"

She waved a hand, impatient with herself for not being able to sort out what she was thinking, put it in an order that would make sense to Grant, and express herself coherently. "A hybrid. Hollywood may have the idea, but the execution is going to require horsepower, in terms of computer programming, in terms of mainframe capacity. Have you seen him this excited before?"

"In college," Grant admitted. "Then again when we rented the first office in Silicon Valley, in the remains of a startup that had gone bankrupt. Then when he introduced his smart watch. And again when he broke ground on the Bonds headquarters. We dragged old furniture from our first office out there, piled it up, put a torch to it, and bam—fucking epic bonfire. We shook a bottle of champagne, launched the cork into the next county then realized we hadn't brought anything to pour it into, so we swigged it straight from the bottle, just like college. Had them turn the dirt over, so the ashes are still there. You know Julien. Said it was the past, present, future, all blended together. All very dramatic. Said we should have filmed it for the archives. You know, just in case someone wanted to watch it a hundred years from now."

She laughed. "I hadn't heard that story."

"I'm surprised. I thought it was legend. We got a hell of a ticket. Something about not being allowed to have a fire in the city limits."

"Who knew?"

He shrugged. "They wanted our tax dollars more than they wanted to make a point. And when they sent the fire trucks and police, a camera crew from a local news station was notified. So he got his footage. And yeah, it's in a digital archive. And because he's now a gazillionaire, we didn't get arrested."

"All of those stories have one thing in common," she said.

He waited.

"You. You've been part of all of that. And he needs you in the future every bit as much as he needed you in college, in the early days. He's looking to you, to us, to provide infill and backfill."

"That sounds like human resources jargon—maybe even bullshit."

"I'm not expressing this well." Aria strode to the window. This time, because her brain was moving so rapidly, she didn't experience any vertigo at the sight of the sheer drop off. "In order for him to move onto the next big thing, he needs people he can trust. There will be a hole created in the organization when he turns his focus toward other things. He's smart enough to see that." She turned back to face him. "What I mean is this... You are going to fill the voids he creates. More and more, you're going to be the face of the technology side of Bonds."

"Not interested." Resolutely, he folded his arms.

Stubborn man. No wonder Julien had sent her. At first, she'd thought he was punishing her for the Simon fiasco. Her broken engagement had made headlines, none of them good, for Bonds. If she hadn't been so stunned and upset by his dictate, she would have realized that he didn't behave that way.

Certainly, he could be fucking ruthless if people betrayed him, violated their confidentiality agreement. He treated his people well, but she'd seen him ruin careers of people who'd plotted against him. And he had always known she wouldn't do anything to harm him or Bonds. Sending her to New Mexico wasn't an act of retaliation, it was an investment in the organization's success.

He needed to see if they could work together, if she could coax or coach Grant into being more prominent. The public, as well as the press and business community, would need to trust him.

Turning to her for help wasn't a bad tactic. She'd developed a leadership program in their overseas divisions so that all representatives, no matter where they lived on the planet, were communicating the same messages about Bonds' integrity and how freaking cool the products were.

She'd seen an intense side of Grant. The fact he'd created Molly—and the hologram dog—attested to his creativity. If the world could see that—like she did, like Julien did—then Julien would be free to expand the business. But first, she had to get Grant out of his cave. Realization dawned on her. The cave wasn't just literal, it was figurative, too. The man needed to come back, at least occasionally, to Silicon Valley. Julien was right about other things, too. When people interacted, energy was generated. What had happened between her and Grant was proof of that.

But she recognized the firm set of his jaw. Whatever had brought him here to Los Alamos would take a while to undo. That was okay. She was patient. He hadn't shoved her into a

BDSM scene. He'd allowed it to move at its own pace. She could do the same for Julien and Bonds. "There is no one else," she told him. "You're a cofounder. You understand him. Without you, there would be no Bonds. Julien is smart enough to know it—and so are you."

"This was never part of the deal."

She was willing to bet that Grant leaving Julien's side hadn't been part of the plan, either. To cover her frustration and the fact she wasn't sure how to help, she asked, "So, where were we before the genius interrupted?"

"Talking in circles," he replied. "Probably because I couldn't stop thinking about sex."

She grinned. "Me either." She crossed the room and slid back onto the stool near him. "What have we got?"

Drinking coffee, they reviewed their ideas from yesterday.

Grant pressed a couple of keys and a thick piece of glass rose from the floor. "Sometimes I prefer to work the old-fashioned way."

If glass partitions rising from a hole in the floor were old-fashioned, sure.

He grabbed a set of colorful markers and put them on top of the metal table then picked up an eraser and started to remove old notes.

"Wait!"

"Don't panic. Molly took an image of the work, saved it and created a file. She can project it back at any point."

"Silly me. When I say old-fashioned, I mean I get a notebook and scribble random thoughts, and when I can't remember where I left the notebook, my ideas are gone forever."

"That *is* old-fashioned," he agreed with a disarming grin.

Together, they recreated the thoughts from yesterday, of

how to make Molly functional at a greater level. They added new notes, ways Molly could be improved.

"Don't tell her I agree with you," Grant warned.

They took a short break to head back toward the kitchen for snacks and to brew a third pot of coffee. She noticed the dog in front of the hearth, and it lifted its head when she entered the room. Its tail did a slow thump on the floor. "Shadow," she said.

"Shadow?"

"The dog. He's always there, real, but not real."

"Brilliant and appropriate," Grant approved.

"I can't believe I didn't think of it before now."

"You did well. I've lived with him for months without even coming up with a name. Shadow it is." He nodded.

Outside, the sky was a milky blue. "This is the first time I've seen the sun since I arrived."

"Once the front passes, it will be spectacular."

A few minutes later, drinks refreshed, they returned to the workshop. The forest scene was back, and the sight of their notes, in random colors, with dots connecting them and small drawings invigorated her. "We need to start with a platform that already exists," she said. "Something that's already in a lot of—if not all—homes and build from there. Don't limit it, but consider ones that carry data."

He drew a line that arced. "Name them."

"Internet. Cable. Some appliances already have smart technology built-in."

"Cell phones. Tablets." Grant nodded and wrote, then added, "Alarm companies."

"Alarm companies?" She drummed her fingers on the metal. "That's a hell of an idea."

"We still have the problem of proprietary or closed interfaces."

She nodded. "Unless we work out a deal. Or…"

"Or?"

"Never mind. It seems...ridiculous."

He capped the marker and looked back at her. "That's what the brainstorming process is for."

"I know. But no one wants to be that person. You know, the one where everyone rolls their eyes? Or worse, groans."

"Better you than me."

"Thanks." She shot him the stink eye to let him know how she felt.

He grinned and slid onto a stool across from her.

"We could work out deals with all these different places—or we could build our own. It makes sense in some ways. We already provide music, books."

"Keep going."

"An even bigger challenge is the hardware. How do you think Julien would feel if we asked him to go out and buy an alarm company and a cable company?"

"Yeah." He sat back. "Pick any two from above. Cable and alarm. Satellite and alarm."

"They have hardware already in people's houses. They've got trust established, a business model that could be tweaked, but it wouldn't need to be created."

Grant whistled. "This is a departure."

"Privacy concerns," she added. "And that's just the beginning. We'll be accused of dozens of things. Obscure laws will be dug up. We'll be sued by private industry, by governments, including our own. It's ludicrous to even consider it." She put a hand over mouth, as if that had any hope of stopping the flow of the words. "I can list sixty-two thousand reasons we should abandon this line of thinking right now. Figure out how to market a stuffed animal that lets nervous parents know how their baby is doing at day care. We should enhance the phones, tweak the watch technology. I know... release the tablet in fourteen karat gold accented with diamonds." Anything but dream up a project so filled with problems.

"If we're not going to change the world, what's the point in showing up for work?" he asked.

That wasn't rhetorical. More like the company motto.

"It would enable us to add a million different services. Your music can play through the whole house."

"And if Julien wants to go into movies…"

"*Fuck me.* He could be on everyone's television sets." Grant tossed his pen in the air. "He'll fucking love it."

"And he can talk everyone through the instructions via a hologram."

"If there's a device in the home…"

They were both silent.

"This will take years," he said.

"Eons," she agreed. Her heart was thundering as ideas zipped through her brain, and possibilities blossomed. "Connecting the world. Others will be forced to interact with our interface."

"Better that than us trying to interact with theirs."

Those words could have come directly out of Julien's mouth, she knew. She was beginning to see how much alike their viewpoint was, even though they couldn't be more different otherwise.

"And someone's going to attempt this eventually," he continued. "But it will never end up as well as if we do it."

"This is beyond arrogant," she said. "Audacious."

"Huge."

"Hairy." And that was what Julien demanded from all his employees. If a concept wasn't scary, it wasn't worth the investment of energy. If it was terrifying, all the better.

She picked up her thermal cup to take a drink, but it was empty.

"I could go and refill it for you."

"You're a man after my heart, but I need to sleep tonight." Forgetting the coffee again, she slid from the stool and arched her back. "We need to think this through. We can't take it to Julien at this stage."

"Agreed."

She noticed that the sun was setting on the horizon. Again, they'd worked for hours without either of them noticing. Being here, without constant email and phone interruptions, soothed the brain as well as the body. She understood Grant better. Who could blame him for not wanting to go back, especially with all that that entailed?

Unfortunately, she knew it was part of her job to get him to agree to that. Bonds needed him. Julien needed him. The world needed him. So how the hell was she going to convince him to do that? "It looks so pretty out there with all that snow," she said, glancing at him back over her shoulder. "Cold, but spectacular."

"We can use the hot tub after our session in the dungeon."

Just that fast, he changed her thoughts, derailing work ideas and making her internal temperature climb. Her pulse, already zinging from the brainstorming, became even threadier. "I thought I said I'd pass on that."

"Yeah." He grinned. "But you didn't say yellow."

"Clever man, Mr. Kingston."

"*He likes Your Majesty better*," Molly chimed in.

"Automatic response," he said.

"Julien," Aria added.

"Those privacy concerns are going to be legitimate. Anyway, back to our conversation. Let's start dinner. As I suggested earlier, I'll take you out there. You can have a look around. You can even bring your wine and your objections. Then you can make a decision about the upcoming evening. If you don't want to be the subbie to christen it, that's fine. No pressure."

He made it sound light, fun. And maybe it could be, for a different woman. But she knew herself and him. Grant would snare her in his spell, and soon she'd be trying things she'd never heard of. And she'd be having a spectacular orgasm—or two.

He stood. Since they'd been working for hours without a break and she was hungry, she nodded. "No promises."

"Haven't asked for any."

"Uh-huh," she said.

After leaving the workshop and securing the door, they walked down the hall, and she saw the dog was again curled in front of the fire. "Do you have Shadow on a timer?"

"I enjoy the companionship when I want dinner, so yes. Whatever time dusk is, he shows up. And if I leave the house, he waits in the foyer for me."

Her heart slowed momentarily as it occurred to her how very alone Grant was. Julien was right to seek him out. It wasn't just for the brainstorming or for the fact Bonds needed a more involved second-in-command. This was about Grant himself.

She knew his isolation was self-induced. She was willing to bet it had something to do with his former fiancée as well as grief. He was clearly a man who loved deeply and completely.

"Pasta?" he offered. "Or we could warm up some tamales, though I'd rather make those for breakfast with eggs."

"That sounds interesting. So pasta would be great."

"Baked ziti?"

"Yum."

"Don't be overly impressed. Daniella brought the sauce, so it's homemade, just not in this house."

They settled on a bottle of Chianti, and while she set the table, he opened the wine.

After the pasta was cooked, he mixed it with the sauce and an obscene amount of cheese.

"Who knew heaven could be found at seven thousand, five hundred feet," she said.

"I take it you approve," he replied as he popped the casserole dish into the oven. After they loaded the dishwasher, he poured wine into two plastic mugs.

"Let's go have that look, shall we?"

Now the plastic mugs made sense.

He grabbed her coat from the hook and held it while she shrugged into it.

"Are you always so chivalrous?"

"When the woman matters," he replied.

She looked at him. "Am I being seduced?"

"Is it working?"

His tone was serious, the look in his eyes burning. "Yes," she confessed. "It is."

"Part of my nefarious master plan." He put his coat on then unlocked the door and picked up their wine mugs. "Molly, illuminate the path. Unlock the shed."

"The shed?" Aria asked.

"Only certain people know the truth. Trying not to shock the 'Nillas."

"'Nillas?"

"I'm sorry. That was scene speak. Short for vanillas. Someone who isn't into kink."

He kept a protective arm beneath her elbow as he followed her to the building. "The path might have iced over," he explained.

She wasn't sure a man had ever been this courteous toward her.

"Allow me," he said when he reached past her for the doorknob. "Molly turned up the temperature a while ago so you don't freeze."

The nondescript door swung open, and shock almost made her lose her grip on the drink. "It's…scary as hell." The floor was concrete or stone of some sort. Shackles were attached to the walls. Some sort of X-shaped structure stood in the middle of the room, and it had a light focused on it. A pair of medieval-looking stocks sat off to the side.

Grant put his fingers in the small of her back to encourage her to enter. If he hadn't been blocking the way, she might have run. Instead, he sealed them inside.

"Cue reality," he said.

The room seemed to shimmer. The shackles faded. The stocks vanished. "You…"

He shrugged. "Sorry. I shouldn't have. But I couldn't resist." His smile was irresistible.

She scowled at him. "You know, by this age, most people have outgrown the need to pull pranks."

"No. They really haven't. Think about surprise birthday parties. Or keeping it secret when someone's coming home at the holidays."

"I always peek at my Christmas presents," she reminded him. Because his enthusiasm was irresistible, she glanced around.

The X stayed in the middle of the room

Other than that, nothing remained the same. Walls were painted a dove gray. Blinds covered the only windows, which were on the far side of the space. A gorgeous wooden cupboard of sorts was attached to the wall. It was only about six inches thick, but it was a few feet wide. There were a couple of doors.

"Storage," he told her, "And a bathroom over there with a small dressing area."

She noticed there was also a sink, along with a round table accompanied by two chairs.

"This is the real dungeon," he assured her. "That's called a

St. Andrew's cross." He indicated the X-shaped structure that was painted black and had thick red padding attached.

"You mentioned that when you were telling me about your first experience." She could see why it had made an impact. The thing was at least five feet tall, and there were a number of eyebolts screwed into the wood. Even to a newbie like her, the screws didn't need an explanation. "It's huge," she said. "Intimidating."

"Any more so than last night on my bed?"

"Maybe not," she admitted. "But, I don't know. It seems much more serious." She exhaled. "That didn't make sense, did it?"

"It did. You're finding this a bit overwhelming because it's out of context. Things progressed naturally yesterday. If I'd have brought out the spreader bar earlier, you might have run." He nodded toward the cross. "Try it out," he encouraged. "Get familiar with it."

"What?"

"Step up on the platform. Face it. Spread your arms, your legs. See what it would feel like. Then try it with your back to the X. You can keep your clothes on. You'll be perfectly safe. Even the restraints are still locked away."

She took a long drink from her wine, considering. She was alternately scared and thrilled, as he'd undoubtedly known she would be.

After a deep exhalation, she went to the table and put down her plastic mug before taking off her coat.

As she walked across the stone floor, her footsteps echoed. That, she realized, was real. The surface wasn't uneven enough to be dangerous even in heels, but it added to the ambiance.

Feeling self-conscious, she stepped up onto the platform, facing the cross. The structure was angled slightly back, evidently so that gravity helped keep a submissive in place.

She reached out her arms then spread her legs. The padding was thick, making it more comfortable than she'd guessed. In this position, her legs were no farther apart than they'd been when he'd used the spreader bar last night.

"Visualize me dragging my flogger over your shoulders, down your back."

Since she'd never felt anything like that, she had difficulty with what he suggested. But his voice, low and deep was intoxicating, making her want to picture it. She closed her eyes.

"To me, flogging is a sensuous experience. It's meant to make your body feel alive. Foreplay."

Until his pussy spanking, she would have said that was impossible. But he'd said he intended to demolish her paradigms.

"Now turn around to face me," he said.

She did. Approval was etched on his face, making her glad she was out here with him.

"Now imagine looking at me, your gaze fixed on mine, as I use a light flogger on your breasts and thighs."

Her heart was doing a frantic thud.

"Get yourself in the position you'd be in."

He'd stayed on the far side of the room. Mug of wine in hand, he rested his shoulders against the wall, and he put a booted foot on the wall behind him.

Suddenly, she wanted to please him. She extended herself along the X.

"As safe as you are at this moment, Aria? You will always feel this from me."

For endless seconds, they looked at each other. Earlier she'd thought of him in terms of his ability to weave a spell that drew her in, and that's exactly what had happened. In a short space of time, his opinion had started to matter.

He'd teased her about living dangerously while she was

here. He challenged her as no man ever had—intellectually, physically. And she realized she wanted to experience every single moment. What he was offering, she wanted. No regrets.

He beckoned her forward, and she joined him near the cupboard.

"Go ahead and open it."

The cupboard had two doors and she opened them to reveal a few floggers hanging from pegs. As she expected from him, it was impeccably organized. What appeared to be canes and crops were attached lengthwise. Sets of clamps, cuffs, gags and blindfolds hung from individual hooks. "This isn't an illusion, I take it?" she asked to cover her onslaught of nerves.

"All mine. For you."

"The blindfold and the gags make me nervous," she admitted.

"That I'd ask you to try, at least once. It can have a liberating effect."

"Remember? I peek at presents."

He grinned. "Have you ever closed your eyes during sex?"

"That's different."

"How?"

"I can open them when I choose, not when my Dom says."

The unintentional word hung in the atmosphere.

"I didn't mean it that way. You're not… I mean—"

"Relax. I didn't take it to mean anything in particular," he assured her.

But she suspected he had.

"As for the gag, I'm open to negotiation. If you're wearing it, we'll work out a signal that you can use to communicate with me. Some subs hold a handkerchief or something that they can drop if things become overwhelming or move too fast. Otherwise, you can use a thumbs-up signal or a thumbs-down signal."

"It seems that would take a lot of trust."

"Maybe not as much as you think. Even if you're gagged, you can still make noise. And I'd be listening and watching you intently."

She knew, absolutely knew that was true.

"And honestly? For me, that's more about kink than anything. I like the sight of it. It's sexy and turns me on. The idea of you being helpless and counting on me to figure out what you need? And giving it to you? Heady stuff for me as a Dom."

He hadn't said the words 'your Dom'. But she heard them, nonetheless. She looked at him. "Your cock is hard."

"As you've noticed, it's perennial now that you're around."

He took down a flogger. She'd never seen one before but thought the purple color was gorgeous. The strands were wide and thick. Pretty, but scary.

"Thirty-three inches long," he told her. "Thirty-six tails."

"Is that a lot?"

"It is. Some Doms would start you with something smaller, lighter, fewer strands, maybe a less costly leather. But I like the control I have with this one. I can use it lightly, and if it turns out you have a high pain threshold or simply like more pressure, this can accommodate you. And as we play more and you crave more, we can continue with this one instead of switching."

"So you're trying to say this isn't your average starter flogger."

"Precisely."

Though she suspected it might hurt like hell, its suppleness, combined with the rich color, made it seem innocent. She tucked her hands in her back pockets so she didn't betray the fact her nerves had become mixed up by fascination.

"Turn around," he said. He slid his mug into the cupboard. "Bend over. Spread your legs. Grab your ankles."

After she did, he laid the strands over her shoulder, then drew them back. The leather felt smooth on her skin. He continued down her back, and she sighed at the slow, deliberate motion. It wasn't as if something had ignited in her, it was more like the sensation of being gently awakened.

He gave her a backhanded smack across the buttocks.

"You can't feel the full impact through denim, but you can get an idea."

It stung, but only a little. And the feeling faded as quickly as she'd noticed it.

Grant changed positions. "Ready?"

"Yes."

He landed the flogger on her right butt cheek. "How was that?"

She considered her answer. It hadn't been anything like she'd expected. The impact felt like a heavy thud rather than a nasty sting. "Not as bad as I feared, but that could be because of the jeans."

"Now imagine it on your naked body and me stroking between your legs. You're on the edge of an orgasm, and I just won't let you tip over. Picture it, Aria."

Her breaths came in jagged little bursts.

"Think of your whole body feeling as if it's been touched by a flame. And know I did it to you."

She tightened her muscles to distract herself from the sudden throbbing in her pussy.

"Also know that I want to take you places you've never been. Sexually, sensually. I'm going to make you yearn for me, Aria. For me and only me."

CHAPTER SEVEN

Grant shook out the strands of the flogger and hung it back up while Aria stood and slowly turned toward him.

Her face was flushed, but it was the way her hand shook as she finger-combed her hair that let him know the tiny taste of leather had affected her.

Clearly this had not been one of his more brilliant ideas. He'd thought that bringing her out here would spark her interest and help her get over any perceived fear. They'd talk about bondage, what the equipment was for, what might happen in a future scene.

But when she'd stepped up onto the platform and stretched her arms along the top section of the cross, it'd been as if his brain circuits no longer connected. Ever since she'd exited the plane, he'd imagined her spread in that position, waiting for him. The reality had surpassed any expectation. And she'd been fully dressed.

He had it bad for this woman.

It wasn't just her feminine curves, it was the whole damn

package. Confidence. Brains. Ability and willingness to challenge his thinking.

Now if he could convince her to thumb her nose at Julien and Bonds and come be his sex slave, life would be perfect.

Reality, unfortunately, was much more complex.

Including the fact that Julien had put them at odds with each other. She'd clearly been tasked with getting him back to California and into the company's marketing and PR efforts, and that wasn't happening. "Shall we?"

He grabbed her coat and held it for her, then they picked up their drinks. She took a long gulp before they left the dungeon. Obviously she was as affected as he was.

Inside, Shadow was waiting, and the scent of Italian sauce wafted toward them.

"This could be what heaven smells like," she said.

They regained their easy camaraderie as he pulled the pan from the oven and added another sprinkle of cheese on top.

While she replenished their wine, he tossed together a salad to accompany the pasta. He marveled at how easy she was to be with, how seamlessly they worked together.

Over dinner, they discussed the plan for Bonds, via Molly, to have a greater impact on people's lives, and strategized a way to present it to Julien since the man had zero tolerance for endless slide shows. He demanded that his employees give him something interactive to look at and consider. Problem was, he already knew everything there was to know about Molly.

"The hologram," she said. "Shadow or…something new, I don't know…" Aria scowled as she sorted through the idea. "The hologram can show Julien what it can do. What if… You use a hologram of Julien…" She took a breath. "I know, I know the hologram doesn't work. So, instead, do a projection, sort of like what you do in here with the landscapes.

Wait. This is too complicated. Make him a cartoon, a computer generated image."

"CGI..." He loved the way her brain worked, enjoyed listening to her talk things out, presenting an idea only to discard, or expand on it, all in the space of a couple of seconds. "Yeah. That's possible."

"So we have CGI version of Julien. He can give the presentation himself, as if he's talking to the press of a group of potential investors."

"Synthesizing his voice is a bigger challenge than you might imagine. There's a reason movie studios have actors read the lines and then synchronize them."

"Are you kidding me? The man never shuts up. You have enough words for the computers at Bonds to put something together."

"This is risky. Maybe beyond my skillset."

"I've seen your skillset, remember? It's pretty impressive."

"With computers."

"What?" She paused with the fork halfway to her mouth. "That's what I was talking about." Her cheeky grin said otherwise.

"Let's continue to brainstorm."

They finished dinner, cleaned up the kitchen together, then when she asked if he wanted more wine, he replied, "I don't have more than one drink if I'm going to play with a sub." He didn't intend to push, but he was going to make it clear she had a choice.

"In that case, let's skip the wine." Her voice was low, seductive.

In that moment, he'd do anything to please her. He knew she had no idea of the amount of power she held over him. "Did you bring anything else to wear?"

"Like lingerie? Heels? No. I had no idea I'd need anything like that. Best I can do is thermal pajamas. Or yoga pants."

"Yoga pants? Do you mean hug-your-butt pants?"

"I'll wear them tomorrow."

"Not if we're working, you won't."

They returned to the dungeon, and he brought out a space heater that he placed a few feet behind the cross.

She took off her coat and hung it on a peg on the wall. He put his next to it.

"How do you feel about getting your first flogging tonight?" He took her into his arms.

"Nervous. Like we're out on a first date—or maybe a blind date," she confessed. "Not sure what to expect."

He grinned, wanting to alleviate her anxiety. With a more experienced sub or if he followed a higher protocol, he might weave a different headspace. But he appreciated that he was the first man to dominate her. "I hope I can do better than grope you in the backseat of a car."

"I'm sure you can."

He kissed her until she raised onto her tiptoes and leaned into him completely, then continued until she was breathless. When he looked into her eyes, he saw that whatever awkwardness she'd been feeling was gone.

Intimacy, he realized.

That kiss had brought it all back for both of them, creating a platform to build from. With her, he was seeing a relationship in a different way than he ever had before.

Grant pulled up her sweater then tugged it over her head in a smooth, easy move, baring her skin to his gaze, his touch.

He skimmed his knuckles down her throat and paused at the small hollow.

She parted her lips slightly and kept her gaze on his.

This evening, he reached behind her to unfasten her bra.

"You've done that before," she whispered.

"Maybe I learned a thing or two in the backseat of a car."

Grant brushed a thumb over one of her nipples. "How do they feel?"

"Not at all sore."

"Maybe a pair of lightweight clamps then." He teased her flesh until her nipples were completely hard and she groaned with pleasure. Her responses were like an aphrodisiac to him. The more she gave, the more he wanted. "Why don't you finish undressing while I set up the play area?"

He started toward the storage area then paused. "Better yet, I'd prefer you help me." Typically he handled all the preparation for a scene. He found the acts meditative, allowing him time to think through the nuances of his plan. But at the club he'd seen other Doms instruct their subs to set up the toys. Suddenly he realized the benefit. Her participation would force her to be more involved and keep them interacting so he could get her in the right mindset before he secured the first cuff. "There's a wheeled cart in the storage closet. Fetch it."

She hesitated only a second before doing as he said. "There's a lot of equipment in there. I don't know what most of it is, but my imagination is urging me to take a guess," she said when she returned.

"If we don't get to use it all when you're here, it'll be incentive for you to return." And he meant it.

She didn't respond.

He didn't want to think of her leaving, but she would—probably soon. Even in this short amount of time, he'd grown accustomed to having her around. While he liked it, he was enough of a realist to know it couldn't last. His tastes were demanding, and living in such an out-of-the-way location didn't work for a lot of people. And he had no intention of leaving New Mexico behind.

Refocusing his attention, he removed the purple flogger

from the cupboard and handed it to her. "Hang it right there." He indicated a metal hook on the side of the cart.

After seeing a similar set-up at a club Kennedy had taken him to in Boston, Grant had decided he needed to order one online. There were individual compartments for condoms, trays for clamps and lube, as well as several hooks that accommodated multiple spanking implements.

"This is heavier than I thought," she said, as she put the flogger in place.

"Try it out."

He watched her test the weight then flick it back and forth. Then she switched hands.

"How do you not get carpal tunnel from this thing?"

"Let's try for flogger's elbow."

She grinned. "I'll bet you know about that."

He considered which set of nipple clamps he wanted. The Japanese clovers would remain tight and in place. The alligators had a nice bite. They might come off when he tormented her breasts, which might be an added advantage.

Unable to choose, he instructed her to put both sets in the tray. He skipped over the blindfold for this night's introductory scene, but selected four soft cuffs.

Then, because she had a pensive frown burrowed between her eyebrows, he put a thumb beneath her chin and captured her lips for a deep, deep kiss.

Instantly she responded, wrapping her arms around his neck. This woman… *His.* He pulled her in closer so he could stroke her back and savor their connection.

"Grant…"

He put his palm flat on her buttocks, drawing her in, letting her feel his erection and more, the effect she had on him.

In his arms she became soft, trusting.

"I need…" she murmured against his mouth.

"Take it," he encouraged. He moved their positions a little, jutting out his leg and offering support.

With a soft whimper, she rubbed her crotch against his leg.

"That's it. That's my sub." Grant had never had anything like this before, anyone like *her.* Her softness combined with her strength, might be his undoing.

He held her while she ground her pussy against his thigh. "That's it," he encouraged.

Her whimpers gave way to moans, and his cock throbbed, rising against his jeans. He captured her mouth again, devouring her as she rode him, their breaths becoming ragged.

She turned her head to the side, and he took more of her weight as she rubbed her pussy on him.

This was as sexy as it got. "Come all over me, Aria."

She screamed his name, the word wrapped in a sigh.

Aria's body sagged, and he was there for her, stroking her hair, reassuring her, telling her how much he loved hearing his name as she climaxed.

"I..."

"Yeah," he agreed. Understood. Words weren't needed. "Thank you," he said.

She put a hand on his chest and used it for leverage to ease back. "Generally I get out of my clothes before I have an orgasm."

"Speaking of..."

Her body was relaxed, and desire painted her eyes a deeper shade of green. Her earlier feelings—whether they'd been caused by awkwardness or apprehension—had clearly vanished.

"I'm anxious to have you on the cross." He reached for the top button of her jeans. "Since the floor is cold, but mostly because I'd find it the stuff of fantasies, you're welcome to leave your boots on."

"You *are* kinky," she said.

"Even more than I had realized," he agreed.

She moved to the chair to finish stripping, but she slipped back into the boots.

"Julien was right." He perused her, devoured her with his gaze. "You could rule the world in those things."

"At this moment, I'm only interested in you." She walked toward him, posture erect, hair flowing down her back, one hand on her hip.

"Have mercy. I'm only a red-blooded male. I don't stand a chance."

She paused long enough to trail her fingertips down his arm before walking to the middle of the room to climb onto the platform.

He stood in place, riveted by the sight of her legs, her ass, her confident strut.

"Which way do you want me, Sir?" she asked over her shoulder.

What was the question?

If there'd ever been a better time to be a Dom, he didn't remember it. "Face it," he said. "So I can turn that ass of yours red."

A dozen different thoughts and emotions warred inside Aria as she turned to face the cross. All of a sudden, she understood what he'd talked about previously, when they'd looked at the portrait. Waiting was difficult and revealed true strength.

The reality of being in the dungeon, naked and bound, knowing he planned to beat her, plowed into her.

But he'd obviously been reading her cues, and he'd responded to them perfectly.

It wasn't just physically. It was verbally too. She wasn't sure she'd ever had a man be this in tune with her before. And it all created trust and intimacy, making her feel safe.

She heard the cart move over the uneven floor, and he didn't stop until he was in front of her. Aria realized that, in the future, she'd measure every man against him, not just in terms of breathtaking good looks, but also courtesy, humor, caring and, heaven help her, kink. Was it possible to go back after this? Would she even want to?

"Make yourself comfortable."

She pressed her body against the padding and spread her arms and legs apart. Her pulse started to race, so she drew a couple of steadying breaths.

"Wrists or ankles first?" He picked a cuff from the cart.

"Whatever you please, Sir," she answered.

His nod of approval made her glad she'd remembered the response.

He started with her wrists, wrapping them in cuffs then securing them to an eyebolt. She realized it would have been just as easy for him to stand behind her and do this, so she appreciated that he was letting her watch him.

Her brain told her the restraints were secure, but she couldn't help but test them anyway. She could move her arms barely an inch.

After securing her ankles—not easy, she imagined, with the boots—he stepped back. "This image of you… I'll never forget it."

Their gazes held for a moment before he gave her a curt nod. Then he moved behind her to stroke her back and shoulders. She wondered how he always managed to surprise her.

Tension she hadn't been aware of seeped from her body as her muscles relaxed.

He vigorously rubbed her buttocks then her thighs,

warming her body.

"It's doubtful I'd leave any bruises," he said, "but this will add insurance."

Only then did he move to the cart to pick up the flogger.

"What will you say if it gets to be too much?"

"Holy shit?"

He put the butt of the flogger beneath her chin and forced her head back a little.

"Even though I'll be watching your responses, I won't be able to see your expression." His eyebrows were set in a scowl. "You have a responsibility to me, to yourself, to our scene, to communicate."

"You're right. I apologize." She saw how very seriously he took this, and she respected that he was concerned for her safety. "If it's too much, I'll say yellow."

"Will I keep going if you scream at me to stop?"

"Ah…"

"That's the importance of communicating," he said. "A lot of subs like the freedom to shout no or yell at the Dom to stop, and to them, it's part of the fun. Because we're still getting to know each other, you can be guaranteed that I'll check in with you, but to put an immediate halt to our scene, the only word you need is yellow."

"I understand, Sir."

"What's your favorite number, between five and ten?"

Guessing what was coming, she said, "Five."

She felt the strands of leather rain on her right shoulder. Then he dragged them down, teasing her skin. He did the same thing on her left shoulder. "Mmm." It was better than she'd imagined.

He allowed them to fall on the top of her buttocks.

She pressed her body harder into the padding. Then she heard him take a step back, his boots ridiculously loud on the stone floor.

"Left cheek," he said.

Survival instinct made her clench, but when nothing happened, she forced herself to relax. Though he didn't speak, she heard his words in her head, urging her to keep her body loose.

The first blow was gentle, a tease. When he'd used it on her earlier, through her jeans, he'd warned her the feeling would be different. It was. This was far more sensuous. The connection of leather on flesh was erotic, thrilling, unlike anything she could have imagined. And to think fear might have made her skip this experience.

He gave her four more strokes, each exquisite and unique. There was no way that thirty-six strands could fall in exactly the same way twice.

Then he paused. She allowed her eyes to drift close. "This is nice," she said.

He slid a hand between her legs. As much as the cuffs allowed, she raised onto her tiptoes.

Back and forth, he moved a finger, making her moist, but not sliding into her, and barely skimming her clit.

Before she was ready, he stopped.

"That was enough to be maddening," she protested.

"It was five."

Monster.

"You set the number," he reminded her.

Leaving her frustrated, he used the flogger on her right butt cheek, then he repeated the slow slide between her labia.

The restraints made it impossible for her to move her body enough to have any control and try for an orgasm.

As he had earlier, he stopped touching her. "Would you like to continue? And if we do, say yellow if it's too much."

"Yes, Sir," she said. "More."

He stroked her nape with the side of his hand. "These will be on your back, in a random pattern."

They were far more intense than the first, but also far more rewarding. She felt perspiration dew on her skin. Strands wrapped around her waist, first on one side then the other, aching.

Before she could get into it, it was over, and he was between her legs, keeping up that maddening rhythm. "I… can't do this," she protested. Her body felt alive, demanding.

"I didn't hear yellow."

"No!" She opened her eyes. "Don't stop." That would be the worst. His touches were having a cumulative effect, letting an orgasm form deep inside her.

He chuckled, and the sound rocked her. It spoke of power and shared pleasure.

"Across your upper thighs," he warned.

Each place the leather landed, it felt different. On her rear, it had been thuddy. When he'd hit her back, several strands had wrapped around her sides, biting into her flesh. On her upper thighs, though, the strands fell flat, creating a dull impact. This she could endure, even enjoy.

After a final stroke, he teased her pussy, sinking two fingers deep inside her. She closed her eyes and let her head tip back. "Damn."

She moaned when he pulled out. "I think I hate you a little right now," she said.

"Be careful what you—"

"Ask for. I should have said nine or ten." She pulled against her restraints, aroused, edgy.

"Ready for more now that you're warmed up?"

She wished she could see him to read his expression. "Yes."

"I won't repeat the pattern, but you've had a taste of what you'll receive, forehand, backhand, and the places I'll strike you."

"Is there an orgasm in my future?"

"Guaranteed."

She shrugged, rolled her shoulders and resettled her body against the pads. This was already feeling more comfortable.

He tossed the strands onto her neck. It was a signal, she realized, letting her know what to expect. Communication.

Before she was fully prepared, he blazed across her buttocks. She clenched her butt cheeks. That was so, so much more searing than any other, but as the pain radiated and ricocheted, it heated her from the inside. She liked it.

She relaxed her body when she was ready and he continued.

Aria realized he was watching her and responding to her reactions.

The next few were easier than the first, then he mixed it up with one across her back that took her breath away.

He immediately put a hand between her legs and slipped two fingers into her pussy.

The pain instantly transformed, making her more aroused.

"Oh, God. Oh, God!"

He pressed the flat part of his thumb against her clitoris, and she lifted up on her toes, squeezing her pussy, searching for an orgasm that he kept just out of reach.

"You're so wet. And hot."

"And—"

Rather than satisfying her, he moved his hand from between her legs and continued the beating, leaving her groaning, all but whining her frustration.

"Surrender," he encouraged her.

She had no idea what the hell that meant, but he pressed on, still tormenting her, landing shocking blows on her back, harsh ones on her ass.

Her pussy ached with need, and she wanted him there, taking care of her. And that's when she realized what he meant. She was focused on what she wanted and not on what he was giving.

She squeezed her eyes shut and resisted the impulse to take little pants of breath. Instead she took deep gulps of air. They allowed her to concentrate.

"That's it."

On some level she was aware of the flogging, the painful caress of all thirty-six tails, but she also felt it as an extension of Grant and his dominance.

And then she understood.

Grant and his dominance meant nothing without her submission to it.

The realization magnified her arousal and her need to give him what he required.

She allowed her body to sink into the padding, and she wrapped her hands around the wrist cuffs for support, no longer seeing them as a restraint.

He continued the flogging, and playing with her. She let go of her internal struggle, giving herself over, not just in her body, but in her mind. How long it continued, she had no idea. She just knew she never wanted it to end.

"Come for me."

She hadn't been aware of him touching her, but he was there, everywhere, all at once.

Eyes closed, she allowed sensation to swamp her.

His touch expert and his words demanding, Grant gave her an orgasm that made her scream and scream. Completion blazed through her, overwhelming her. The world became hazy, then black.

She was aware of sensation, but also of a feeling of peace, something she'd never felt outside of meditation.

Her body felt warm, not seared.

Aria knew he was speaking, but the words blurred and sounded nonsensical. Instead, they soothed.

It took some time for her to register that the strands no longer fell over her body and that he was still speaking to her. She realized that he was behind her, his body pressing into hers. He'd unfastened her right wrist and was rubbing her arm.

She moved her head to the side to look at him. "Wow."

"Welcome back." He pressed a kiss to the side of her neck.

"I feel like I went on a rollercoaster ride."

"In a way, you did."

She stretched out her fingers then shook her arm while he released the left one.

In under a minute, he'd removed the cuffs and carried her to the chair. He sat, holding her in his lap.

"I liked that," she admitted, burying her head in his shoulder, in his formidable strength.

"So did I," he agreed. "How about a soak in the hot tub?"

"That sounds awesome." Her body felt relaxed from the aftermath of the sensual arousal, but there was an undercurrent of fatigue from the tension of getting ready to leave California, flying, getting to work right away, and the unnatural ways he'd spread her body and tied her up.

"You can stay here. I'll be right back with a few things," he said.

She frowned. "Why don't I just go with you?"

"I thought we'd use the outdoor hot tub."

"Are you kidding me?" Another surprise. "In this weather?"

"It's cold," he agreed. "But not snowing. I'll keep your sexy little body warm."

"Outdoor hot tubs are for summer nights," she protested. "Not when there's snow on the ground."

"You certainly have a lot of rules, Aria."

She wondered if that was true and if so, what that meant for her, her future. With a little jolt of pain, she realized he might be right. All her life, her parents had encouraged her to focus on the future, attend the right schools, land the right job, establish her work credentials, get married, buy a house. She hadn't taken the time to figure out what she wanted. Instead, she'd followed the path that had been set for her.

It had been instinct that had stopped her from taking the final step and walking down the aisle. But until now she hadn't realized that her actions had been motivated by what she thought she should do rather than what was right for her. "Well, as if I don't have enough of my own," she replied, "you keep adding some, too. About orgasms, what position my body should be in, what I should call you during a scene, what I should wear—"

"Or not wear. All true." He shot her a disarming grin. "But you have to admit, where my rules are concerned, I'm right. Those nipple balls? Hotter than hell."

The image floated through her mind. It wasn't the balls that she remembered. It had been the lustful hunger in his blue, blue eyes.

"And the orgasms? The way I've made you think about them has made them more powerful. Admit it. Admit it, Aria."

She blew out a frustrated breath.

"Say it."

"Fine. Yes, Sir. You're right."

"My rules are much better than yours." He grinned. "Wait here for a minute."

She picked up her sweater and draped it around her shoulders, more for comfort than anything else since he had the place so warm. Even though the perspiration was evaporating, she didn't feel chilled.

She thought about putting away the toys and tidying the dungeon, but she honestly didn't have the energy to move. Even folding her clothes was beyond her.

For a few minutes, she closed her eyes and relaxed, something that had become foreign to her over the last few years. She was always on the go, heading to work or the gym, continually connected via email, telephone, video conferences.

All of a sudden she realized she'd kept herself busy, maybe so she didn't have to think or question her life. The knowledge was a bit sobering.

A few minutes later, Grant returned. The sight of him, in a robe, tantalized.

In jeans, a T-shirt, boots and a leather bomber jacket, he seemed so in charge. Dressed like this, with who-knew-what underneath his robe, he was mouthwateringly sexy. So many facets. And she appreciated them all.

He put a pair of his beach sandals on the floor near her. "I know they're too big for you," he said, "but they're better than nothing." He held up the extra terry cloth robe he'd brought. "This, too. Honestly, Aria, the idea of having you in my clothes is a bit of a turn-on."

"And I thought it was you wanting to get into my pants," she returned.

"Don't think I won't."

His words were every bit an intriguing promise.

"Stand up. I want to look at your body to see if I marked you." He extended his hand.

Aria wasn't sure why this seemed so intimate, but it did. He'd flogged her, fucked her, tied her up, bathed her pussy after sex. But it seemed he knew exactly the things to say that made her aware of his command over her.

She accepted his hand.

"You are unbelievably sexy." He continued to draw her toward him and placed a gentle kiss on the top of her head.

This part of the BDSM experience rocked her. The flogging had actually hurt at times, especially when some of the tails had wrapped around and bitten into her skin. But before she'd even protested, there'd been another sensation. And he'd mixed it all up with tenderness. The combination of consent, pain and gentleness was heady stuff, feeling like a rush of wine or the most potent of drugs through her system, leaving her lightheaded.

"Let me see your backside."

Slowly, she spun.

"Stop."

He traced lines along her back. "This one is gorgeous. It wrapped around, here…" He moved his fingers along her ribcage. "And this one…" He ran his thumb across the upper part of her left thigh. "How do they feel?"

"Fine. I'm not sure what you're asking."

"Do they hurt?"

"Not any longer. The first one did initially, but I don't even remember the one on my thigh."

His hands were on her shoulders, and he turned her to face him again. "I can't tell you how much the sight of these appeal to me."

Yielding to instinct, she responded, "Thank you."

He hissed in a breath, and his eyes darkened with simmering desire. In that moment, Aria saw the power she had over him. It was not all about him, she realized. He might command her, but she affected him equally.

"I've gotta have a picture of you in them," he said. "On the cross with your head tipped back and your body open for me. I'll project it on the wall of the workshop. You're much more inspiring than a landscape."

She shook her head, but she realized he wasn't joking. She'd never been with anyone who'd given her so much approval. This man was proving irresistible, and she wondered how in the hell she was supposed to leave him.

The way her thought process had changed in such a short time astounded her.

Several days ago, she hadn't wanted to leave the mild weather and high energy of her California lifestyle. She and Grant had made a lot of progress on the work she'd been sent to accomplish. No doubt the enforced break from her normal responsibilities had been good for her. She felt more rested, more invigorated than she had in a long time.

She recognized that her interaction with Grant was the reason. No doubt his home and its location in the spectacular mountains of New Mexico were part of it, but it was more about the man himself. He'd changed her life, introduced her to things she'd never known existed.

After she convinced him to take a larger role at Bonds—something Julien might also have to help with—there'd be no reason to stay any longer.

The idea of going back to her previous life left her chilled in a way that had little to do with the evening temperature.

"Hot tub," he said, as if reminding them both.

She sat to remove her boots then slid her feet into the sandals he'd brought for her. "You're right. They're ridiculous. I feel as if I'm wearing a clown costume or something."

He laughed. "They're adorable."

"I don't think I've ever been called adorable."

"Let's go." He plucked the sweater from her shoulders and held the robe for her.

"I can't believe I'm even considering this."

He opened the door after she was huddled beneath the terry material.

Cold air swirled in around her ankles. She shivered and pulled the lapels tighter across her chest, keeping her fingers buried in the warmth. "This is insane. *You're* insane."

"In that case, let's go to the edge of madness together."

How could she resist an invitation like that?

"Move it," he urged.

CHAPTER EIGHT

"Magic," she said.

Grant brought his head forward and looked at Aria through the steam. He'd chosen the lighting on purpose. There was enough that they could move around the yard safely, but not enough to interfere with the ambiance.

She appeared to be bathed in an ethereal glow.

Since the beating, her demeanor seemed different, more relaxed—accessible. With every new facet, he wanted to know more.

"This was a good idea," she continued.

"One of my many."

"That's what I meant to say, obviously," she teased back. Then, softly, hardly above a whisper, she said, "I can't believe how clear it is out here."

The storm had passed, taking all the clouds with it. Because there were few neighbors and no real city in view to create any distortion, the sky seemed to stretch endlessly, with a million stars sparkling in onyx.

"I'm rarely far enough away that I can appreciate how vast it is." She fell silent for a minute. "I may notice a full moon, but it's almost as if I forget how inspiring it is, how small you can feel beneath it. It's easy for me to get caught up in work, my responsibilities and to-do lists and forget that all this exists."

"I think we need room, space to breathe."

"Has it worked as well as you'd hoped?"

He considered her, thought carefully about his answer. He'd told her about Kathleen, about why he'd moved here. But since Aria had shown up, he was seeing things differently. "I'm still the same person I was when I left California. I'm starting to realize that I use work to escape." The knowledge made him a little uncomfortable.

"I'm with you. Your comment makes me wonder what life might be like if I took work less seriously, kept it in a better perspective."

"For a while, today, we have," he reminded her.

"And, I don't know about you, but it made me more creative."

"Amazing, isn't it?"

"Did it have a similar impact on you?"

"It did," he admitted. But what would it mean for his life if he were to make a change?

They were quiet for a few minutes. At least for him, he was looking at his choices through a different lens.

Eventually, she spoke. "The flogging…" She trailed off, hesitated. Then she closed her eyes and rested her neck against the rim of the tub. "It wasn't at all like I'd imagined."

He waited, letting her find her way. He hadn't been sure she would want to talk about what they'd shared, but he was certainly curious to know what the experience had been like for her.

"I appreciated the fact you started slow. And you playing with my pussy kept me from thinking about what you were doing. But then, I'm not sure what happened. At some point it was if I wasn't even there. Peripherally, I was aware of what you were doing, yet... It was as if it were happening to someone else and not to me. I didn't feel pain. Just...darkness. Not in a scary way."

"Subspace," he said. He'd never been with a woman who'd achieved subspace under his lash. Then again, he'd never been as in tune with anyone as he was with her. It pleased him, and it gratified him.

"I'm not sure what you mean."

"Some might argue whether it exists or not, but there's no denying what you experienced. Have you ever been so absorbed by a task or project that you lose track of time? You can emerge an hour or more later and have no recollection of what happened?"

She finally looked at him. "Of course. It happened this afternoon when we were bouncing ideas off each other, brainstorming how to take Molly to a larger consumer base."

"Same thing, I imagine. You get lost. But from erotic stimulation, mostly a beating. People I've heard talk about it call it bliss. Floating. I've generally heard that it happens through a beating of types—whips, canes, spanking. Makes sense to me that flogging is a good vehicle to achieve subspace simply because it can last longer. My hand would get tired on your ass pretty quickly, probably before you achieved subspace. Maybe with a paddle or a hairbrush," he mused. With a cane or a crop, he'd need a light hand. Not that the experience could be repeated. It was a combination of her headspace, her relaxation and his ability to intuit what she needed and to coax and nurture her trust.

"Sounds kind of Zen."

His experience of it anyway. "The pursuit of it makes it evasive. The non-pursuit of it is the only way to achieve it."

"The eternal conundrum. Isn't that what you call it?"

"I'm surprised you remember."

"I've listened to every word you've uttered, Grant."

He believed her. "Stay with me tonight. In my bed."

She was silent for a minute.

He wished he could read her expression better. She couldn't have any idea how much her response mattered to him. Until he'd issued the invitation, even he hadn't known. He wanted her in his bed, next to him, where he knew she was safe.

"I'd like that."

A few minutes later, he climbed from the water. He held her robe while she slipped into it, then they hurried into the house.

"Go ahead and take a shower and make sure you stay warm," he encouraged her once they were inside the house. As always, Shadow was there, waiting. On some level, he must have recognized his lack of companionship. Why else would his first hologram have been of a dog? He'd told himself it was easier to manipulate the image of an animal, but that wasn't the truth. Until now, he hadn't wanted to face that truth. "I'll straighten the dungeon—for your next visit."

She nodded.

"Feel free to use the master bathroom."

"Are you kidding? Even if I lived here, I'd use the guest shower. It's amazing."

Still in his robe, he headed back outside to tidy up. When he put away the unused nipple clamps, he was already picturing a future scene.

He picked up the flogger—his new favorite toy—and hung it back in its spot before closing the cupboard doors. After returning the cart to the closet, he nodded his satisfaction and told Molly, "Temperature at sixty degrees."

"Yes, Your Majesty."

"Can we override that response?"

"Ask the genius. He says it amuses him to annoy you."

Probably some truth to that. He gathered Aria's discarded clothing and the fuck-me-now boots. He was definitely going to take a picture of her in them. Stuff of masturbatory fantasies.

When he returned to the house, he grabbed the bottle of wine that they'd been drinking and carried it and two glasses to the bedroom.

Aria was still in the shower and he shouted at her to join him when she'd finished.

"Will do."

Grant poured two glasses of wine and set them on the dresser before heading for the shower himself.

He was already out, dried, and dressed in a pair of lounging pants when she entered his bedroom.

She had a towel around her body and was using a second to dry her hair. "Sorry I took so long. Tankless heater. Not sure if I want one or not. I might never make it to work on time if I had one," she admitted. "And I was wondering if you had a T-shirt I could sleep in? I don't want to scare you off with my thermal pajamas."

"I'm tough. It would take more than that to frighten me away."

"Don't be too sure," she cautioned.

He grinned.

"They're that scary," she said. "I didn't really anticipate I was coming here for mind-blowing, amazing sex."

"Mind-blowing?" he repeated.

"And amazing."

"I take it milady is pleased?"

"And I'm concerned that His Majesty is missing out."

"I was afraid I might have worn you out." He was prepared to beat-off in the shower later, if needed.

"Maybe," she said. "Maybe not." Her gaze had that same, melted jade quality.

Christ. A single look from her caused testosterone to flood his system. She could wrap a bow around his dick and lead him anywhere. And he'd have a stupid grin on his face while he followed. Julien had been right about that, too. Dangerous women were fucking sexy. "Middle drawer of the dresser," he said to cover his reaction. "Pick anything you want."

She selected a soft, gray one that dwarfed her shoulders. It covered her ass. Just. Better than any lingerie.

"Good choice. A T-shirt makes it easier for me to grope you."

"That's what I was hoping you'd say."

Their gazes met. Her honesty appealed to him, another thing that kept him hard. He was definitely hungry for this woman.

He put her damp towels in the laundry basket.

"Is one of those for me?" she asked, indicating the wineglasses.

"It is." He gave one to her then plumped the pillows and turned down the comforter.

"I didn't know people actually did that. Well, except for fancy hotels."

He shuddered. "You sleep under your comforter?"

"I have about a million bad habits."

He wouldn't mind keeping her around long enough to discover them all.

"A mint on the pillow would make it perfect."

"You and your chocolate."

"Not sure why we're wasting time on the Molly project."

"*Yes?*" Molly interrupted.

Aria laughed. "Sorry."

"Standby, Molly," Grant said.

"I miss all the fun."

"As you were saying?" he prompted, fetching his glass.

He held Aria's glass while she climbed onto the bed, then she did the same for him. Together they propped themselves against the headboard.

"We should forget the hologram. People need a real robot. Like a droid."

"Something to get you chocolate so you don't have to go to the kitchen."

She grinned.

"Or someone," he corrected.

"You don't have to go, really. I'll manage without it. Even if red wine is the perfect accompaniment."

"That's entrapment," he said.

"Is it?" She shrugged. "I wouldn't know. I'm no legal expert. I'm afraid I don't know the exact definition of the word."

"A perfect sub would find out what her Dom wanted."

"I'm sure you're right." She blinked her eyelashes exaggeratedly.

"How old were you when you learned that trick?"

"I don't know. Seven?"

Maybe she did have some idea of her power over him. And rightfully so. Any woman who responded so perfectly to him could have anything she wanted.

"Dark chocolate is best."

"You may not know the law, but you certainly know your desserts."

"I'm fluent."

"Yeah. I remember."

He put his glass on the nightstand on the way out of the room.

Since he didn't know exactly what she'd be in the mood for, he brought back a few different selections. Her smile made the effort worth it.

She slid her glass onto the nightstand so she could unwrap a single, foil-wrapped piece of chocolate.

Watching her take a bite, close her eyes, savor it, followed by the sound of her soft whimper? Damn. She made chocolate into sex.

She licked her fingers, then her upper lip.

"You did that on purpose," he accused.

"Could have," she agreed, reaching for her wine. She pulled her legs toward her and rested the glass on top. "I'm definitely beginning to see the benefit of less work and more play." She hesitated. "So, about this submissive thing…"

He wondered where she was going, whether she was going to be serious or whether she wanted to continue the slow, tantalizing seduction. Either way was fine with him.

"Tell me more about it."

"What do you want to know, exactly?"

She turned her body a little so she could look at him better. "This chocolate thing is what I'm asking about. And the whole way you were taking care of me after the scene in the dungeon. It occurs to me that I really don't remember you getting me down."

He took a drink before answering. "I'm happy to get the chocolate for you, and that has nothing to do with any D/s relationship that might exist between us."

"D/s? Is that what it's called?"

Aria had responded so easily, so completely to his lead that it was easy for him to forget she had no previous experience. "This part of it, yes. Dominance/submission. The term BDSM is large and encompasses a lot of different things. Not everyone practices everything. Some are just into the bondage or the sadomasochism. And even in the D/s realm, there are degrees, from high protocol—meaning rigid expectations—to something less formal. A lot of people practice it in the bedroom only. Others live the lifestyle all the time.

Each couple works out their own rules. So, yes, you can still be submissive to me while I get you chocolate."

"I'm not saying I want to be," she hedged.

"I'll get you dessert, regardless," he promised.

"Whew. I was concerned." She took a sip from her glass, and he waited, wondering if she had other questions. If she weren't intrigued on some level, she wouldn't ask.

"So... I could choose to have a beating and a rockin' orgasm."

"You could. But not all Doms are as generous with that."

"The whole ratio thing," she mused. "Like my one dozen—"

"Surely two dozen by now."

"At least," she said. "To your miserly few."

"Few?"

"Couple?"

He raised his eyebrows.

"It is a little lopsided," she agreed, tracing her finger around the rim of the glass.

"If you go to clubs," he explained, "or play parties, you may find Doms who are willing to engage in a scene." Even as he spoke, the idea of another Dom lashing her, coaxing a response from her, mind and body, made something go hard in his chest. "Often, sex won't be a part of it. In fact, in some clubs, it's not permitted."

"To me, the two seem indelibly tied."

"Because of the way I introduced it. But they are to a lot of people. There are some who enjoy a good rousing spanking and that's enough for them. And there are celibate D/s relationships. There's no right way or wrong way to do any of this. Every vanilla couple does things their own way—so do kinky couples."

"Kinky couples," she repeated. "I like the way that sounds."

Yeah. So did he.

"The other day, we talked about dick worship."

"Cock," he corrected with a grin. "Cock worship."

"I'm curious what that would entail."

He was instantly erect. And he wanted her. "It might start with the sub's hand."

"Oh?" She put her down her glass.

For safety reasons, he did, too.

She placed her hand on his cock, and it was all he could do not to moan and let her know how much she affected him. "And the sub would very carefully watch the Dom's reaction to see what he liked," he said.

"Like this...?" She stroked him.

This time, he did groan. His words rough, he added, "She might make her grip a little tighter..."

For a second, she released him. Suddenly he comprehended how important touch was, understood why she'd been upset when he'd left her alone while he'd fetched a mirror.

Aria got onto her knees and faced him. She looked at him through those impossibly long eyelashes.

"Would she tell him how much she liked his cock?"

"She might. Yes."

She stroked him, looked at him, teased him. "Would she casually mention how much she liked it when he fucked her?"

"Unless he forbade her from talking, he would probably enjoy that." He felt a drop of pre-cum on his cockhead.

"Would she ever use her mouth on him?"

"She would. And she'd ask permission. She might even beg to please him."

"Please?" she said softly.

Suddenly, it was all real, him and her.

He climbed from the bed and she scrambled off, too.

"Take off the T-shirt," he said.

She pulled it off and laid it on the mattress.

"Kneel for me, Aria."

She did, and, as he'd earlier instructed, waited for instruction.

"Lick my balls."

Gently, then with a little more firmness, she did. He put one hand behind her head, to cradle it.

The best she could at the angle, she continued looking at him. Her compliance aroused him even more.

With unimaginable tenderness, she sucked one testicle into his mouth, laved it then moved on to the other.

Thoroughly she licked his balls. And she pressed a finger against his perineum. He jerked.

"How did you like that?" She moved her finger back a little to tease his anus.

It could take less than ten seconds to lose control here.

"Suck my cock, little subbie."

"Yes, Sir." The words were sexy, and so were her actions.

She ran her tongue around his cockhead and simultaneously stroked his shaft, even as she pushed the flat part of a finger against his ass.

"You are one hot woman."

"I like to suck you," she said. "The way you taste."

She stroked him with her hand and drew him farther into her mouth with each motion. She took him deeper than any other woman had, and he felt his balls draw up tight.

He'd already known this woman was dangerous to him, but he'd had no idea the exact amount of her power until this moment. He tightened his grip on her, knowing he was close. "Stop."

Ignoring him, she continued.

"Aria…"

She drew up a little and looked at him.

"Stop."

"Please," she asked. She pressed her thumb against the sensitive place on the underside of his cock. "Let me please you. Let me show you how much I want you."

He nodded. "Finish me off."

Aria went to work, sucking, licking, swallowing as she jerked her hand up and down. She kept a finger from the other hand against his anus, increasing the pressure just a little, shoving him over the edge.

He ground his back teeth together and thrust his hips forward as he ejaculated into her mouth. She continued to suck, until she'd gotten every drop.

"Yum," she said when she finally looked up.

At some point, he'd put both of his palms on the side of her head.

The last tremor went through him, and he gently pulled her head back. She could not have done that better, even if she'd been the most perfectly trained submissive.

He helped her to stand, and he tugged her into his arms, holding her close. *How the hell am I ever going to let her go?*

"Ah! Aria, there you are," Julien said when she walked into the workshop.

In the ten days she'd been at Grant's house, Julien had checked in at least once a day. And she should be used to it. But seeing his face, much, much larger than life, still took her aback.

"What's going on?" She slid onto a stool, put down her mug of coffee and offered the other one to Grant.

"Thank you," he said with a smile.

Already she recognized that look.

To anyone else, it might appear to be a casual or grateful gesture. But she'd seen the way he'd perused her. His gaze had taken in her whole body, and he'd drawn his eyebrows together to communicate approval and a promise that he was thinking about the evening ahead.

"Tell me that's not a caffeinated beverage," Julien said.

"Mine even has vanilla spice creamer in it," she said, "with a few chocolate chips, too." She prepared to enjoy his shudder. He didn't disappoint. "Grant had something he had to put into the blender for breakfast. Spinach, I think."

"Kale," he corrected.

"They're not the same thing," Julien added.

"They're green and taste better warmed up with butter and salt. But it should counteract the caffeine, right?"

"You'll ruin your adrenal glands."

"But I'll get more work done in the meantime."

She and Grant clinked their mugs together.

In the time she'd been at his house, they'd had fallen into an easy routine. Midday, one of them would take a break, brew a second pot of coffee and bring back the manna for the other.

If Julien hadn't intruded, Grant would be showing his appreciation right then.

"I was telling Grant we're ready to begin beta testing Blanca's app," Julien continued, as if the conversation hadn't taken a side street.

"Already? That was fast," Aria responded.

She'd given the project to David for assignment and it surprised her that Julien would take an interest in a project this size when movies beckoned.

"I pride Bonds on being like a speedboat. Fast. Responsive. Able to spin. Turn on its axis in a millisecond."

"Does a speedboat technically have an axis?" she asked, amused.

"I have no idea," he responded, frowning.

"Grant?"

"It's irrelevant," Julien interrupted. "You understand my point."

"When a beautiful woman is involved, a man will move the heavens," Grant agreed.

"That was poetic," she said.

"Thank you."

"I'm hoping Blanca will go on a date with me, to show her gratitude," Julien continued.

She looked at Grant.

He shrugged.

Julien's focus on Blanca's project explained a lot about his disheveled appearance. He was seated behind the desk in his Cupertino headquarters, a glass of something that could be carrot juice in front of him.

He was unshaven, and his button-down shirt was a bit rumpled. If her guess was right, he hadn't gone home yesterday. He'd probably napped on the bed behind a partition in his office.

Which wasn't all that unusual. Despite admonishments to his staff to rest and take their vacation time, he often spent the night at work. The mattress, she had been told, boasted fourteen hundred thread count sheets.

"What's the next step?" Grant asked.

"I can reach out to her," she said. "Let her know where we're at, give her an update, let her know what to expect."

"You need to focus on your current project," Julien replied. "And testing protocols will be initiated with the mainframe."

"That's Bonds speak," Grant said.

"Bonds speak?"

"Basically...it means his reason is subterfuge."

She grinned. "Bullshit?"

"Exactly. He wants an excuse to call Ms. Montoya. And it has to look as if it's business. You're one of his top people, you're very, very busy, but the project matters so much to you that you sent it to the boss for personal attention."

She could only guess how personal. "How long have you two been reading each other's minds?"

"Since college," Grant said.

Julien shrugged and took a drink of his juice without wrinkling his nose. No matter how unhealthy, she personally preferred her artificially sweetened, potentially adrenal-gland killing coffee. More and more, she was learning to appreciate each moment, the more delicious, the better.

"So how's your project coming?"

She waited to see if Grant would reply.

Eventually, he did. "Slow. It's evolving. We're hoping to have it put together for you soon."

"Most important thing is to relax," Julien coached them. "You can't force genius."

"Helllllllo, Genius."

At the sound of Molly's voice, Julien grinned.

"You've given her some interesting verbal cues," Grant said.

"She does like having her...*components* adjusted."

Aria rolled her eyes. "I'm beginning to wonder if you two mentally left college."

They looked at each other. Simultaneously, they shook their heads.

"Every time I ping you, I hope you're not there," Julien admitted, and he actually sounded a bit disappointed.

"We could pretend," Aria said. "Maybe actually get something productive done."

"Nah. Molly would tell me the truth. Isn't that right?"

"Helllllllo, Genius."

Julien's grin was the last thing they saw before the wall went blank.

"He didn't even say toodles," she protested.

"The bastard," Grant sympathized.

Since the afternoon was overcast, they'd again selected the sunny Caribbean as their work background picture. She decided she might want the projection ability in her California office and her apartment.

The idea of going back gnawed at her.

Grant was starting to mean something to her, and she was enjoying the introduction into BDSM.

But reality loomed and there was no denying it.

There were business trips she couldn't skip. As much as she adored Grant, she wanted to see her parents, her friends.

They'd made progress, and it had been exciting to work together and to play together. But that was all it was.

Grant had made it abundantly clear he wasn't leaving New Mexico, no matter what Julien demanded. He'd resisted all her attempts to get him to do practice presentations. When he'd moved to Los Alamos, he'd clearly cut off the old part of his life. Maybe he hadn't come to heal. Maybe he'd run.

"In front of people, Julien's a natural," he'd told her.

"Julien's *not* a natural," she'd countered. "He gets out there, begins to talk, builds to a crescendo. He has an idea of what he wants to say, but he uses a scriptwriter."

"No he doesn't."

"The hell he doesn't. Every word he says in public is vetted. Mostly, though, he lets his passion shine through. He's more awkward than anything, but no one cares… Well, except for the haters and the handful of critics who love to tear down Bonds so they get readers. You know, the ones who go to bed with a thesaurus so they can find new ways to insult our latest technological feat. But the truth is, people want to be excited, so he gives them that. Our products aren't gadgets. They're a way to make lives better. He believes it, so he communicates that—the idea, the hope, passion."

As she'd spoken, she'd paced across the workshop, and he'd sat there, seemingly captivated, but also unmoved. When she'd asked what he'd thought, he'd said he'd consider it then had changed the subject.

They'd spent the rest of that day with tension worming between them, until he'd taken her to bed, tied her up, and communicated in a way that made words unnecessary.

And now, his gaze was riveted on her as she took a drink of her sugar-laced, cavity-causing coffee.

"You didn't really put chocolate chips in there, did you?"

"Really I did. Would you like a taste?" She offered the cup.

"Yeah. Put it down and come here."

That was her favorite kind of taste, as well...

She went into his arms, and he kissed her deeply, gently at first. He didn't need to coax her response, she offered it. From the moment their tongues touched, desire arced through her. At times he was soft and gentle, expressing reverence. At others, he was demanding and urgent, but always, he expressed his moods, his intentions through his touch.

He tugged her sweater up and off.

"Here?" she asked.

"Here."

At the desire that made his eyes smoky, she trembled.

She toed off her shoes and shucked her jeans and undergarments as he fished a condom from his pocket and pulled off his clothes.

"What do you want, Aria?"

"Fuck me, Sir," she replied.

He nodded.

Over the days, she'd become more comfortable with him and his demands, and in fact, liked them. He refused to allow sex to be perfunctory—something that happened in bed at night before two people rolled over and went to sleep.

With Grant, she'd learned, arousal constantly smoldered, just waiting for a spark to take it to flash point.

In moments, he had her against the glass window. She spread her arms and braced her hands on the steel beams.

The view took her breath, and so did the freezing cold sensation when he put a hand in the middle of her back and pressed her forward, flattening her breasts on the frigid pane of glass, making her nipples harden.

"Spread your legs."

She did and he stroked her pussy, arousing her. He dipped a finger into her pussy, making her damp, and he drew some of that moisture backward to lubricate her ass. Gently, he inserted one finger in her anus, then he brought in his other hand, filling her pussy with four fingers.

Aria couldn't see his reflection in the window, but she inhaled his scent, that of command and musk.

She was lost as he fucked her cunt, her ass.

Vertigo and passion tilted her world, making her scream.

He had her on the knife-edge of danger, and she felt his sheathed cock at the entrance to her pussy.

Somehow, he managed to keep a finger in her ass, stretching her as he drove his cock up into her, filling her. The double sensation overwhelmed. "I need…"

"Tell me," he whispered, demanded, breath warm on her ear.

"To come. Please," she said. He thrust in her hard, and her thoughts vanished. All that remained was raw need. "Please, Sir?"

"That's it. Come for me, Aria."

Convulsing on his hard cock, she came.

She continued to rise onto her tiptoes then bend her knees, inviting him, urging him. Each thrust brought him deeper, reignited her desire.

He changed positions, putting one hand in front of her to support her lower abdomen so he could keep her still.

She heard his breathing change, felt a telltale pulse in his cock.

For a moment, he went rigid.

"Yes," she urged, hot for him again. "I want... Fill me, Grant."

With a final, shuddered breath, she felt him come, filling her and pushing her into a second orgasm.

He collapsed against her and, for a moment, she supported the combination of their weight before he seemed to find his bearings.

Slowly, he moved the hand that he'd put in front of her, and he pushed it against the support beam then eased himself back.

His cock slid from her, and he withdrew his finger from her ass.

"I'm not sure how that position was even possible," she told him.

"Me either."

His hands were on her, helping her to stand.

"That was a hell of a way to get me over the fear of falling off the edge of your house," she said as he turned her to face him.

"You did go over the edge, metaphorically."

"Twice," she said, outlining the hard planes of his jaw.

Together they left the workshop. She no longer felt like working. Besides, she knew their creative conversations would follow them wherever they went. It was part of who they were.

As she usually did, she headed for her shower. She was shocked when he followed her.

"It's big enough for two," he told her as he scooped her up

and sat her on the countertop. "Molly, shower on. Temperature at a hundred and one."

"That's pretty steamy," Aria said as the water flowed from the shower ceiling.

"It'll be steamier when you're in there with me."

"We're not done?" she asked, her breath constricting again.

"Aria, we're just getting started."

CHAPTER NINE

"Let's mix it up," he said.

Aria glanced up. Grant was standing in the doorway of her bedroom, one shoulder propped against the jamb. With his damp hair, freshly shaven face, sexy boots and tight jeans, he made it impossible to think. "What do you mean?"

"Roads are clear. We've been stuck here for a few days. We need some groceries, so I figured we could drive to Santa Fe, walk around the Plaza, have dinner then pick up supplies on the way back."

"Now?"

"It's less than an hour away. We can use the time in the car to talk."

She wondered if he'd sensed the restlessness that was starting to crawl through her. "You've talked me into it," she said. "Give me twenty minutes?" She'd need that long to dry her hair and get dressed.

Within thirty minutes, they'd passed the Montoyas' restaurant. "Julien has a thing for Blanca," she said. "Who'd have guessed?"

"Probably neither of them," Grant replied. "Sure as hell not me."

She settled back, adjusted the lumbar support then turned up the seat warmer by a degree before grabbing her cell phone to check email. "This highway is pretty narrow," she said. "And gorgeous."

As they drew closer to Santa Fe, she noticed more Kokopellis. "He really does represent fertility?"

He glanced at her. "Look it up."

With a shrug, she picked up her phone and asked for the meaning of Kokopelli.

Grant grinned as the response confirmed what he'd told her all along. "Anything else you doubt me about?" he asked.

"Fine," she said. "You were right."

"Three of my favorite words."

"Humility is a virtue."

"Like you wouldn't brag if you were right?"

"That's different," she insisted.

It took a few trips down narrow streets before they found a parking spot.

"Saint Francis Cathedral," he said, pointing out a stunning, historic church.

It looked very different from the surrounding adobe buildings, making it stand out more in contrast.

The rest of the Plaza fascinated her. In front of the Palace of the Governors, a number of Native American vendors from various pueblos had braved the cold to display their pottery and stunning pieces of jewelry.

She bent to look at a sterling silver bracelet that had an unusual, green-colored stone set into it.

"It's hand hammered," the vendor said.

Aria admired the filigree. It was both delicate and sturdy.

"Candelaria turquoise," the vendor continued.

"That's turquoise?" she repeated, looking at the woman.

"From a mine in Nevada. It's beautiful, as well as unique."

"It is," she agreed. Even the small veins of brown added to its beauty.

"Try it on." The woman, her hair secured in a long, gorgeous braid, picked up the piece and offered it to her.

Putting it on would be the first step to falling in love, she knew.

Grant was no help. He nodded encouragement.

"Did you make it yourself?" Aria asked.

"For you," she said, jokingly.

Aria offered her wrist and the Native American woman slipped it on.

Even in the weak winter sunlight, the silver seemed to sparkle, and Aria had never seen a stone that color before.

"This shade of green reminds me of your eyes," Grant said. "And it even sounds like your name. Calendaria." To the woman, he added, "We'll take it."

"But... Wait," Aria protested. "I don't even know how much it is."

The woman named a price that was fair, but Aria's instinct was to haggle, just a little.

"Done," he said, extracting his wallet from his back pocket.

"Grant," she warned. "Don't." Her heart began to thunder. Except for an engagement ring, a man had never bought her a piece of jewelry. "I can buy my own things."

"Of course you can. I just happen to want to do it for you." He handed the woman two crisp bills.

"I..." Aria looked at him, then the bracelet and finally back to the vendor who was smiling delightedly. She sighed. "I'm not sure what to say."

"How about thank you?" he suggested, putting his wallet away. To the vendor, he said, "She'll wear it home." He shook hands with the vendor, accepted her business card and a velvet pouch to store the gorgeous silver piece.

With his hand under her elbow, he guided her away from people, toward the gazebo across the street in the town center. "It's beautiful."

"You still shouldn't have bought it for me." She lifted her wrist to admire it, though.

"It was my pleasure."

"It was too much money."

"Not in the least," he countered. "Every time you wear it, you'll remember this day. And it'll be tied to memories of me."

Her breath hitched.

"You'll remember New Mexico. You'll remember your first taste of submission. More than anything, this is a symbol of that."

"That's a lot of symbolism in one bracelet."

"It is," he said. "That's why I wanted you to have it."

Even if he hadn't bought her a remembrance, she would never forget him. "I appreciate the thought." Aria leaned into him, wrapped her arm around his neck and kissed him. "I love it."

"Just be glad it didn't have a Kokopelli on it," he replied, slapping her hard on the ass.

She yelped and giggled, enjoying their interaction.

He tucked her arm into the crook of his elbow and guided her back across the street to a sidewalk. Since she'd been in New Mexico, the days had started to lengthen slightly. But it was still dark early, and one by one, people were drifting away from the plaza, toward the few restaurants. Stores were starting to turn off lights and lock doors and the Native Americans began to put away their wares.

"Dinner?" he offered.

They wandered into a small restaurant that specialized in seafood.

"Seems odd," she said, "in the heart of the Southwest."

He nodded agreement as he accepted a menu. There'd been numerous awards posted in the window, so they'd agreed to give it a try.

It wasn't just ordinary seafood, she realized as she took her first bite. The fiery, spicy-sweet prawns served with chile polenta were exquisite, as was the wine the waiter had suggested to accompany the meal. "I'll admit, I was a skeptic," she said. "When you live on the coast, it's hard to believe anyone else can do fish well, but this was incredible."

And so was the Wicked Mexican Chile Chocolate Cake served with a side of cappuccino ice cream.

"Fabuloso!" she exclaimed.

"Again proving you are fluent in dessert," he said, before taking a drink of strong piñon coffee.

After dinner, they wandered around the darkened plaza to work off some calories before settling in for the thirty-five minute trip back to Los Alamos.

They barely made it before the grocery store closed for the evening.

As they wound their way back up the mountain, she fell silent. Their day had been exquisite, and she'd always cherish her bracelet. But all-too-soon the visit would be over, and the time with Grant would become nothing more than a memory. His gift had been tied with a bittersweet ribbon.

"You're quiet," he observed, sliding her a glance across the darkened compartment.

"Carb coma, I think," she hedged.

"I've got a remedy."

"Do you?" Aria shook off the sudden melancholy.

Inside, Shadow was waiting, and Molly turned on the

lights as they went toward the kitchen. "I'm getting used to this welcoming committee," Aria admitted.

"We'll get your apartment set up. You can be our beta tester."

"I love the idea. Does Shadow come in any other breeds?"

"I'd never thought of it," he said as he put the milk away. "What's wrong with…whatever he is. A Labrador, I think."

"Nothing. But we had a cocker spaniel when I was growing up, and I've always wanted another."

"I'll consider it. Now, for tonight…"

Work projects were suddenly shoved to the side. "Yes?" she asked.

"Go to my bedroom, take the duffel bag out of the closet, lay out the toys on the bed, then kneel on the floor with the blindfold on and wait for me."

She forced out a breath. When he'd mentioned a blindfold on a previous occasion, she'd told him she wasn't sure about it. She knew that saying the word yellow would get her out of anything she didn't want to do, but in the last day or so, she'd also decided to try as many new experiences as she could. As he'd said, she hadn't known she'd like having her pussy spanked until she'd experienced it.

"Oh, and Aria?" He folded his arms across his chest in that formidable, Dom-like way that melted her resolve. "I want you naked."

"Yes," she whispered. "Of course, Sir."

It amazed her how much that one word changed her mindset, helping her slip from a day of work and an enjoyable afternoon out to a woman who craved her man's touch.

She started down the hall. Then, realizing he was watching, she exaggerated her movements. If he was going to accuse her of sashaying, she was going to behave in a way that would find her guilty as charged.

The sound of his guttural groan was all the reward she needed.

With a saucy grin, she stopped at the entrance to his room, turned back toward him and blew him a kiss.

"You've just earned your first ever punishment," he warned her.

Good.

Excitement and nerves collided, winding her tight. She entered his closet for the first time. The space was enormous, big enough for two or more people to peacefully coexist. His stuff barely took up a quarter of the space. She did notice, however, a pair of athletic shoes in a cubby. The neon color was so bright she was afraid it would blind her. She remembered seeing a picture of Grant, Julien, Reece and Kennedy all wearing them. It was hard to believe that four such accomplished men would put such garish shoes on their feet before going out in public.

Worrying that Grant might come into the room and find her not ready for him, she found the duffel on top of a shelf and pulled it down.

Her mouth dried as she took out each item and laid it on the bedspread. Cuffs. Two different blindfolds, one with lace trim, another made from leather. There was a paddle, a flogger made with stringy pieces of rubber, and an egg-shaped vibrator.

As she considered the toys, any doubts about Julien's motivation were erased. All along, he'd been trying to set them up. She hated people meddling in her life, but there was no doubt that the time away had been worth it. She had more energy. She'd been more creatively challenged than she had in years, and Grant had shown her that there were men out there who were worth waiting for. Ending her engagement had been difficult, but now she was convinced she'd made the right—the only—decision.

She undressed, but she decided to leave the bracelet on. It seemed fitting.

Then she considered the blindfolds. The choice was easy. Leather. The scent of it, the feel of it, the way it would fit against her face. No doubt he'd like that one.

Exhaling to settle in, she knelt.

BDSM was part ritual, she realized as she put the blindfold over her eyes. The instructions, the touches, the verbiage…it created its own intimacy and relationship.

Being unable to see made her hearing keener, and she listened for his movements. She was reminded of the portrait on the easel. Originally she'd suggested that he had it there as a warning to potential subs. But now she thought of it as so much more. She related to the woman in the picture—her trust, her resolve, her transcendence.

Eventually, inevitably, Aria heard him.

Her heart did a slow thud.

She shook her head back, letting her hair fall down her back, and she placed her hands on the back of her neck, still waiting.

As he came closer, she thrust out her breasts, spread her knees farther apart and waited. Patience may not have been one of her greatest virtues, but she was learning.

His footsteps stopped. She inhaled, smelling the leather blindfold then…him. Even though she couldn't see, she squeezed her eyes shut, savoring the anticipation.

"Stunning," he said softly. "I'd imagined what you might look like, but I'm not brilliant enough to have filled in all these details. Your breasts are gorgeous."

"Thank you," she whispered.

"And how's the blindfold?"

"I'm okay with it."

"I mentioned you'd earned your first punishment," he said.

But she wasn't worried. There was no anger in his voice, only the thrum of desire on his vocal cords. "Yes, Sir."

"No fear?"

"None," she admitted. Then, thinking, she asked, "Should there be?"

"Perhaps."

His response made her stomach plummet.

"I like the choice of blindfolds," he said.

"Thank you."

"What shall I spank you with, subbie?"

"Your"—she bit back her instinctive response—"choice, Sir."

"I wonder what you might have said if you hadn't remembered the correct response?"

He moved behind her, and it was all she could do not to twist him to follow him. Ridiculous, she knew, given the fact she couldn't see anyway.

"I might have said, your hand, Sir, but I'd never be so bold."

"What did you put on the bed?"

"A paddle, Sir. A leather one." Either way, she wished he'd get on with it. She was a bundle of excited nerves.

"Stand," he told her.

He put his hands around her waist to help her up.

"You couldn't be any more perfect," he said.

She dropped her hands to her sides and waited.

He obviously sat on the bed, and he drew her over his knee. Desperately, she put out one hand, trying to touch the floor with her fingers.

"I've got you," he said, clamping a strong arm around her. "And if you don't struggle, you won't fall."

She was very much aware of her precarious position with her naked butt upturned over his lap. But it was hot and sexy at the same time, made more so by the scratch of his denim jeans on her soft skin. The fact he was fully dressed while she was completely naked added a sense of vulnerability.

"Is your pussy already wet?"

"Yes," she whispered, horrified.

"Just from the anticipation?"

She nodded.

"Then I wonder what you'll be like in a few minutes when I've punished you for your submissive sass?"

His words, the harsh tone, made her squirm. "Why don't you find out?" Quickly, she added, "Sir," knowing it was too little and much too late.

He laughed. "Goading me?"

"You're killing me," she admitted. "I need you, Sir."

"And now you can wait."

She flailed her legs in mute protest.

He jostled her, sliding her from his knee, setting her upright and holding onto her until she found her footing. "Damn it," she protested.

"We'll start over," he said.

Other than clenching her back teeth, she didn't show any further frustration.

"Better," he said. "I'm adding the nipple balls."

Aria reminded herself that she'd endured them before. As long as he talked, touched, reassured, she could tolerate anything.

"Put your hands on your hips."

Once she'd complied, he gently squeezed each nipple until they were aroused then attached the balls.

She was almost dizzy with arousal.

"Fuck. They do make you even more gorgeous. Now, would you like to behave like a perfect submissive, or shall I clamp your cunt, too?"

"Ah… I've learned my lesson, Sir."

"Back over my knee then," he said, helping her back into position.

This time, she kept her mouth closed.

He stroked her ass with his fingers.

In silent entreaty, she spread her legs to give him better access to her pussy, desperate for a single touch.

He ignored her.

She bit her upper lip to keep her mouth shut.

Before she was completely ready, he blazed his open palm on her ass. She arched her back and gasped. That had damn well hurt.

But the pain vanished immediately and she never considered asking him to slow down or stop. She wanted this.

His words from the first day replayed in her head. *Live dangerously.*

He gave her at least another half dozen swats, on her ass, on her thighs, moving quickly, not letting her absorb one before going onto the next.

It sparked a fury of arousal.

Only then did he stroke her pussy, quickly, harshly, shoving her to the edge with no relief.

"Punishment," he reminded her.

And it wasn't enough.

The next spank made her go stiff. He'd placed it just beneath her buttocks, and it had been harsher than the previous ones. He'd apparently moved on to the paddle, and its pain was different, more like the flogger, but broader, more concentrated.

It sounded different, too. Louder and hollower. She loved it.

Aria tossed her head from side to side, letting him know how much she approved. "Yes," she whispered, but wasn't sure she'd said it aloud.

He moved at a measured pace, working his way up with

each strike. She no longer noticed the pain in her nipples, just the throbbing sensation on her butt.

Grant held onto her, keeping her in place, making her aware of his masculine power.

Damn. On so many levels, Grant got to her. Maybe Julien had been right when he'd said that Simon was the wrong kind of man for her.

She heard the echo of something thudding against the hardwood floor, and she realized he was fingering her pussy, fucking her with his fingers.

Then he moved her onto her back and she heard him unfasten his belt buckle, then the sound of his zipper. Even though she was blindfolded, she was aware of him taking a minute to roll on a condom.

He pulled her into position, her legs spread, knees draped over the edge of the mattress.

"You're wet," he said.

And he was hard. He impaled her in a single thrust.

The pain from the spanking, the bite from the nipple balls, the fury of his thrust combined to shove her headlong into a shuddering climax.

She bucked against him, and his hands were everywhere —on her clit, her breasts, prolonging the torment and driving her forward again as his cock swelled with arousal.

He pinched an already abused nipple and she surged forward.

"I... I..."

"Come," he urged.

The word and his own orgasm were enough to make her shatter again.

By slow measures, reality returned, and she became aware that he'd taken off the balls.

"Close your eyes," he told her before removing the blindfold.

She blinked several times to let her eyesight adjust to the light in the room. It was then she saw he hadn't even managed to get all the way undressed.

He sat next to her and pulled her against him.

"How was your first punishment?"

"Anything but incentive to behave," she confessed.

"As I thought. In that case, no more punishments for you. I'll only do something like that if you're very, very good."

"Very, very good?"

"Extraordinarily so."

She settled her head on his shoulder. "I liked that."

"Yeah. You may be ready for more."

More? There was more? "In that case, I'll be extraordinarily good," she promised.

"What do you think?" Aria asked.

The video on the screen faded. This time, instead of a soothing landscape, the Bonds logo was displayed. Despite the fact it wasn't 3D, it seemed to float above the wall.

Grant tapped his index fingers together. "It's astounding. But is it enough?"

In the three weeks that she'd been at his house, their original idea had taken shape. The underlying concept was solid, but there were still hundreds of unknowns. The success of Project Molly depended on Julien's ability to make deals happen, either by acquiring companies or working out agreements with them. And mostly, it rested on Julien's interest. Bottom line, if he didn't like it, it didn't get developed.

This presentation was their only chance.

And given the fact Julien had become very interested in

movies, he might scoff at this effort—or maybe not. He'd always liked being the star.

With help from their labs, they'd created a CGI image of Julien and added the sound.

Molly had spoken for herself during key parts. And they'd had Julien's own theme music play at the beginning.

Still…

"What can we do different? Better?"

She slid from her stool and paced to the window, something she had done regularly since the day he'd fucked her up against it. She still hadn't ventured onto either deck, but he hadn't given up on that.

"Honestly?" she asked. "I think we're there. We've gone through the objections."

In fact, during some clandestine video conferences, they'd run it past a few of their senior engineers. They'd added several dozen more concerns.

Bottom line, no one thought it was insurmountable.

He studied her.

"The video is solid. It's not Hollywood, but it's not bad."

And it was a sight better than endless slide shows.

The trouble was, the closer they were to the end of the project, the closer she was to returning home. Other than the fact that, greedily, Grant wanted to keep her, there was no reason for to stay.

Having her here had been natural, and more, he enjoyed her company. And the sex? Beyond anything he could have imagined.

He wasn't able to fool himself, though. Good sex enhanced a relationship. It wasn't the basis for one.

"You have to be the one to introduce it to him."

"We can do it together."

"He's looking to you," she reminded him.

That had been their biggest source of discontent during

the past few weeks. The more she and Julien pressed Grant to take a bigger role, the more he protested. He liked his life. He had never agreed to be anything other than an engineer. Being cofounder hadn't come with expectations of him taking a stage.

He reminded her of it again.

"Oh, please. Look at you when we're in a scene. That's a stage. You create the whole thing, set it up, script it."

At that, he grinned. "You give me too much credit. It's mostly extemporaneous."

"You're good at it," she persisted. "Presenting Bonds' products is the same thing. C'mon, Grant. You wrote almost that entire video."

"That was easy." He waved her off. "All I did was put words in Julien's mouth and let him talk about Molly."

"Exact same thing as talking to an audience." Then she put her hand on the table and leaned toward him. "You're better looking than Julien."

As if that meant anything to him.

"Less arrogant, too. People are going to like you more than they like him."

"Julien is a natural."

"And he pisses off as many people as he engages."

"I could be exactly the same."

"You're not."

"A genius is trying to reach you."

The interruption startled him, and she stood up straight.

"What are we going to tell him?" she asked.

He put his finger across his lips then pointed up.

She nodded, indicating she understood. Through Molly, he was most likely already listening in.

"Hello, Julien," he greeted. "What an unexpected surprise."

Julien didn't even pretend to engage in any pleasantries. "What don't you want to tell me?"

"Are we ready?" Grant asked, glancing at Aria.

Obviously she'd meant what she'd said earlier. Other than giving him a thumbs-up, she said nothing. He was on his own. So be it. "Video on."

"Ah, Aria, you're looking beautiful, as always."

She gave an exaggerated curtsey.

"It's the boots," he added. "I told you it was going to be the boots."

"Hands off," Grant said.

Both Julien and Aria looked at him. Aria's mouth formed an O and she frowned.

"It's like that, is it?" Julien asked.

His own reaction shook him. He'd never been possessive with a woman before, and certainly not with a coworker—and most definitely not with Julien. The man, to Grant's knowledge, had never been in love. He never flirted with other men's women, except in an overt, friendly way. Julien might be an asshole at times, but he was never dishonorable.

Despite the silence, looks cast his direction and an innate desire to pass it all off and move on, Grant remained resolute. Instead, he looked at Julien and responded, "Yeah. It's like that."

"Understood. My sincere apologies."

Aria continued to stare at Grant, and when he directed his gaze toward her, she wrapped her arms across her chest.

The action made the bracelet even more prominent.

He hadn't been completely honest with her when he'd bought it. To him, it was more than a stunning piece of jewelry. The Candelaria turquoise reminded him of her eyes, yes. That and the fact the stone sounded like her name had both been reason enough to buy them. Her joy in handling the piece had been palpable. And still, there'd been more. He saw it as a gift of his appreciation for her having shared the first steps of her submissive journey with him. At least to him, it would forever be a reminder of that.

After a few more seconds of awkward silence, Julien spoke again, "Is that what the great debate is about? Whether you were going to tell me that the inevitable had finally occurred?" He made a show of looking at his fingernails then he rubbed them on his Oxford shirt.

"Could you be any more of an ass?" Grant snapped. This whole fucking thing was making him edgy. And Aria was still too damn far away from him.

"Probably not," Julien said. "Though I do try. Constant battle. Always raising the bar."

Grant knew he was overreacting. This was his best friend, one of the most loyal, trusted people he'd ever known. But where Aria was concerned, rational thought didn't always prevail.

"How about I just fuck off?" Julien asked with an easy grin. "I'll check in with you tomorrow. I really do want all the delicious details."

Before Grant could respond, the screen had gone blank.

Silence hung thick, heavy like a shroud.

"I owe you an apology," he said eventually.

He took a step toward her, but she rubbed her arms, silently communicating her need for space.

"That was crass. I was out of line. What happens between us is no one else's business." *Crap*. He sensed he was bungling this, making it worse, but the truth was, when his heart was engaged, he only knew one way to behave. "Not even a step above a Neanderthal."

She expelled a shaky breath. "I want to tell you it's okay. But..." She didn't seem to be any better at this than he was. "I've never slept with a coworker, even on the road where there's plenty of opportunity. And there are good reasons for it. We've blurred the lines, and I had a big part in it." She paused. "That made things messy."

"To me, they're not. And to be clear, I'm not apologizing for having a relationship with you."

Her eyes widened.

"Nor am I apologizing for demanding your submissive obedience."

She put a hand on her chest.

"In fact, despite all that, I'd do it again. I love having you in my arms, under my lash, on my cross. I cherish you, Aria, and this relationship we share." Even if it meant getting entangled. Even if it hurt when she left. Even if loneliness devastated him. "But I am sorry if my reaction to Julien's comment embarrassed you." He met her gaze. "Forgive me?"

"You make it difficult not to." She gave a tentative, half-formed smile.

It was polite, he saw, more than sincere.

Slowly she lowered her hand. "I think I'll go and exercise for a bit. I need some time alone."

He nodded.

Maybe he could be a bigger fool. But as she put her palm on the scanner and waited for the door to open without ever looking back at him, he wasn't sure how.

CHAPTER TEN

Shock had left her reeling and needing a little bit of time alone.

Though she'd said she needed to work out and it would do her mind and body a lot of good, she really didn't feel like it. Instead, she went to her room, took off her clothes and slipped into a robe as well as the sandals she'd never returned to him.

She thought he might follow her outside, but she was grateful that he respected her request.

Aria dropped the robe onto the ground then walked down the two steps into the hot tub. The water soothed and healed—her body, at least.

Her heart was another story.

Trying to hold onto her equilibrium, she closed her eyes and tipped her head back.

At least a week ago, she'd acknowledged to herself that she was starting to care for Grant. She'd known that he appreciated the way they worked together as well as the way she responded to him in bed. They'd both also understood the relationship would draw to a natural close.

Grant's reaction to Julien had been all male, smacking of territorialism. It had felt awkward in front of her boss, but then again, Julien continually stuck his nose into her business.

The real problem for her was that she was going home soon, and she would be leaving a man, the first man, she genuinely cared for.

Cared for? It was more than that. Much more, she reluctantly admitted.

She loved him.

Freaking loved him.

Damn it.

She pressed her hands to her face, futilely hoping she could keep emotion at bay.

No doubt he had affection for her as well, but it wasn't on the same level as hers. Clearly he'd let Julien know that she was physically spoken for at the moment, but emotionally was a different matter. Grant's heart was still enshrouded by misplaced guilt and grief. No way would she offer her emotional vulnerability to a man incapable of returning it.

No doubt, they made a talented team. And she was having an amazing time learning about submission. Like him, she didn't apologize for that. The only thing she regretted was that she'd allowed her emotions to get mixed up in the equation.

Stupid.

Damn it. She was smarter than this. She should have kept her heart under tighter control. Should have constantly reminded herself that this was a short-term situation, that, yes, of course, sex would happen when two people spent this much time in close, enforced quarters. Sleeping together had been inevitable, but becoming entangled hadn't been.

Even if all that hadn't been true, he was an extraordinarily complicated man, with his heart shrouded by loss.

So, what happened next?

Even if he wanted to do a long-distance relationship, she'd have to refuse. Phone calls and occasional weekends weren't going to be enough for her, especially when combined with her travel schedule. And her parents were in California. She wanted time with them, too.

Julien could not have been more wrong. A man like Grant was definitely not for her.

She took her hands from her face. Pretending reality didn't exist wouldn't help anything. She sank into the tub a little deeper, letting the heat soothe away the sudden knots that had formed in her shoulders.

After a few minutes, she exhaled deeply, resolved to enjoy the remaining time she had with Grant. And she warned herself that she'd have to keep her heart locked up.

He wasn't around when she went back into the house, and she breathed a sigh of gratitude. She showered then dried her hair. After freshening her makeup, she dressed. "Molly?"

"Yes, Princess?"

Princess? She wondered which of the men were responsible for that response. "Where's Grant?"

"His Majesty is in the kitchen."

She went to find him. He was in front of the stove, and he turned toward her.

He swept his glance over her.

"Julien was right," he said.

She propped her shoulder on the entryway. "About?"

"The boots."

She rolled her eyes. She appreciated his version of an olive branch, letting her know they didn't need to talk about it, that he was allowing them to go back to the easy camaraderie that had been the hallmark of their time together.

"I still want a picture of you in them."

"Dream on."

"I was afraid you'd say that. I opened a bottle of Malbec." He nodded toward the counter.

She joined him in the kitchen and poured each of them a glass. "What's for dinner?" This was something else she would miss. At home she grew tired of takeout and eating at restaurants, but she simply didn't have the energy to prepare dinner when she arrived home after a long day. And since it was just her, she often couldn't see the point of cooking for one person.

"Nothing fancy. Beef stir fry."

She wrinkled her nose. "Which means it has green stuff in it."

"And there's still some of the chocolate cake that we picked up last time we were in town."

"I may forgive the green beans."

"They're sugar peas."

"Oh. Is there a difference?"

Despite her fears, the food was delicious. In fact, she speared a sugar pea from his plate.

Afterward, he said, "There's a full moon tonight. The deck is a perfect place to see it."

"I was hoping you hadn't realized I still hadn't been out there."

"Live dangerously," he reminded her.

He grabbed jackets for both of them then slid open the doors.

"Can I see it from here?" she asked, frozen in the doorway.

"What we did in the workshop was far more frightening than this."

Vertigo fluttered, despite his reassurances. "But you had me the whole time," she replied quietly.

"I still do." He reached a hand toward her. "Always will."

Making a funny face, as if that would stop the glass from breaking beneath her feet, sending her plummeting hundreds of feet to the canyon floor, she took that first, tenuous step.

Closing her eyes, still holding his hand, she took another.

Even though she spent all day touting astounding engineering feats, she didn't trust this deck. "That's as far as I'm going." No way was she going to the edge.

"Look up." He pointed at the full, bright orange moon.

He moved behind her, wrapping his arms around her. As she relaxed into him and glanced skyward, the paralyzing fear receded. "It's stunning," she agreed. "I've never seen anything like it." No matter what, she still couldn't relax. Survival instinct was battling with rational thinking, and no way would rational thinking prevail. "I'm going back in. Next time, you can bring my cell phone and take a picture." She wriggled from his grip and hurried back into the relative safety of the living room.

"Was it as scary as it appeared?" he asked as he rejoined her.

"Honestly, Grant? I'm learning that illusion is often more frightening than reality. For all of us." Frustration was still there, even though she'd tried to set it aside. "You can pretend things are a certain way, but that doesn't mean they are. Distortion is a trap." She knew he was listening without hearing. "Bonds needs you." *I need you.* "Your enthusiasm. Your brain." She exhaled. "You're not doing yourself any favors by staying out here, cut off from the world, from living, from breathing and experiencing...yeah, all the risk, the fear, the joy, the failure. It's what makes us human."

"You're in dangerous territory."

"Am I?" she asked. "And? So what? Do you want me to be scared of you? I'm not. Of your power over me, maybe. But not of you, of your temper. Despite your Neanderthal display earlier, you're a damn honorable man."

"You don't know me." Restrained energy all but crackled in his eyes, made more ominous by the pulse ticking in his temple.

Even though they were only several feet apart, Aria remained in place, not yielding to the temptation to change the subject, heed his warning. She knew she might never have another chance to say what she was thinking. "Come back, Grant. Don't let the craziness of your relationship with Kathleen define you or your future. You made mistakes. She made mistakes. I've made mistakes. It's something you did, not who you are."

"You don't know what the hell you're talking about."

"Actually, Grant, when it comes to this, I do." Her heart thundered. She hurt for him, for his loss, but she ached for herself, as well. "You apologized to me earlier, and I owe you one, as well. But I will tell you what I'm not sorry for. I'm not sorry we fucked. I'm not sorry things got messy. I'm not apologizing for having a relationship with you." She echoed his earlier sentiment.

He shoved his hands into his back pockets.

"Nor am I apologizing for any of my submissive actions. I, too, like being in your arms, wondering what you'll do to me next, knowing the exquisite pain will take me somewhere I've never been. But I am sorry that you care for me and that you're terrified because you don't know what the hell to do about it."

Her eyes filled with tears. "It scares me, too. And I don't know what the hell to do, either." She blinked rapidly. "There are never cue cards to tell me what to say, and I'll be damned if I can figure out how to act. But since I arrived here, I've been taking your suggestion and living dangerously. I'm willing to get past my screw-ups. I'm willing to learn and grow and take a chance on what I want, even if I end up devastated in the end."

She brushed past him to hang up her coat.

Suddenly, she felt exhausted and, at the same, time, restless. She was done here. But she was still trapped. She'd never exposed herself to another human being that way. On the other hand, she'd never felt this way. The worst thing was the realization it didn't matter. Grant had walled himself off so completely that she didn't know where to begin the excavation.

Aria went into the kitchen, poured herself a glass of wine then said, "If you'll excuse me...?" She didn't wait for an answer.

For the first time in days, other than to get clothes, she went into her bedroom and closed the door.

She called her parents to let them know she'd be home soon, though she didn't commit to their invitation to join them for Sunday brunch. After checking up on the progress of the project for Blanca, Aria tried to focus on work emails. All the while, Aria was hyperaware of his moving around the house and the unbearable ache deep inside her, somewhere that, until now, had never been touched.

This was the feeling she'd been waiting for. *This* was what love was.

She just hadn't known how bad it would hurt.

Several hours later, he knocked on her door.

Aria told herself to pretend to be asleep, ignore him, tell him to go away. But that kind of behavior was for a stronger woman. She remained on the chaise as she called out, "Come in."

"Stay the night with me?"

Over the rim of her empty wineglass, she looked at him. Her heart stopped. Considering the idea was insanity. She knew she should say no, leave the already existing wedge where it was. It would make the inevitable parting easier. But damn, she wanted nothing more than one more night, no matter how bitter the emotional toll.

"I'll even let you steal another T-shirt."

With a half-smile, grateful he'd dissipated the tension, she replied, "How can I resist?

Still standing in the threshold, he extended his hand. She rose and crossed the room to accept.

Courteously, as well as a bit possessively, he placed his fingers in the small of her back as they walked down the hallway to his bedroom.

This felt as natural as it did uncomfortable, the juxtaposition adding to the underlying upset deep in her.

"Give me a minute?"

She changed into one of his T-shirts and curled up in his bed, waiting for him while he showered and toweled off. The intimacy wouldn't last, but its seductive spell was compelling nonetheless. As she'd said to him a minute ago, how could she resist?

When he came back, his fresh scent aroused her. That damnable lock of blond hair, now damp, fell over his forehead.

And the confounded man had skipped a shirt. His lounge pants rode low on his hips, and she hungrily drank in his sexy abs and broad shoulders.

She would miss him—and especially this.

He climbed into bed next to her. He sat with his back against the headboard and said, "Come here."

For two seconds, she thought about protesting. She needed to protect her heart. Suspecting it was already too late, she snuggled into his lean strength.

"Molly, lights off."

The full moon provided enough illumination for her to make out his shape and to create atmosphere.

"I want you," he said.

Her insides melted, taking her resolve along with it. "Yes."

"Put your hands above your head."

After she'd done so, he stripped off her T-shirt.

He was always the Dom, and that was something that was always very right between them. Other issues didn't exist here, only each of them and the moment.

She did what he requested, and he kissed his way down her body, from her mouth, to the column of her neck, her breasts, her abdomen, then…there…

Twisting her hands together, she lifted her pelvis, silently asking for more.

He licked her pussy.

She desperately wanted to touch him, dig her hands into his hair.

"Remain in position," he told her.

"Yes, Sir," she whispered, letting her eyes close.

He parted her labia then pulled back the hood of her clitoris. Then he moved his tongue rapidly over the swollen flesh.

With a scream, she ground her hips into his face.

He was merciless, sliding a finger into her, then a second, licking as he fucked her, searching for and finding her G-spot.

"Come for me."

She tossed her head as he wrung it from her. But before she could relax, he demanded a second and a third, leaving her drenched with perspiration, panting from the exertion. "I… Grant! Sir!"

"Remain where you are," he told her as he slowly withdrew his fingers.

There was barely enough ambient light for her to make out what he was doing. He went to the closet for a moment, and when he returned, he was gloriously naked, his cock jutting out powerfully.

Her mouth dried.

Everything about this man turned her on.

He sat next to her on the edge of the bed. "Nipple clamps," he informed her.

She'd followed his orders and kept her hands above her head and she watched his every move. His eyes were dark, expression unreadable. He frightened her, just a little, in the best possible way.

He didn't ask permission to put the clovers on her, instead, he sucked each nipple until it was hard and ready then he put the clamps in place.

She gasped at the pressure. "These are worse than the others."

"You can do it."

Aria wasn't as convinced as he was.

"Think about something else," he encouraged her. "Like the way I'm going to fuck you. Ride you. Make you call out my name."

Maybe for the last time. The unspoken words didn't dampen the sizzling heat, and it amped up her urgency.

He reached for a condom and rolled it on. "Turn over. I want you on all fours."

Because of the clamps, she moved gingerly. Then he was there, helping her, touching her, arousing her.

Her breasts swayed, weighed down by the metal. Every part of her body prickled with awareness.

He teased her with his fingers, and it only took him seconds to make her forget everything except the hunger for his possession. "Do me," she encouraged.

As usual, confounding her, Grant insisted on setting the pace.

By slow measures, he entered her. On the first stroke, he inserted just his cockhead, then, on the next, he went a bit deeper.

She was desperate for him to take her completely. Silently, she pressed back her hips, forcing him deeper.

He slapped her left hip and she yelped.

"We can start over if you'd rather."

"No!"

"Then…?"

She dragged in a breath. "Whatever you please, Sir."

"Oh, fuck," he said, words sounding as if he'd dragged them through rusty nails. "You, Aria. You."

He grabbed both her hip bones and yanked her back as he slammed into her.

"Yes!" *Finally.*

He pounded her pussy, and she cried out.

This was what she needed…the passion to match her seared internal feelings.

Her breasts swayed, making the clovers tighter, adding a layer of exquisite pain. Then he reached beneath her to grab the chain. He fisted it, yanked on it.

Agony shot through her, and she screamed, arching her back.

He went in deeper and an orgasm slashed through her.

She'd never felt anything as intense, as hungry.

Though she hadn't told him what she needed, he'd known, and he'd given it, responding to her urgency with his own.

She felt his cock harden further. Unbelievably, the sensation made another climax unfurl in her. It gnawed at her, and she whimpered.

"Wait this time."

She turned her head to the side and clenched her eyes shut, fighting to hold on.

Grant continued to pull on the clamps, igniting nerve endings.

"I…" Can't wait, she wanted to say. But the words weren't there.

"I want to hear my name. Now," he said.

He grabbed one of her shoulders and held her tight as he went still.

Then suddenly, he thrust into her. The friction and permission were a powerful combination. He pulsed his heat into her and she screamed his name.

She wasn't sure how long it went on, but at some point, his weight and her exhaustion claimed her and her arms went weak. She dropped onto her elbows.

He pulled out his cock and was there for her, capturing her, rolling her over onto her back.

"Let me get those clamps off you."

As bad as they felt, she knew that taking them off would be worse.

She should have known better.

Her considerate Dom fingered her clit, distracting her as he plucked off the clovers.

She snuggled onto her side.

"Wait a minute," he instructed.

He went into the bathroom and returned with a washcloth. He bathed her pussy then helped her back into the T-shirt. Even more tenderness that she was going to miss.

Eventually, he climbed in behind her and pulled her tightly against him, making it clear she was going nowhere.

She could stay like this forever, and the realization that wasn't possible made her heart beat a frantic staccato. Seeming to sense her distress, he uttered soothing sounds and pulled her close, tucking her beneath his chin, protecting her.

Aria realized she'd never had a man so in tune with her before.

His breathing, his touch, comforted her. She drifted off, and when she woke up, he was standing next to the bed, holding her coffee mug, waving his hand above it to waft the scent her direction.

"This one's yours," he told her.

"Heaven," she said with a sigh. She scooted up and back, resting against the headboard.

"Julien has already tried to reach us."

It hadn't taken reality long to intrude.

"I told him we'd get back to him in an hour. I was afraid of waking you without coffee, though."

"Julien partnered with you because you have a brain," she agreed.

He sat on the edge of the bed, a serious frown between his eyebrows. "You doing okay this morning?"

She knew what he was asking. It wasn't just about the sex, it was about the interaction yesterday. "I'm okay." Despite her resolve to enjoy their time, she knew it would be better for her mental state if she left. Now that the project was done, except for the presentation, there was no reason to stay, especially since there was no future in it.

He brushed her hair back from her face. For a moment it appeared he was going to say something, but, obviously changing his mind, he stood. "Tamales and eggs?"

She hesitated, giving him space to say something. Hoping. Praying. But he didn't. It was as if he'd never heard her words the previous night. "Sounds heavenly."

At the door, he paused. "I liked waking up with you in my bed."

"I did, too." Even if it would never happen again.

He walked away.

Fuck. With a sigh, she put down the cup. This was getting more and more difficult.

While he made breakfast, she showered and dressed for the day and pretended everything was okay. She just had to hold the fractured pieces of her heart together for a little longer.

She picked at her breakfast, moving it around her plate, even though it was delicious. Then there was no more reason to stall.

"Let's do this," she said.

They went to the workshop and placed the call to Julien, video already on.

Nerves and excitement twisted inside her as they waited for him to answer. He'd said he had other things ready to present this year, and that was a good thing. The 'Hello, Molly' project, as they'd named it, would take months or years to fully implement. At best, she knew, it was risky. At worst, it could be a financial blunder unlike any other, even if Julien approved it.

Mostly, though, she was proud of what they'd put together, and she knew it mattered to Grant, as well.

Julien finally connected with them.

He was sitting on the white couch in his office, his arm spread along the length of the back, some sort of ugly green concoction in a glass in front of him. Wisely, he didn't mention her boots.

"We have something we want to show you," Grant stated.

"Oh?" Grant leaned forward.

"On the screen."

"If all you two have is a fucking slideshow, I'm firing you both." Scowling, he stood. "I'm fucking selling the company. Starting over. Just stab me in the gut and skewer me through the heart with a—"

Julien's theme song rocked the space, all but jiggling electronics off the metal table.

A thousand miles away in Cupertino, California, Julien shut his mouth.

She took a drink of coffee to cover her smile.

"Okay. So maybe your slideshow won't suck pavement."

"Rocks," she corrected, elevating her voice to be heard. "The saying is suck rocks."

"There's rocks in pavement," he shouted back, unconcernedly.

Grant exchanged looks with Aria. "You got this," she mouthed.

The CGI version of Julien walked onto the screen, every motion accurate. It should be. They'd copied imagery from one of his presentations.

"Well, shut me the fuck up," he said.

The theme music gradually faded, and, on the screen, the CGI Julien said, *"Once every generation, if we're lucky, something comes along that's so big, so crazy, so unimaginable that you wonder why no one thought of it before. World, I'd like you to say Hello to Molly."*

"Hellllllo, Genius."

"Ah..." Aria exchanged glances with Grant. They hadn't realized that Julien's voice, though synthesized, would still reach through the electrons to reach her.

"Standby," Grant told the computer.

As the movie went on, Julien sat down, leaned back, listened, watched. A minute or so in, he took out his pad and scrawled notes on it.

Toward the end, Julien finished with, *"Imagine a world where all this is possible. Your world. Only better."* His theme music increased in volume. The CGI image vanished, then words appeared. *The future. Here. Now.* Almost imperceptibly, the O in 'Now' morphed, becoming the Bonds logo. A moment later, the logo was in 3D and the music ended.

Julien sat on his couch, unmoving. After ten full seconds, he said, "This is fucking outrageous. All that passion." He balled a hand. "That enthusiasm. The vision."

She knew then that they'd nailed it. That was exactly how he approached life, made decisions, selected projects. And that's what he communicated to the world. That's what had made him nearly invincible, maligned as well as adored.

"It's crazy," Julien continued.

Grant nodded.

"Years to accomplish."

"And infinite opportunities to make it better, add more," Grant said.

She began to see how much this mattered to him. But was it enough? Enough to galvanize him to leave Los Alamos and his past, even for short times, to lead its development and creation?

"Its success or failure will have epic repercussions."

"So…?" she prompted, unable to wait any longer.

"You've blown me away," Julien admitted. "I wasn't expecting this. And I do like the movie."

"The…movie?" she asked, her heart sinking. She thought they'd been discussing the 'Hello, Molly' project. And Julien had been appreciating his having his perfection projected onto the big screen.

"I was a storyboard, wasn't I?" he continued.

She rolled her eyes. "The team at Bonds has it, yes."

"You've set the standard in presentations."

"And the actual idea?" she prompted.

"Oh, that." He took a drink of the smooth green concoction. "Of course, it's stellar," he said matter-of-factly, as if that had never been in question. "It will need someone to head it."

She and Julien both looked at Grant.

"I'm available as a consultant," he said.

He'd answered all her questions. Julien's, too, she assumed.

"I'll gather a team," Julien said, "show them the video, invite them to participate." He drummed his fingers on the side of the glass. "Ben Marley."

"He fumbled the last debut," Grant interjected.

"People learn from their mistakes," Julien replied with a casual shrug. "Svetlana's inbound from New York City later today," he said to Aria after looking at his smart watch. "Are you ready to come home?"

There was no need to stay now that they'd made the presentation. David, her second-in-command, had filled in long enough. Though she'd known her time with Grant was winding down, she hadn't suspected the end would be so abrupt.

Aria hazarded a glance at Grant. His jaw was tight, and she couldn't read anything in his expression.

"According to her potential flight plan, she would arrive in Los Alamos around seven o'clock," Julien continued. "It'll give you time to pack, wrap things up. You'll be home by nine."

Slowly, she nodded. "I'll be ready."

CHAPTER ELEVEN

Grant waved his airport badge in front of the security camera. A moment later, the arm lifted and he drove onto the property.

Julien's hybrid plane, the spectacular Tornado, was already there, waiting for Aria.

All afternoon, he'd wanted to say something—express emotions—but hadn't.

Instead, they'd spent a few minutes in the workshop after ending the call, discussing how well things had gone, congratulating each other.

But tension had made the air thin.

He knew she wanted him to accept a great role at Bonds, maybe even head the 'Hello, Molly' implementation team—and he was the natural choice. Aria's talents were best utilized where she was. But Grant…

He wasn't an idiot. He knew what Julien wanted. The man had mentioned Ben Marley's name as division leader on purpose. Grant had wanted Marley fired after the phone fiasco, but Julien had remained steadfast, stupidly so in Grant's opinion. Julien generally had little patience when people failed, especially when it happened so publicly and spectacularly.

But Marley had admitted the fuckup, accepted responsibility and worked tirelessly to restore the public's confidence.

Grant maintained it shouldn't have happened in the first place.

So mentioning Marley as a potential division leader had been calculated to piss Grant off, and it had worked. Mostly because he hated being manipulated, and Julien had been doing more meddling than usual lately. Julien could take his fucking brilliant ideas and shove them up someone else's ass.

When he'd lapsed into silence, Aria had excused herself, saying she'd needed to pack.

Since there'd been a lot of the day left and no reason to continue working together, he'd returned to the workshop.

Later, they'd headed to town and had an early dinner at the Montoyas' place.

For the first time since the meeting with Julien, Aria had been animated, asking Blanca about the app, how the beta testing was doing then, boldly, she'd asked about Julien.

"He invited me to have dinner with him," Blanca had confessed.

Aria had pretended to be surprised. "Are you going to do it?"

"Have dinner with a billionaire in San Francisco? Are you kidding me? He's going to send a plane and a pilot." Then she'd grinned. "I didn't tell him I'm bringing my sister and my mother."

Grant and Aria had exchanged glances, and they'd both laughed.

"Priceless," Aria had said.

"I'm not letting him get any ideas. If he thinks he can get me to do the bedsheet wiggle with him, he's wrong."

"Are you going to tell him?" Aria had asked after Blanca had pushed send on her phone app and left the table.

"Hell no."

"Me either."

They'd enjoyed that laugh, but had spent the rest of the meal talking in general terms about world events and the upcoming opening of the Bonds' store in Boston.

"I'll be there," she'd said.

Instead of replying, he'd paid the bill.

Grant parked the SUV inside the designated area and watched an airport employee push the stairs up to the Tornado's side.

Time seemingly warped, vanishing and stretching endlessly at the same time.

He left the engine running, and she made no move to exit the vehicle.

There was so much he wanted to say, needed to say. And fuck it, he couldn't find the words.

Last night, he'd held her after they'd made love. He'd wanted to confess how much she meant to him, how much her submissive trust had jolted him, how her presence invigorated him, energizing his creativity. But then, as now, he'd had no idea what to say.

The truth was, it didn't matter how much he cared. He was a selfish prick. He'd have extreme expectations of her as his cherished submissive, and she'd made it clear she wanted to make her own choices.

Over the last week, he'd noticed that the enforced isolation had started to bother her. The trip to Santa Fe had helped, but even that hadn't been enough.

She had a company to lead, and Bonds needed her as much as she needed the stimulation. He refused to be arrogant and ask her to give that up.

In the dim lighting, he saw that she wore his bracelet. He told himself that was enough.

"You were an amazing host. Thank you," she said, turning to him with false, sunny brightness.

"Aria…" Since he didn't know what else to say, he kept his mouth shut.

When Julien had sent Aria to him, he'd had no idea what to expect. In a matter of weeks, she'd upended his life, made him question his decisions.

She leaned forward, pressed her lips to his.

He couldn't help himself. He dug his hand into her hair, dragged her closer, devoured her, as if he were a man desperate, hungry.

He inhaled her fragrance, that of promise and hope.

And he tasted her.

Their physical connection was intimate. And hoped she understood his silent communication.

As she ended the kiss, slowly drawing away, she brushed back hair from his forehead. "You know, when I first touched down here, I thought it seemed a bit remote, hostile. I couldn't wait to leave."

"And now?"

Slowly, she lowered her hand. "It was restorative. I enjoyed working with you. And…" She paused. "The experiences have left me changed, helped me see the world in a different way. I'll never forget that."

"Neither will I," he admitted. "You know you're welcome here anytime."

"I may take you up on that."

Her words though, rang hollow. They were nothing more than courteous, something people said when words were meaningless.

She opened the door and grabbed her briefcase and

purse. He fetched her suitcase from the back of the SUV and dragged it toward a waiting airport employee.

Aria started up the airstairs. At the top, she paused. He expected, hoped, she'd look back, but she didn't.

Within two minutes, the main entry door was closed and the engines powered up.

Grant stayed there a long damn time, watching until lights from the plane were no longer visible.

He drove back home, to the emptiness, the familiar companionship of loneliness.

Shadow waited, and Molly had turned the lights on, bright, as if he still had company.

An unfinished bottle of wine was in the fridge, along with a piece of chocolate cake. No matter where he looked, there were reminders of Aria and what they'd shared.

Her absence cut a hole in his heart.

Unable to decide what to do, he did what he usually did. He went to his workshop. And he stayed until the sun came up. Then he went to bed, slept restlessly a few hours, then got back up and repeated the process.

Days later—he couldn't say how long—Julien's theme song made the walls bounce. He pushed a button on his keyboard to ignore the intrusion.

Apparently undeterred, Julien tried again—and again.

After Grant had rejected the call four times, Julien stopped.

Grant continued to ignore the outside world. His housekeeper brought food and did the laundry, but even after Kathleen, he hadn't put this much distance between him and other people.

At some point, fatigue triumphed over insomnia.

He headed for bed without showering, without removing his clothes.

"I cannot believe I failed so spectacularly."

"You? This really isn't about you," Aria said, nodding her assent as Julien filled her glass with a very nice red wine. She sat across from him on the white couch in Bonds headquarters. This visit was different in tone. Last time, he'd been behind his desk. When he'd told her she was being sent to Los Alamos, she'd felt as if she were being punished, exiled at the least. "And that's a bit of an exaggeration. You got Grant unstuck and 'Hello, Molly' came out of the three weeks. I'd hardly call that a failure. Besides, you got to be in a movie."

"I did, didn't I? It needs to go in the archives, so that when we're done, everyone can see its evolution. This, Aria, is history in the making." In his usual way, he then changed the topic. "I should send it to my mother. But then she'll want a Molly."

"We should get her one. We need more beta testers, and we need people who won't go to the press."

He nodded, seemingly thoughtful. "But then she'd have an excuse to call me every day."

"Yeah." She looked at him pointedly. "It is annoying that some people call every day."

Either he missed the point or ignored it. She was willing to bet on the second.

"How are you doing?"

"I'm back," she hedged. Now it was she who was intentionally missing the point. Because it still hurt too damn much to talk about, she diverted the topic. "I told David to take off Wednesday for a long weekend so he and his family can go to southern California for a few days."

"Have transportation see if the Tornado is available."

"Are you kidding me?"

"He deserves it. Now." He rolled the globe of the glass between his palms. "I see you've perfected the art of evasion. So tell me how you're doing."

"I'm good."

"You're not."

"Then why did you ask?"

"Because I want the details."

Aria shook her head. "You really are an asshat."

"King of them." He waited, then he sighed. "He hasn't called you, has he? No text. No email."

She inhaled to disguise her hurt. "Could you aim for something other than the jugular?"

"I tried. You dodged. So, you can either spill it so we can cauterize the wound or I can keep digging around until it really bleeds."

"Even for you, that image is a little graphic."

"I was reading a script earlier to see if we want to acquire it. High body count." He shivered. "With a kick-ass female lead. If she'll wear leather—"

"Don't mention the boots."

"Right. The boots. Bad. If she'll wear a body suit, I'll start filming tomorrow."

"I'm pretty sure it doesn't work that fast."

"Anyway." He waved his finger in a circle in the air. "You were saying."

"I'm okay."

"You fell in love," he countered.

And because Julien was the only one who might understand, she admitted, "All the way."

He gave a delicate shiver. "Did you tell him?"

"More or less."

He regarded her until she squirmed uncomfortably.

"No. It wouldn't have made any difference. He has expectations, thinks I couldn't live with them. He needs to figure this out." She'd repeated that to herself a hundred times a day even though it provided no comfort.

At work, she'd been almost useless. Then at home, she'd start something and be unable to finish it. She'd spent time with her parents, but she hadn't been communicative. Her mother had been concerned about her health and had pressed her palm to Aria's forehead to check her temperature. Even though she'd promised that she was okay, her mother had made a pot of soup and had sent it home with her.

She hadn't been sleeping well, either. When she went to bed, she tossed and turned, longing for the comfort of his arms.

"If it helps any, he hasn't talked to me either."

She leaned forward. She'd been hoping Julien would fill her in. But she hadn't asked because she hadn't wanted to seem as desperate as she felt. "It's been over a week," she said.

"I'd worry more, but I spied on him."

She choked on a drink of wine. "You what?"

"Oh, come on. He should be grateful. It was either that or I was jumping in the Tornado myself."

"You made the right choice."

"All this is very good. He didn't even act this bad when the twit ran away."

"Kathleen?"

"If he'd done his research, he would have known she had a penchant for drama. Award winning. I used to make popcorn before reading her social media posts."

Once again, he'd left her speechless.

"He may be morose and feeling sorry for himself, but he isn't doing more than working too much. Even Grant will get tired of that. If not, I'll blast him out of there when I have my date with Blanca."

"Oh?" An evening with Julien was just the thing to change her focus, save her from another night at home alone, aimlessly wandering her apartment, wondering what the hell she'd done wrong or what she could have done differently.

"I was planning to send Svetlana by herself, so that she can stop en route across the country. But if Grant continues to possum for much longer—"

"I think you mean a mole or a gopher."

"I do?"

"Lives underground?"

"Right. As I was saying, I'll go with Svetlana to collect Blanca."

She took a drink to hide her smile. It was going to be very interesting when he found out Blanca was bringing family members and had no intention of doing the bedsheet wiggle.

"By the way, did you see that Simon is getting married?"

"What?" Because she suddenly didn't trust her grip, she put down her glass.

"I was saving that savory morsel."

"Turns out your former fiancé is not lovelorn. He proposed to a college sweetheart while you were away. The banns have been posted, and the joyful union will happen this spring."

"That was fast." While the news surprised her, it didn't upset her. The feeling of guilt that she'd been piling on herself eased a little. He'd said he wasn't devastated by the breakup, and obviously he'd just been trying to spare her feelings. Absently, she wondered if he'd been thinking about the other woman the whole time they'd been planning their marriage. "How the hell do you know all this stuff?"

"Every morning I get an email notification if something appears on the Internet about people I'm interested in."

"And Simon is on that list?"

"Aren't you glad?"

They talked about business for a while, discussed their plans to debut Molly at Aria's apartment then Julien invited her to accompany him to the upcoming opening of the Bonds store at Kennedy's new building, the State Street Plaza.

When they'd finished the bottle of wine, he called for a car.

As she was walking to the elevator, she saw several new pieces of art on the wall. "Are those frames from the movie storyboard?"

He grinned. "I am a handsome fellow, aren't I?"

She punched the elevator button.

As the doors whisked closed behind her, he shouted out, "Don't give up! I'm betting on the boots."

She wanted to believe Julien—desperately, desperately wanted to believe him. After all, he knew Grant better than anyone else on the planet did. But at the days dragged, she told herself she was behaving like Grant had been. Morosely going through life, not savoring or enjoying.

She opened the door and said, "Hello, Molly."

"Good morning, Princess."

She grinned at the word princess. Someone, either Grant or Julien, had tweaked the response.

But then she realized the greeting was wrong. "It's evening, Molly."

"It's twelve-o-seven a.m. in California, Princess."

She checked her phone. "Right." And that was a good start. "Lights on. Forty percent. Shower on, one hundred degrees."

So far, Molly could only do a few things, and not all of them reliably. Like this time—the heater kicked on, and the water in the shower was about forty degrees. As for the lights, all of them came on.

Aria overrode the heater, adjusted the light dimmer switches and turned up the temperature of the shower water before jotting a note on her phone and sending it via email to the development team.

As she stood in the shower, she replayed the time with Julien. Being in his company, subject to his bizarre thought processes and offbeat humor, had helped her put things in perspective, as had the news that Simon had moved on. Ironic that she was still wallowing.

Determined that, even if she felt like hell, she would fully reengage, she finished her shower and went to bed. Before she fell asleep, Julien's words echoed in her head.

"I'm betting on the boots."

CHAPTER TWELVE

"A *genius is trying to reach you."*

This time, Grant answered. He figured ten days of solitude was long enough. If he were honest, he'd admit even he was sick of his own company. Julien's intrusion was a welcome distraction. "Video on."

From behind his desk in Cupertino, Julien frowned. "Well, don't you look...*well?*"

"Sorry to disappoint," he said drily.

"It's not disappointment, actually. It's just... I was hoping to see Blanca."

"And I'm not giving you a reason. So it is a disappointment."

"All that green chile—and a hot tamale." He sighed.

Julien mentioned nothing about Grant's lack of communication or the situation with Aria, and Grant was eternally grateful. That was the basis of true friendship in his opinion.

He didn't need recriminations. He had enough of those.

"We're having some problems with Molly."

"Tell Ben Marley."

"I would. But it's the one at Aria's place."

"Not my project."

"Of course not. But I shot you the code that went wrong."

Ignoring any forthcoming argument, Julien beamed the code straight onto Grant's glass work screen, superimposing it above the notes he'd been making on the hologram project. Despite his best intentions, Grant glanced at it. "After midnight?" he asked.

"Does it say that?"

Julien could write code as well as any of the greatest minds who'd graduated from the most prestigious technical universities.

"Third line," Julien said.

Grant saw it. And changed a one to a zero. Other errors jumped, and he corrected them as well. "Anything else?" he asked the genius.

"Headed to Boston in two days. Aria is going with me."

"And?"

Rather than answer, Julien changed the subject, mentioned the script he was considering then ended the conversation.

Grant steepled his fingers and gently touched the tips together repeatedly. Julien might think he was a genius, but this time Grant was a step ahead of him.

He'd spent the first three days of Aria's absence throbbing with loneliness. The portrait in his bedroom had seemed to mock him, which was most of the reason that he'd avoided going to bed.

But after that…

He'd started to right his world.

He'd begun eating again, sleeping on a regular schedule, working when the muse struck, exercising, soaking in the hot tub.

Even though it was frigid, he'd gone for a hike in Bandelier National Monument, and that was where he'd found peace.

With the blistering wind biting his skin, things had become clear.

He had been letting Kathleen and their tumultuous past ruin his future. Aria was nothing like his ex. He'd blamed himself for Kathleen's car wreck, the anguish of waiting while she'd been checked out at the emergency room. For days afterward, he'd waited on her, doted on her, but nothing had made her happy. He'd told himself it was the shock, but it hadn't been.

Kathleen hadn't been able to put sanity ahead of tantrums.

In retrospect, he'd been an idiot to try as many times as he had.

While Aria's words had been harsh the night before she'd left, she'd been more accurate than he'd been willing to admit.

In the cold light of an endless winter night, he'd finally faced it.

But there was another truth, as well. She needed a strong, complex man. And he damn well intended to step up and be the man she needed.

He wasn't sure if things could work out with Aria, but he had a few ideas. And the woman was forever telling him she liked to make her own choices. So it was damn well time that he gave her a few to select from.

In the years that she'd worked for Bonds, Aria had never been to a store opening. She'd seen pictures, heard rumors, watched videos. Even though she'd visited almost every store, she'd never been there for an actual opening.

Julien had never missed one.

He guided her through the back door of the Old Bronwyn Building to a freight elevator that would whisk them to the eighth floor, where they were meeting Kennedy Aldrich and Mackenzie Farrell for dinner.

"I had no idea service like this actually existed," Aria said.

"It does when you own the building."

"This is yours?" she asked.

"Kennedy's. Or rather, his family's."

She'd selected a black cocktail dress, but Julien was wearing dress slacks, a white Oxford shirt, a sloppily looped tie and, of course, hideously colored athletic shoes.

Just the reminder of Grant gave her a pang of loneliness.

But she reminded herself that he'd moved away to avoid exactly this kind of scene.

She decided that, just for an hour, she wouldn't obsess about where he was or what he was doing, who he was with or whether he missed her as much as she missed him. She ignored the nagging voice that told her she'd need to make the same deal with herself an hour from now.

"Through the doors, down the hall then take a left," Julien said when the elevator stopped at the eight floor.

"Good evening, Mr. Bonds, Ms. DeWitt. Right this way," the maître d' greeted without Julien ever supplying a name.

Unbelievable.

Kennedy and Mackenzie were already in the private dining room, and Kennedy stood to greet them. Like Julien, he too, was wearing blinding neon shoes. They were so bright her eyes momentarily watered.

"I figured it would be quieter over here," Kennedy said after they were all seated. "You've already got a hell of a crowd gathered for tomorrow's opening. They're spread out on three different floors. Some people brought tents and set up two days ago."

"It's the giveaways," Julien said.

"It's the opportunity to meet the genius," Kennedy corrected, "and get their electronics personally signed."

"Well, totally right," Julien agreed. "I'm just too modest to say so."

"Modest," Aria agreed.

"Besides, you can take in the sight of the whole building from here," Mackenzie added. "And it's something to behold."

"The future Mrs. Aldrich is correct," Kennedy said.

"You finally gave in?" Julien asked. "Oh, my dear sweet Mackenzie, I was hoping you'd make him suffer a little longer."

"She lifted the moratorium." He reached across the table, picked up Mackenzie's hand and kissed her near the ring.

"I may swoon," Julien said, fanning himself with a napkin.

"I think I missed something." Aria looked between Julien and Mackenzie.

Mackenzie grinned. "I told Kennedy he couldn't ask me to marry him for three months."

"Felt like three years," he added.

"But he had my engagement ring."

"I wouldn't have been able to wait, either," Aria confessed. "May I see it?"

Mackenzie showed off the stunning square-cut diamond.

"I've never seen anything like it. It's beautiful. When's the wedding?"

"This summer," Kennedy said.

"No date yet," she corrected, leveling a steely glare at her fiancé.

Aria suddenly liked the woman. She knew what she wanted, was willing to wait.

"Well, at least it will stay interesting," Julien said. "Unlike my love life."

"What? You have a love life?" Kennedy asked.

"No."

"Do tell," Mackenzie encouraged. "I want to hear."

"I had a hot tamale date. I thought."

Aria reached for her glass of water and took a long drink.

"I sent the Tornado for her."

"Impressive," Mackenzie replied. "Have you done that for a woman before?"

"I did it for three."

Kennedy frowned.

"At the same time."

"I'm lost," Mackenzie admitted.

"Blanca," he said.

"Of Los Alamos restaurant fame? The one you've named the new app after?"

He had?

"*Si.* I thought it was love. I sent the Tornado. Imagine my surprise when I showed up at the airport and her mother and sister were with her. Something about no bedsheets wiggling for me."

Mackenzie laughed so hard she pressed her hand against her mouth.

Aria looked at the State Street Plaza building. The structure was a visual masterpiece. "This view really is something."

"Something, indeed," Mackenzie agreed, recovering enough to be a good hostess and help redirect the conversation from Julien's devastation.

"We're pleased," Kennedy said. "Quite pleased."

Julien had already told her that the State Street Plaza was the crown jewel in the Aldrich Real Estate Holdings empire. Over the years, construction had undergone numerous delays.

And now, with the addition of a spire, the architecturally stunning twisted glass building had clawed its way into the record books as the tallest structure in Boston. Nothing had prepared her for the way its shape would create the optical illusion that it was moving.

They chatted about the building and business, and the athletic shoe company Kennedy had invested in.

"Don't tell me," Aria said. "Walking on air."

"Precisely," Julien said.

Mackenzie rolled her eyes.

Clearly, the shoes were a man thing.

After dinner, a car had whisked them to the back of the State Street Plaza. Kennedy had arranged for rooms there and explained that there were a couple of back ways around. He'd added that the building had been designed to accommodate egos even larger than Julien's.

"Is that possible?" Aria had asked.

Every bit of her suite was stunning. She'd never stayed in anything like it and probably never would again.

As she did often, she thought of Grant, wishing he was here to share it with her.

Loneliness raked its way through her insides.

Reminding herself that her hour was up and that she could allow herself to think of him again, she went to take a shower.

Memories washed over her and, this time, she surrendered to them.

She remembered him touching her pussy…

And she slid her fingers between her labia.

She remembered the way he'd squeezed her nipples before placing a clamp or the metallic balls…

And she twisted her nipple.

She remembered him telling her that he wanted her to wait for her orgasm…

Slowly, lightly at first, then faster and quicker, she moved her fingers over her clit, into her pussy. She fucked herself with her fingers, stretching, filling, as if he were there.

The orgasm built, and she forced it back, holding onto it as he might demand.

"They belong to me now."

Even in her mind, she was his to command.

Tears formed, then spilled as she jerked her hips forward and climaxed all over her hand.

She dropped her head forward and allowed the water, the heat, to soothe her.

Worn out, she crawled into bed, curled into a ball. She finally fell asleep once she imagined she was wrapped in Grant's arms, and she slept until Julien's theme song shattered the silence.

He invited her to his room for room service breakfast, and he promised he had coffee—lots of it.

He also had an unreasonable amount of energy. What he didn't have was flavored creamer.

Fortunately, she discovered he did have a plate of chocolate croissants.

After breakfast, they agreed to meet again at eight. They'd go down to the store opening together. A trio of security guards would meet them outside the service elevator and ride down with them. They'd use back of the house routes, emerging into the retail space on the third floor.

"You have security?"

"Precaution. Necessary evil at times. I hate it."

She nodded.

Back in her room, she showered and got ready, dressing in a skirt, a sweater and her favorite boots.

"Betting on them, are you?" Julien asked when she met him near the elevator.

"Better than your shoes."

"Like walking on air," he said with a sigh.

The security guards joined them.

As they descended, a hum of voices met them, even from outside the elevator.

The doors slid open and the noise grew louder.

"Ready?" he asked.

"I can't believe how exciting this is."

"This, Aria, is why we do what we fucking do. We make the world a better place. Never forget it. Never forget why we do what we do."

The security guards flanked them, and a partition she hadn't noticed slid open.

Suddenly, they were in the midst of hundreds of screaming, yelling people.

Julien pulled a permanent marker from his pocket and started autographing anything put in front of him. It took them twenty minutes to make it to the front door. A ceremonial key was stuck in the lock. The thing was huge, with a showy, great big red bow on it.

Inside the sparsely stocked wooden and glass and chrome two-story retail space, a platform had been set up. Reporters were already near it, waiting along with a film crew. *Shocking.*

She knew he'd make an announcement, broadcast through speakers, then they'd go inside the store. Employees and some of his first-ever customers would join them, along with winners from a lottery set up over the previous few days. Mackenzie and Kennedy would be on hand. Another of Julien's college friends, Reece, along with his new wife, Sarah, would also be there to congratulate not only Julien, but also Kennedy, on the opening of the building.

Was she the only one who noticed the only key person missing was Grant?

If Julien wasn't concerned, she told herself she wouldn't be, either.

With the precise timing that was a hallmark of everything Bonds did, his theme song rocked the entire building. Some people made an entrance. He could make one after he'd already been signing autographs for twenty minutes.

At the top of the hour, the music silenced, and so did the crowd. Julien turned on the lapel microphone.

He strode through the area, shaking hands as he said, "I'd like welcome you to the opening of Boston's Bonds at the stunning State Street Plaza. Without you, Bonds wouldn't exist. Come inside. Let us change your world."

He cut the mic, moved to the front door. Amid flashing lights and people crowding around to take pictures and video, he turned the key. Then with a smile and a cheery wave to the crowd, he opened the door and ushered her through.

They waited for a few minutes while lottery winners and loyal fans were brought inside. All the while, he worked the crowd, listened to people's ideas, held court.

Then, from the podium, he talked about the impact their products had on lives. One fan shared a story of her extended range phone making a call when others couldn't, and it had enabled her to save a life. Another shared a small story of a child finally understanding a math concept through one of his apps.

Finally, he introduced Kennedy. "Thank you for building such a supremely cool place for me to have a store."

Kennedy thanked Julien for signing the building's first lease. He presented Bonds with a ceremonial certificate.

. . .

Tenant #1.

Then Julien introduced her, said they'd be seeing more of her at future events.

She waved, made a small curtsey.

Then he continued. "Most of you know, if you're here today, that Bonds wouldn't have been possible without Kennedy's initial belief and investment."

Kennedy remained silent.

"And you know that I'm not the real genius behind the company."

A number of people clapped. There was a wolf-whistle, too.

"You, asshole! Off with your head!" Julien called.

The crowd roared.

He never tried to speak over people, instead he waited until things quieted.

"And you know that the person who worked night after night in the early years was Grant Kingston."

Her heart stopped. She hadn't been expecting that recognition for Grant.

"Nothing would be possible without Grant hanging out, putting together components, taking shit apart—wait. Did I say that out loud?"

The crowd cheered raucously.

"Ladies and gentlemen, the man, the legend who was Bonds and is the future of Bonds—Grant Kingston."

He emerged from the crowd and went to the podium.

Her pulse swarmed in her ears. The world seemed to vanish beneath her feet. She didn't hear a single word he was saying. Damn Julien. All along, he'd known Grant would be here, and he'd said nothing. *Nothing.*

Grant began to speak, and it didn't matter what he was saying, she realized.

He was communicating passion, raw, unharnessed passion. He held the crowd, and her, captivated.

She drank him in, that misbehaving lock of hair that fell across his forehead. Those blue eyes that seemed to look not at her, but into her.

The arms capable of such tenderness and such precision with a flogger.

And that voice…

He wrapped up each person individually the way he had her.

No matter the passage of time or space between them, she was as stunningly in love now as she had ever been.

Her heart resumed a normal pattern, and she was able, finally, to hear as he spoke of the past and hinted at the ways that Bonds intended to change the world. He didn't name the 'Hello, Molly' project, but he invited the crowd to imagine a world that might one day exist.

In his own way, he paced, rocked back and forth, gestured. And she didn't mind the hideous shoes one bit.

And then…

Shadow walked from the back of the room and climbed up onto the podium.

Her knees sagged.

He'd done it. He'd created a hologram that looked and behaved like a living creature.

The dog barked.

"Sit."

The dog stood still, wagging his tail, tongue lolling out of his mouth. And people cheered.

In mock frustration, he turned back and looked at it again.

The dog wagged its tail.

He raised a finger. With a soft growl of protest, Shadow sat. Then when Grant went closer, Shadow lifted a paw to shake.

"Bonds fans, say hello to Shadow, the world's first holographic pet." As he'd spoken, he allowed his voice to rise to a stunning crescendo.

The roar of the crowd shook the store.

Across the room, he sought her out. She gave him a thumbs-up before she joined everyone else in the clapping.

Shadow bounded up the stairs to meet a holographic image of Julien, then security opened the door to let the first fifty people through the door.

CHAPTER THIRTEEN

Grant clamped his hand on her elbow and drew her to the side of the room. It wasn't private, and it wasn't quiet. But to her, no one else existed.

"Are you able to escape from this place?" he asked.

"I have a room upstairs."

"Can I have a minute of your time?"

"I don't know." *Yes.* This was either her dream coming true, or potentially another devastation. "You may have to earn it."

He grinned.

As he often had, he placed his fingers against the small of her back as he guided her to the exit.

Julien stopped them on the way out. "It was the boots," he said.

"Don't push your fucking luck," Grant snapped.

Julien smiled then turned and posed for a picture while he held one of their first-generation tablets.

She and Grant didn't speak until the elevator arrived. She had nothing to say and too much to say all at the same time.

The moment the doors closed, sealing out the din, he had

her up against the back wall. He grabbed her hands, pulled them over her head.

He looked her into her eyes.

She couldn't breathe or think. God help her, she needed this.

"Give me a word," he said, voice raw with the same kind of passion she'd heard downstairs.

"Yes," she said.

He took her mouth. He kissed her, ravaged her, loved her.

Then he put a hand between her legs and stroked her pussy through her tights. She closed her eyes, linked her hands around his neck then gave him the surrender he demanded.

When the elevator slid to a stop, they composed themselves and smiled at the people entering the car.

"I apologize," he said as they walked down the hall. "I've been thinking about that for weeks."

She waved her key in front of the card reader and the lock snicked.

He reached around her to open the door then he followed her in.

The space suddenly seemed smaller than the elevator had. She didn't offer a drink, and she kept him in the small sitting room area. With how combustible she was with him, she wasn't going near a bed.

"You said I had to earn a minute of your time." To his credit, he moved to the small bar area rather than crowding her.

"You do," she said. "You can start with some explanations. Why are you here? At the event? And in my room."

"It's the boots."

She tried to smile and failed.

"Well, actually, it is. I haven't been able to stop thinking of you. The first few days after you left, I was pissed. At you. At me. I felt you wanted something I couldn't offer."

She leaned against the entertainment center. "That's probably true."

"And I knew you had every right to demand it. It was me who was too fucked up to deliver it. After that…" He paced. "I pulled my head out of my ass. I wanted to be the kind of man who deserved a woman like you. Honestly?"

She waited.

Earlier, at the opening, he'd timed his words and actions to generate enthusiasm and energy. Now, he allowed his voice to drop to reveal the depth of his emotion. "I didn't trust that I could do it. I'd become myopic, shutting out everyone else. I knew you were right. So was Julien. But it took a lot for me to face it. I needed to be sure I could let go of the past. Not very noble."

"You told me a long time ago that courage can look very different, given the circumstances," she reminded him.

"Your strength inspired me, motivated me."

She waited for him to continue, wanting to be sure he was willing to talk, really talk, before she took a risk by opening up to him again.

"The way I reacted that day, in the workshop, when I was an ass after what Julien said about your boots…" He exhaled. "That's when I knew. I'd never felt jealousy like that before. I realized I cared about you, didn't want to let you go, but damned if I knew how to keep you. Any relationship we have will be complicated. If you're even interested. But I figured that choice needed to be yours, that I shouldn't make it for you. So I'm here." He dragged a hand through his hair. "And none of it's as easy as I'd like it to be. But you're worth it." His voice cracked.

"Grant…" Emotion choked her up.

"I was always honest about the BDSM. I won't live

without it. We would have to negotiate, maybe reach compromises, but we can define it. It doesn't have to define us."

She nodded.

"As for living… I want to keep the Los Alamos house for a retreat."

She blinked as she tried to keep up with what he was saying. He was talking in terms of a future for them, of ways for it to work.

"But I will be taking a more active role at Bonds. We can travel together. And I'm willing to live in the city."

His words were everything she'd hoped for, and they momentarily overwhelmed her. "I'm not sure what to say."

"I've missed you, Aria—in my bed, my house, my life. Come here."

She went into his arms.

There were a million unanswered questions, a million things to sort out, but to her the only thing that mattered was the effort he'd already gone through—for Julien, for himself, for her.

He picked up her hand. While tracing the outline of her bracelet, he looked her in the eye and said, "I love you, Aria."

"I…"

"Tell me you love me. Say yellow, or tell me you love me."

Her lips twitched. "I love you."

"If you'll have me, I'll work every day of my life to be the man you deserve."

"There's nothing I'd like more."

EPILOGUE

"I've fantasized about having you back home since the day you left," Grant told her when they were inside the dungeon at the Los Alamos house.

Home. Aria drank in the word, savored it and their relationship. "Me, too, Sir," she admitted.

"I want you on the cross."

Aria shivered.

He stood there, arms folded, every inch a commanding Dom. As always, when he slipped into that tone, those actions, her brain circuits seemed to fire off more responses. It was as if she became a different person, with heightened expectations and responses.

"Undress," he said.

She kicked off her pumps and shimmied from her skirt.

He hissed in a breath. *"Fuck me.* You wore that on purpose."

"Me?" she asked innocently. She was wearing a lacy garter, stockings and a sheer thong. Oh yes, she'd done it on purpose. The last time she'd been here, she hadn't had anything sexy to wear. Yesterday, she'd taken a long lunch break and spent an obscene amount of money on lingerie. Now, seeing the way his cock pressed against his blue jeans, she realized every penny had been worth it.

She continued, drawing up her blouse to reveal a matching demi bra that cupped her breasts and exposed her nipples.

"Turn around slowly. Let me admire your body."

Aware of his rapt attention, she dropped the blouse to the stone floor as she followed his orders.

No matter how many times they were together, it was always as thrilling as the first. He always expressed his appreciation, and he always demanded everything she had to offer.

"I might have to fuck you before I flog you, little Aria."

She smiled. "As you wish, Sir." She'd been pissed when Julien had insisted she needed a strong man, but it turned out, damn him, that he'd been right. She craved Grant's lash as much as his love.

"Take off the thong and go to the cross," he said, words hoarse.

Which meant he was going to let her keep the rest of her lingerie on.

Aware of her power, Aria sauntered. Their love only made scenes hotter, more explosive.

Her relationship with Grant didn't resemble anything she'd been taught to want. It was unique, dynamic, demanding. Perfect. It was what she'd been looking for without knowing it.

"This time, I want your back to the cross."

"Oh?" Even though she felt a little ripple of trepidation, she did as he'd said, extending her arms and legs, drawing in breaths to calm herself while she waited.

He collected the rolling cart then went to the cupboard.

Damn him. She realized he'd made her go to the cross so she couldn't see what he was doing.

That didn't surprise her. He liked to prolong anticipation, drive her a little mad.

Over the months, he'd perfected the art.

After the store opening in Boston, they'd spent weeks sorting out the details of their new relationship. He'd flown to California with her, and they'd started house hunting in Cupertino. They'd gone through over thirty homes before finding one he would agree to. It was away from neighbors, had a six foot privacy fence and a garage where he could beat her.

Even after they'd purchased the place, he hadn't been willing to move in until his workshop had been set up, there'd been a state of the art security system installed and 'Hello, Molly', version 2.0 was operational.

She'd accepted that he was never going to be an easy man to please—complex, complicated, confounding. But she'd realized she would rather be challenged than bored. Her father respected him. Her mother wondered if he was a bit too intense—she liked him, but saw through to his depths and had admitted she was glad Aria's father was easy to deal with.

Grant spent a lot of time with Julien, but he'd refused to have an office at 1, Bonds Street. And he hadn't been willing to compromise, despite Julien's repeated requests. There were plenty of conference rooms he could use if he needed to be there for any extended period but, as part of his agreement to be more involved, he intended to do his tinkering away from any interference.

Now, finally, they were back at their real home—in Los Alamos—for a long weekend. Grant had instructed the upgraded Molly to block all incoming calls, even those from Julien. They'd picked up tamales and *tres leches* cake on the way through town—and they'd ordered it and paid for it online.

It was hard to believe she'd once been furious with Julien for sending her out here. And now she treasured the escape —the stunning beauty, the sight of spring and the solitude with her Dom. Recently, Grant had insisted it was time they got married, but she'd asked for a little more time. They'd gone through a lot of changes, fast, and she didn't want to plan a wedding in the midst of it. Besides, the journey to a more submissive relationship was challenging enough to negotiate.

He'd reminded her that the bracelet he'd bought for her in Santa Fe was symbolic of their union, a reminder of her journey into submission. She'd promised she would always wear it. And she'd honored her word by never taking it off.

Finally, finally, he turned to her and wheeled the cart across the floor. She didn't see the flogger hanging there, instead, she saw a crop. It had an oversized red leather flapper, shaped like an apple.

She spread her fingers in nervous reaction. "That looks a little vicious, Sir."

"I imagine it will be."

Aria shuddered.

He selected four cuffs and started with her feet. Then he traced the stone on the turquoise bracelet.

Their gazes met, locked.

"I cherish you," he said.

"Show me."

He kissed her gently, coaxingly. She wrapped her arms around his neck. The first time they'd met, she hadn't known what he meant when he'd said he used Dominance to show his subs how much they meant to him. Now she understood, totally… When they were in a scene, she was the center of his focus. Nothing existed except them. With his words—his touch—he showed his love.

He slowly ended the kiss and finished securing her to the cross. Then he picked up a pair of alligator nipple clamps.

As he always did, he rubbed her body, teasing to increase blood flow and prepare her. After he sucked on each nipple, he attached the nasty things.

She drew a shuddering breath. These only clamped a bit of her nipples, and they bit far harder than the clovers he usually selected. "These are evil," she said.

"But they look sexy as hell with that lingerie."

Which meant that, unless she said yellow, they were staying in place.

She wriggled, trying to get used to the sensation, but it didn't help. Then, totally confounding her, he added a blindfold.

Something inside her settled as she focused her other senses on him.

"Perfect. So good."

She heard the swish of the crop as he tested it, and she froze. They'd never played with one before, and the sound startled her.

He teased her with the flapper, gently bouncing it off her midriff, her belly, her breasts.

She groaned. "That's..."

He continued the light motion.

"Incredible," she finished.

Then he changed up the rhythm, striking her harder, then softer, raining blows all over her body. He beat her inner thighs with a brutally loving staccato that she surrendered to. Then he moved higher, striking her pussy.

She screamed and allowed the bonds to support more of her weight.

He was relentless, pitiless as he blazed her, igniting her clit.

When she was sure she was about to reach her limit, he moved back down over her thighs, allowing her to breathe and settle before he began to crop her breasts, the edge flirting with the clamps.

She tried to back away, but her movements intensified the sensual agony.

"God, you're beautiful with the red marks—my marks."

"Yes, Sir. Give me more."

He went on, varying the location and the intensity. And he continually affirmed his love and approval. She was hungry for more, aroused, wanting an orgasm.

Earnestly he used the flapper on her nipples and she felt one of the clamps rip off. She screamed. The pain ignited her. "Please…"

"Tell me."

"I need to come."

"In a minute."

She clenched her buttocks, fighting it, fighting herself.

He cropped the other breast until the second clamp yielded and clattered to the floor.

"I can't wait!"

"You can." He continued to use the leather erotically on her inner thighs, her breasts, her pussy.

"Sir! Grant!

She heard something hit the floor and then she felt him spread her labia, followed by the touch of his tongue on her clit. Then he inserted a finger in her pussy. Without warning, overcome, she orgasmed against his mouth.

"That's my perfect sub. I love you, Aria. More and more."

He unfastened her, ripped off the blindfold then helped her down from the cross. She wrapped an arm around his neck and rested her face against the strength of his chest.

The air was summer-warm on her bare skin, and she'd never felt more loved or adored. He carried her inside the house to their bedroom where he put her on the bed.

"Fuck me," she said. "Please."

"Demanding sub." But he was smiling.

He undressed while her pussy continued to throb. The climax had not satisfied, it had merely dulled the ache.

Sitting on the edge of the mattress, he traced a few of the marks on her inner thighs. The gentle abrasion brought back a flood of desire.

With gentle motions, he teased her cunt, played with her clit, made sure she was slick for him.

"I want to look at you," he said.

She nodded.

He moved between her legs. He rested his weight on one elbow and secured her wrists with the other hand, putting a thumb on the piece of turquoise. "You're mine."

"Yes."

He entered her quickly and surely, possessing her.

She cried out and moved so she could wrap her legs around his waist.

"Perfect."

As promised, he kept his gaze on her, reassurance and forever in his gaze.

Then, under the onslaught of emotion and physical sensation, she closed her eyes. She screamed his name as she shattered.

"Yeah," he said. "That's it."

She felt the change in him as her pussy muscles constricted around his cock. He got harder, thicker.

Aria opened her eyes and pulled one hand away so that she could bury it in his hair.

His jaw became rigid and his breaths came in ragged bursts.

Shockingly, another orgasm built in her. This man, *her* man… Thought splintered.

"Aria!" He broke her name into three distinct syllables.

Responding desperately, she lifted her hips to urge him deeper, and he accepted the primal invitation, taking, commanding.

Then he came, the force urgent and hard.

She pulled her other hand away so she could cling to him, keep him there another second until she came again.

He reached between them and found her clit, pushing hard and making her come right before he took her mouth.

Even though they'd been together months, had made love every day, it had never been this powerful. She didn't know how it was possible that he made it better and better, but the more she turned to him, relied on him, rose to his challenge, the more meaningful the connection became. "Forever," she whispered.

"And a day," he demanded in return, brushing her hair back so they could read each other's expressions.

"Yes, Sir," she whispered. "And a day."

◊ ◊ ◊ ◊ ◊

Thank you for reading Command. I hope you loved our reclusive Grant and the determined Aria. (And Hello, Molly. Honestly, I want one! Hello, Molly, run my bath and pour me a glass of prosecco!)

I love Julien Bonds, too, and his stories are coming soon. Yes, the Genius needs more than one story. Of course he does.

You can enjoy another glimpse of Julien in Hold On To Me, a Hawkeye novel featuring a sexy as sin bodyguard who is also a deliciously Dominant cowboy. When Elissa refuses protection even though her life may be in danger, Jacob tosses her beautiful, reluctant body over his strong shoulder. He's going to do everything to keep her safe…and I guarantee you some very steamy scenes at his ranch house.

DISCOVER HOLD ON TO ME

I invite you to meet the Titans…a secret society of the world's most powerful and dangerous alphas. In Billionaire's Matchmaker, Rafe Sterling needs a bride, stat. And he wants Hope Malloy, the very woman hired to find him a bride. Trouble is, she doesn't date clients, and especially not one who is as terrifyingly ruthless as the Sterling heir…

A ruthless Dominant billionaire marriage of convenience romance, with a touch of intrigue.

★★★★★ A flawless five-star read! ~New York Times Best Selling Author Angel Payne

"It was all things hot and steamy. And I want more of these Titans!" ~Amazon Reviewer

DISCOVER BILLIONAIRE'S MATCHMAKER

Continue reading for an excerpt from HOLD ON TO ME

HOLD ON TO ME

CHAPTER ONE

HAWKEYE

"No fucking way, Hawkeye." In case that wasn't clear enough, Jacob Walker tipped back the brim of his cowboy hat and leveled a stare at his friend and former commander across the small, rickety table that separated them.

The stench of cheap whiskey and loneliness hung in the air—as putrid as it was familiar.

Through the years, they'd held dozens of meetings at this kind of place. Didn't matter which fucked-up hellhole they were in—Central America, the Middle East, Texas, or here, a small, all but forgotten Colorado mountain town, a place with no security cameras, where neither of them were known.

As usual, Hawkeye dressed to blend in with the locals—jeans, scuffed boots, and a heavyweight canvas jacket that could be found on almost every ranch in the state. He'd added a baseball cap with a logo of a tractor company embroidered on the front. Today, he also wore a beard. No doubt it would be gone within an hour of his walking back outside into the crisp, clean air.

At one time, Jacob thrived on clandestine meetings. The

anticipation alone was enough to feed adrenaline into his veins, and he lived for the vicarious thrill.

But life was different now.

After a final, fateful job in Colombia that left an American businessman's daughter dead, Jacob walked away from Hawkeye Security.

He returned to the family ranch and a world he no longer recognized. His grandfather had died, no doubt from the stress of managing the holdings by himself. Though Jacob's grandmother never uttered a critical word, he knew she was disappointed that he'd missed the funeral. He wasn't even in the same country when he was needed the most.

When she passed, he stood alone at the graveside, the only family mourner, like she'd no doubt been a few years before.

Spurred by equal measures of guilt and regret, he poured himself into managing the family's holdings as a way to redeem himself. Then, because of his loneliness and the horrible dreams after Colombia, he did it as a way to save himself.

"The op will take less than a month." Hawkeye shrugged. "Give or take. I'll give you three of our best agents—Johnson, Laurents, Mansfield. You can man the gate, rather than just utilizing the speaker box. Another on perimeter. One for relief. You have the space and a bunkhouse."

Jacob shook his head to clear it of the ever-present memories. "Is there a part of my refusal that you don't understand?" Of course there was. When Hawkeye wanted something, nothing would dissuade him. That willful determination had made him a force on the battlefield as well as in the business arena. "When I quit, I meant it." He took a swig from his longneck beer bottle. "No regrets." The words were mostly true. There were times he wanted the camaraderie and wanted to flex his brain as well as his muscles.

There was also the sweet thrill of the hunt. And making things right in the world.

Rather than argue, Hawkeye removed his cap long enough for Jacob to get a look at his former boss. Worry lines were trenched between his eyebrows. In all his years, Jacob had never seen dark despair in those eyes. "Yesterday, Inamorata received what appeared to be a birthday card from her sister."

Ms. Inamorata was Hawkeye's right-hand woman and known for her ability to remain calm under duress. She could be counted on to deal with local and federal authorities, smoothing over all the details. Rather seriously, Hawkeye said she batted cleanup better than any major leaguer.

Jacob told himself to stand up, thank Hawkeye for the drink, then get the hell out of here while he still could. Instead, he remained where he was.

"There was a white powder inside."

Jesus. "Anthrax?"

"Being tested. She took appropriate precautions and received immediate medical assistance. Antibiotics were prescribed as a precaution." Hawkeye paused. "There were no warning signs that the piece of mail was suspicious."

Meaning the postmark matched the return address. The postage amount was correct, and there was nothing protruding from the envelope.

Jacob knew Inamorata and liked her as much as he respected her. He took offense at a threat to her life. "Received at headquarters?"

"No. At her home. So whoever sent it has access to information about her and how to circumvent our protocols."

Slowly he nodded. "Any message?"

"Yeah." Hawkeye paused. "Threats to take out people I care about, one at a time."

"The fuck?" Instead of sympathizing, Jacob switched to ops mode. He didn't do it on purpose—it was as immediate as it was instinctive. No doubt Hawkeye had counted on Jacob's reaction. "Anything else?"

"There was no specific request. No signature." Hawkeye paused. "I've got profilers taking a look at it. But there's not much to go on. Tech is analyzing writing and sentence structure, tracking down places the card could have come from. FBI has the powder at its lab. Profilers are trying to ascertain the type of person most likely to behave this way."

All the right things.

"But we don't have the resources to take care of our clients and have eyes on everyone who's a potential target."

At this point, there was no way to know how serious the threat was. A card was one thing, a physical attack was another.

"I don't give a fuck who comes for me."

Over the years, their line of work—cleaning up situations to keep secrets safe, protecting people and precious objects, even acting as paramilitary support operators overseas—had created a long list of enemies.

"But I can't risk the people I care about." Hawkeye reached into a pocket inside his jacket and pulled out a picture. "I need you to take care of her."

"Oh fuck no, man." Jacob could be a sounding board, analyze data, but he didn't have the time to return to babysitting services.

Undeterred, Hawkeye continued. "Her name's Elissa. Elissa Conroy. Twenty-eight. My plan was to have Agent Fagen move in with her and accompany her to work."

Makes logical sense. "And?"

"She refused. Then I decided I'd prefer for her to be away from Denver, out of her normal routine in case anyone has been watching." After a moment's hesitation, Hawkeye slid the snapshot onto the table, facedown.

Hawkeye knew every one of Jacob's weaknesses. If he glanced at Elissa's face, the job would become personal. She wouldn't be a random woman he could ignore.

Jacob looked across the expanse of the room, at the two men talking trash at the nearby pool table. Above them, a neon beer sign dangled from a tired-looking nail. The paint was peeling from the shabby wall, and the red glare from the light made the atmosphere all the more depressing.

"Her parents own a pub. Right now, she's running it on their behalf while they're back home in Ireland for a well-deserved vacation. Her father has just recovered from a bout with cancer, and they're celebrating his recovery."

Of course Hawkeye crafted a compelling narrative. He knew how to motivate people, be it through their heart-strings or sense of justice. At times, he'd stoke anger. His ability to get people to do what he wanted was his biggest strength as well as his greatest failing.

Never had his powers of persuasion been more on display than when he'd gotten his Army Ranger team out of Peru, despite the overwhelming odds.

From the beginning, the mission had been FUBAR—fucked up beyond all recognition. They sustained enough casualties to decimate even the strongest and bravest. Relentlessly Hawkeye had urged each soldier on. Despite his own injuries, Hawkeye had carried one man miles to the extraction point.

What happened immediately after that would haunt Hawkeye and Jacob to the end of their days, and it created a bond each would take to the grave.

"You've had some time on the ranch. I assume you're a hundred percent?"

Physically, yes. But part of him would always be in that

South American jungle, trying to figure out what had gone so horribly fucking wrong.

Hawkeye nudged the photograph a little closer to Jacob.

"Who is she to you?"

Hawkeye hesitated long enough to capture Jacob's interest.

"Someone I used to know."

Jacob studied his friend intently. "Used to?"

Hawkeye shrugged. "It was a long time ago. Right after we got back from Peru." He stared at the photo. "She helped me through the rough patch."

Tension made Hawkeye's voice rough, and he cleared his throat.

"Shit." Jacob cursed himself for not walking out the moment Hawkeye asked for help. "It—whatever it was between you—is in the past?"

"Yeah. She's a smart woman, recognized damaged goods and was astute enough not to follow when I walked away." He shrugged. "To tell the truth, she's too damn good for me. We both knew it."

"It's over?"

"There never was anything significant. She's a friend. Nothing more. But if anyone's intent on hurting me..." With great deliberation, Hawkeye flipped over the picture.

Jacob couldn't help himself. He looked.

The woman was breathtaking. She was seated on a white-painted carousel horse, arms wrapped around its shiny brass pole. Dark, wavy hair teased her shoulders. But it was her eyes that stopped him cold.

He was a practical man more accustomed to making life-and-death decisions than indulging in fanciful poetry, but that particular shade of blue made him think of the columbines that carpeted the ranch's meadow each summer.

Her smile radiated a joy that he wasn't sure he'd ever

experienced. Longing—hot and swift—ripped through him. Ruthlessly he shoved the unfamiliar emotion away. He was seated across from Hawkeye, discussing a job. Nothing more. If he accepted the assignment, it would be his responsibility to keep her safe and ensure she had plenty to smile about in the future.

"After this, Commander Walker, we'll call it even."

"Even from you, that's a fucking cheap shot." Jacob didn't need the reminder of how much he owed Hawkeye. Nothing would ever be *even* after the way the man rescued Jacob's mother from the inside of a Mexican jail cell.

Unable to stop himself, Jacob picked up the photo. Hawkeye's gamble—his drive deep into the Colorado mountains—had paid off. Jacob couldn't walk away. Elissa wasn't a random client. She was a woman who'd shown compassion to Hawkeye, and that shouldn't have put her at risk.

With a silent vow that he'd care for her until the shitstorm passed, Jacob tucked the picture inside his shirt pocket.

Hawkeye lifted his shot glass, then downed his whiskey in a single swallow.

"Sir? It's closing time." Elissa summoned a false, I'm-not-exhausted smile for the cowboy sitting alone at a table for two in her mom and dad's Denver-area pub. The man had been there for hours, his back to the wall. From time to time, he'd glance at the baseball game on the television, but for the most part, he watched other customers coming and going. More than once, she was aware of his focused gaze on her as she worked.

When he arrived, he asked for a soda water with lime.

Nothing stronger. Minutes before the kitchen closed, he ordered the pub's famous fish and chips.

Throughout the evening, he hadn't engaged with her attempts at conversation, and he paid his bill—in cash, with a generous tip—before last call.

Now he was the last remaining customer, and she wanted him to leave so she could lock up, head for home. She needed a long, hot bath, doused with a generous helping of her favorite lavender Epsom salts.

If she were lucky, she'd fall asleep quickly and manage a few hours of deep sleep before the alarm shrieked, dragging her out of bed. After all, she still had to run her own business while taking care of the bar.

Over the past few days, exhaustion had made her mentally plan a vacation, far away from Colorado. Maybe a remote tropical island where she could rest and bask in the sun. A swim-up bar would be nice, and so would a beachside massage beneath a palm tree.

But she was still stuck in reality. She had to complete the closing checklist, and that meant dispensing with the final, reluctant-to-leave guest.

With a forced half smile, she tried again. "Sir?"

The man tipped the brim of his cowboy hat, allowing her to get a good look at his face.

She pressed her hand to her mouth to stifle a gasp.

He was gorgeous. Not just classically handsome, but drop-dead, movie star gorgeous.

His square jaw was shadowed with stubble, but that enhanced the sharpness of his features. And his eyes... They were bright green, reminding her of a malachite gemstone she'd seen in a tourist shop.

In a leisurely perusal, he swept his gaze up her body, starting with her sensible shoes, then moving up her thighs, taking in the curve of her hips, then the swell of her suddenly aching breasts.

When their gazes met, she was helplessly ensnared, riveted by his intensity.

The silence stretched, and she cleared her throat. She was usually a total professional, accustomed to dealing with loners, as well as groups out celebrating and being rowdy, or even the occasional customer in search of a therapist while drowning their sorrows. But this raw, physical man left her twitterpated, her pulse racing while her imagination soared on hungry, sexual wings.

Andrew, the barback, switched off some of the lights, jolting her. After shaking her head, she asserted herself. "It's closing time, sir."

"Yes, ma'am." The cowboy stood, the legs of his chair scraping against the wooden floor. "I'll be going, then."

His voice was deep and rich, resonating through her. It invited trust even as it hinted at intimacy.

An involuntary spark of need raced up her spine.

Forcing herself to ignore it, she followed him to the exit. Instead of leaving, he paused.

They stood so close that she inhaled his scent, that of untamed open spaces. She tried to move away but was rooted to the spot. She was ensnared by his masculine force field—an intoxicating mixture of raw dominance and constrained power.

Desire lay like smoke in his eyes. In a response as old as time, pheromones stampeded through her. She ached to know him, to feel his strong arms wrap around her, to have his hips grinding against hers as he claimed her hard.

Dear God, what is wrong with me?

It had been too long since she'd been with a lover, but this cowboy was the type of man who'd turn her inside out if she let him. And she was too smart for that.

"Ma'am." Finally he thumbed the brim of his hat in a casual, respectful farewell that made her wonder if she'd imagined what had just happened between them.

"Thanks for coming in." Her response was automatic.

"I'll see you soon." Conviction as well as promise laced his words, and it shocked her how much she hoped he meant it.

After locking the door behind him, she stood in place for a few moments, watching him climb into his nondescript black pickup truck. It resembled a thousand others on the road, in stark contrast to its intense, unforgettable owner.

The barback tugged the chain to turn off the Open sign, reminding her of the chores still ahead of her.

It was past time to shove away thoughts of the stranger.

She checked her watch. A few minutes after one a.m.

It had been a long day. *Another* long day. With her parents still on vacation, the responsibility for running the pub had fallen to her. That wouldn't have been so bad, but Mary, the nighttime manager, had called in sick. And Elissa's freelance graphic project was due at the end of the week. Sleep had been in short supply for the past month.

Month?

Actually, it had been more than a year. Her father's cancer diagnosis had upended her family's world. The emotional turmoil had taken its toll as they all fought through the terrifying uncertainty and fear.

After his final chemotherapy treatment, her parents had departed for a much-needed break.

Andrew continued walking through the area, switching off the neon beer signs. "Everything's done. Clean and ready for tomorrow."

"Not sure how I would have managed without you." For the first time ever, he'd ended up waiting on several customers, and he'd done a good job. "Why don't you go ahead and leave?"

"I'll wait until you're done and walk you to your car."

"That's okay." She shook her head. It had been busier than usual for a Tuesday, more like she'd expect closer to the weekend. "I still have to reconcile the cash register, and that will take some time. You worked your ass off this evening. Go see your girlfriend."

"It's our one-month date-iversary. I didn't know that was a thing until this morning, and she warned me I better not screw it up." Clearly besotted, he grinned. "I don't mind staying, though, for a few more minutes."

"Go."

He glanced toward the rear exit. "If you're sure..."

"It's your date-iversary. *Go.*" She made a sweeping motion with her hand.

Grinning, she turned the deadbolt once he left.

After turning off the main dining room lights, Elissa retreated to the tiny management office. She sank into the old military-surplus style leather chair behind the metal desk. Determined to ignore the clock on the wall, she counted the cash, balanced the register, then ran the credit card settlement.

Once everything was done and the bank deposit was locked in the safe, she sighed, part in relief, part in satisfaction.

Finally.

As usual, she straightened the desktop and gave the office a final glance to be sure everything was where it needed to be.

Satisfied, she released her hair from its ponytail and fed her fingers through the strands to separate them, part of her ritual for ending the workday and easing into her off time.

Then she reached for her lightweight jacket. Even though it was summer, Colorado could still hold a chill after the sun set. Finally she slung her purse over her shoulder before plucking her keyring from a hook in the wall.

She let herself out the door, then secured the deadbolt behind her.

There were only a handful of vehicles in the parking lot, and she headed toward hers at a quick clip.

As she neared it, a figure detached itself from the adjoining building.

She struggled for calm, telling herself that the person wasn't heading toward her. But as she broke into a jog, so did the figure.

Frantically she ran, hitting the remote control to unlock the car, praying she could make it to safety before the assailant reached her. As she grasped the door handle, he crowded behind her, pressing her against the side of the vehicle.

"Get away from me!"

When he didn't, she screamed.

"Calm down."

Fuck. She recognized his gruff voice. *The cowboy.* For a moment, she went still. But when he pressed her harder against the car, fear flared, and she instinctively fought back. "Get the hell off me!"

He was unyielding, and her strength was no match for his.

"Hawkeye sent me."

Elissa froze. *Hawkeye?*

Of course he'd sent someone. She should have expected it when she refused to let him provide her with a bodyguard.

Years before, she'd met the wounded military man when he returned from an overseas mission. The first few times he'd come into the pub, he'd been quiet, drinking whiskey neat, staring at a wall while occasionally flinching.

They'd gone out a number of times, and she'd cared about

him. But no matter how hard she tried, she couldn't connect with him on an emotional level. He kept more secrets than he shared. But the one thing she learned was that the need for revenge consumed his every waking thought. In the end, it had been impossible to have any kind of relationship with him.

When he informed her that he'd started Hawkeye Security, she wasn't surprised. And when he came to say goodbye, she tearfully stroked his cheek while wishing him well.

She had been stunned when he called her to tell her she was at risk. Someone from his past threatened the people he cared about. Before hanging up, she dismissed his ridiculous concerns. Their halfhearted relationship was so far in the past that no one could possibly believe that she meant anything to Hawkeye.

"You're going to need to come with me."

"Oh hell no." Her earlier attraction to the stranger had vanished, replaced by anger. She made her own choices and didn't appreciate his heavy-handed tactics. "Tell Hawkeye I said both of you should fuck off. Or better yet, I will."

"I'm not sure you understand." His breath was warm and threatening next to her ear.

And now she understood why he'd spent so many hours at that table. He'd been studying her, planning the best way to bend her to his will.

But Elissa answered to no man.

"You're in danger."

"I can take care of myself. Now get off me, you..." *What?* "Oaf."

"As soon as you give me your word that you'll get in my truck without creating a fuss."

Realizing physical resistance was futile, she allowed her body to go limp and concentrated on tamping down her adrenaline long enough to outwit him. She needed to think and escape his unbearable presence. "How about I'll go home and stay there?"

"Not happening."

"Look..." There was no way she would yield to this oversize, determined goon, even if he was pure masculine perfection. "I'll agree to have one of his employees stay with me."

"He made that offer. You turned it down."

Damn you both. Why hadn't she just agreed to Hawkeye's suggestions?

"Let me be clear, Elissa..."

Despite herself, the way he said her name, gently curled around the sibilant sound, made her nerves tingle.

"He made it my job to protect you, and he signed off on my plan."

"Care to fill me in?"

"Yeah. We'll go to my ranch until he gives the all-clear."

Unnerved, she shivered. "Ranch?" That was worse than she could have imagined, and fresh panic set in. "I demand to talk to Hawkeye this instant."

"Demand all you want, little lady."

She refused to leave town, the pub, and be somewhere remote for an indeterminate amount of time with the cowboy shadowing her twenty-four seven. "No. No." She shook her head. "It's impossible. I'm needed here. And Hawkeye knows it." Struggling for breath, she pushed back against him. "We can work something out, I'm sure."

"You can take it up with him."

"Now we're getting somewhere. Let me get my phone out of my purse." *And figure out how to get in my car and drive like hell.*

"Not until we're on the road." He looped his massive hands around her much smaller wrists and drew them behind her.

"Ouch! Release me immediately!"

Though he didn't hurt her, his grip was uncompromising. "As soon as you agree to get in my truck without struggling."

"Look, Mr.—" *God. I don't know your name.* And like the asshole he was, he didn't fill in the missing information.

"We're done talking."

She stamped her foot on his instep, and he didn't even grunt, frustrating the hell out of her.

"Please get in my truck, Elissa."

Since he was immovable, she tried another approach, pleading with his better self. "I'm begging you. Don't do this. Let me go home." Elissa turned her head, trying to see him over her shoulder. Because of his hat and the darkness of the moonless and cloud-filled sky, his expression was unreadable. "You can follow me to my place." The lie easily rolled off her tongue. Anything to get away.

"Within the next five seconds, you'll be given two options, Ms. Conroy. One, you can come with me willingly."

"And the other?"

"You can come with me unwillingly."

"Option C. None of the above." With all her might, she shoved back, but he tightened his grip to the point of hurting her.

As if on cue, a big black truck—his, no doubt—pulled into view. Since he didn't react, it obviously meant Hawkeye had sent more than one person to deal with her. "This is absurd."

The vehicle, with no lights on, pulled to a stop nearby.

"I'll need your keys, Ms. Conroy."

She shook her head in defiance.

"Always going to do things the hard way?"

Since he was still holding her wrists, it was ridiculously easy for him to pry apart her fingers and take the fob from her.

"Has anyone ever told you that you're annoying as hell?"

A woman slid from the cab of the still-running pickup

and left the driver's side door open a crack. A gentle chime echoed around them, while light spilled from the interior, allowing Elissa to make out a few of the new arrival's features.

Dressed all in black, she was about the same height and build as Elissa. She even had long dark hair.

"Perimeter is still clear." Then in a cheery voice, she went on. "I see you haven't lost your way with the ladies, Commander."

He growled, all alpha male and frustration. "You're here to help, Fagan."

"That's exactly what I'm doing."

The cowboy eased his hold a little.

"Sorry for the caveman's actions, ma'am. I'm Agent Kayla Fagan. And I'm afraid Commander Walker needs a remedial training class in diplomacy."

Walker. First name? Or last? "Diplomacy? Is that what you call an abduction?"

He remained implacable. "I have my orders, and Ms. Conroy wasn't interested in talking."

Bastard. "His behavior needs to be reported to Hawkeye."

"I'll let you do that yourself," Kayla replied. "But honestly, I'd like to listen in."

"Get out of here, Fagan." He kept his body against hers while somehow managing to toss her keys to Kayla.

"Wait! You look so much like me you could be my double."

"That's the plan. Fagan will make it appear as if you're following your normal routine this evening while we get away. When we're on the road, you can talk to Hawkeye and make a strategic plan for opening the bar." Walker's tone was uncompromising.

The infuriating men had planned out everything.

Kayla opened the car door and slid into the driver's seat.

"Time's up, ma'am."

"Could you be any more condescending?"

"As I said, we can do this the hard way or the easy way. Your choice."

Determinedly Elissa set her chin. "I'm not going with you."

In a move so calculated and fast that she had no time to react, he took her purse from her, then yanked her around to face him. As if he'd done it a million times, he swept her off her feet, then hauled her into the air.

The Neanderthal tossed her over his shoulder, and she landed against his rigid body with so much force that breath rushed out of her lungs, stunning her into silence.

"The hard way it is."

ABOUT THE AUTHOR

I invite you to be the very first to know all the news by subscribing to my very special **VIP Reader newsletter**! You'll find exclusive excerpts, bonus reads, and insider information.

For tons of fun and to join with other awesome people like you, join my Facebook reader group: **Sierra's Super Stars**

And for a current booklist, please visit my **website**.

USA Today bestselling author Sierra Cartwright was born in England, and she spent her early childhood traipsing through castles and dreaming of happily-ever afters. She has two wonderful kids and four amazing grand-kitties. She now calls Galveston, Texas home and loves to connect with her readers. Please do drop her a note.

ALSO BY SIERRA CARTWRIGHT

Titans

Sexiest Billionaire

Billionaire's Matchmaker

Billionaire's Christmas

Determined Billionaire

Scandalous Billionaire

Ruthless Billionaire

Titans Quarter

His to Claim

His to Love

His to Cherish

Titans Quarter Holidays

His Christmas Gift

His Christmas Wish

Titans Sin City

Hard Hand

Slow Burn

All-In

Titans: Reserve

Tease Me

Titans Captivated

Theirs to Hold

Theirs to Love

Theirs to Wed

Hawkeye

Come to Me

Trust in Me

Meant For Me

Hold On To Me

Believe in Me

Hawkeye: Denver

Initiation

Determination

Temptation

Bonds

Crave

Claim

Command

Donovan Dynasty

Bind

Brand

Boss

Mastered

With This Collar

On His Terms

Over The Line

In His Cuffs

For The Sub

In The Den

Collections

Titans Series

Titans Billionaires: Firsts

Titans Billionaires: Volume 1

Billionaires' Quarter: Titans Quarter Boxset

Risking It All: Titans Sin City, Boxset

Hawkeye Series

Here for Me: Volume One

Beg For Me: Volume Two